Mae and Me

BY TYLER DAVID RIGDON

FISHER
BOOKS

New York | Michigan

First edition, 2026
This edition published by Fisher Books in 2026
ISBN: 979-8-9943970-1-5
Published by Fisher Books

Ebook published by Indy Pub in 2026
ISBN: 979-8-2958-7467-3

Cover art by Joseph Pennell
Cover design by Riva Olson-Adler

For more by Fisher Books please visit:
linktr.ee/fisherbookspublishing

For more by the author please visit:
linktr.ee/tylerrigdon

Printed in the United States of America

"Two things above all else arouse love;
great beauty and a good name."
-Don Quixote

Mae and Me

PART I

Chapter One

How I Came to Write This Book

"In those days we ruled the neighborhood. Mae moved into my apartment on 7th and A that summer and we never got any sleep. And we liked it. We stayed out late circusing Alphabet City until we couldn't stand, and then I'd be up early in the morning to write. While I wrote she went out 'scavenging,' or at least that's what she called it—that is, to capture ideas, to keep the sketchbook full. In the afternoon I'd be done writing and she'd come home and she would begin to paint. I couldn't write in the afternoon because of the heat and she couldn't paint in the morning, so we never had to work at the same time. One might think it would be best for a couple to work at the same time, so that they could spend their free time together, but that wasn't so. Because we were both movers. Once I got writing, I couldn't sit still. I was up and pacing over the apartment, stepping and sliding and humming; shirtless, eating, singing and swearing my way through every thought, every line. And when Mae painted, she danced. She closed her eyes between brushstrokes and twirled, one, two, three perfect pirouettes and then back to the canvas she went, where she let love out. If we had worked at the same time, we'd have collided, so for that, I stepped out in the afternoon to allow her to work. In those afternoons I walked, read in the park, and day-dreamed of Mae. And in the evening when she finished her work and we could finally be together, we drank. We did a lot of drinking and Avenue A was very good for that."

This is the first paragraph of my new book. If you haven't read that book, stop now and read it before continuing on with this one. Presently (as I write these words), the manuscript for that book is being formatted by a very famous Parisian publishing house. Printing is to follow. It is set to be on the shelves on the first of May.

It wasn't easy getting it published. I had tried first in New York and didn't have any luck. I was shut down by every major publishing company in Manhattan, most of them having some very strong words for me along the way. Rather than sustain my abuses, I did what every great artist must do when they feel smothered by the strangling arms of New York and left the city. I had to travel halfway across the world before I got someone to read more than one chapter of that book. In Paris they practically fell to the floor and kissed my feet when I brought them the manuscript. It was the love story they'd always been looking for, they said. A perfect culmination of all the great love stories before it, and a catalyst for all that would attempt to come after it.

Now I'd always known that my book would be bound for greatness, as it was born from a *true* love story, and true love stories are always more unbelievable and alive than fictional ones. My book was born from a love more passionate than anything Shakespeare could have thought up, more volatile than Hardy, more noble than Tolstoy, and more mysterious than Alstwin. This love was an unpredictable love. A messy, screaming, bleeding-hot love that can only occur between real people. Books could never hold such force. Except mine. And nobody would have been able to write such a book. Except me. Yes, reader, I was made to write that book. No writer past or present is as educated on the intricacies and histories of the *romance* as a *form* as yours truly. My whole life had been in preparation to write that book; reading every romance I could get my hands on, from the dainty dimestore paperbacks of my youth to the colossal soul-shaking offerings of Austen and Sir Henry James.

I've spent more hours reading romances than I have spent *dining* in my life. I am the world's greatest student of all things romantic. It has even been said by some (namely my French colleagues) that I am romance itself, and when one becomes the very quintessence of the force that possesses him, he has no choice but to do the very thing that so exercises the full power of his enlightened state. So naturally, I decided to write that book. To write the greatest love story ever told—to be the flyer of the flag, the cantor of the creed—now *that* is romantic. And that is what I'd always set out to do.

I don't mean to lead you on, reader. I don't mean to tease you. This isn't that book. This book is the story on how I came to write that book. How I came to *find it*, as Mae likes to say. You see, that story always lived inside of me. I felt it for years. I chased it, I kissed it, I lost it several times only to find it again, and the final time that I'd found it, I realized that I was never meant to write it alone. I needed her to do it with me. I needed her to show me where it was and how to tell it. Oh, magical Mae! How I love you now more than I ever have! I thank you in all that I do for revealing to me the secrets of this life, for standing by me as I probed our love for the words that would become our *opus*. Without you, I fear I'd have never written again.

Here she is, with me now along the Seine as I write these words. We are enjoying a light dinner at our favorite restaurant, anticipating the publication of that *tour de force* that bears her very name: *Mae and Me*. Yes, my book was inspired by a real woman, and believe me now when I tell you, her name really was Mae, the sweetest, softest, roundest, easiest name in all of romance. Can you believe it? This is just what I mean when I say that only real life could have arranged itself as such: For the perfect story to be lived out by the perfect storyteller.

Now it is certainly a *long story* about how Mae and me met and how I came to write my book. A story full of ambition, gusto, heartbreak, coincidence, passion, agony, misunderstandings, betrayals, midgets, and perhaps divine intervention. It certainly isn't for the faint of heart, nor for the disbeliever of miracles. For that reason I believe it would be courteous and responsible of me (if not later required) to relate in this companion volume how and why that book came to fruition in the first place. It seems that a great deal of fine artists are silent on their most acclaimed works, seemingly leaving it up to the public for interpretation, but I won't have that. I've decided that rather than risk the intellectual integrity of my finest hour—and the world's greatest romance—falling victim to the biased and degenerative ignorance of our indulgent and desensitized generation, I could publish this book here, recounting all that went into my labor, so as to be honest, clear, and empirical about just what means what. All great works have their detractors, so let ours only detract from the truth if they must, not from their speculative notion of what that truth may or may not be. With that disclaimer, we can now talk about beginnings.

One appropriate place to begin would be two years ago. I was alone then. It was the springtime when the first phantoms of her love crossed me in the night. It was then that I came to realize the weight of the story I would soon have to tell. Or perhaps some three years before that would be a more fit place to commence our tale, that is, my moving to New York City. I knew I was moving to the city to become a writer, and I knew I was moving there to find love. But that begs the question, Why? Why did I want to write and why did I know it must be about love? Well, we must go back even before that for the answer to these questions. Back to my very first encounters with love by way of an intense, unforgettable teenage affair with a certain girl who has long escaped my life, but whose fleeting impressions still haunt my heart to this day. For it was that girl, and our story that made me dependent on love. It was through her that I knew I would grow to write a great romance, because through her, romance was the only thing that I came to know.

So without further ado, I offer in this document a glimpse into the life of the world's next fine novelist. He had humble beginnings, and suffered through the proverbial throes of heartbreak, identity crisis, and rejection as all great artists do, but he is as you see him now: the ruler of his own world and a known conqueror of others. Though, before he learned to write romance, he had to learn how to live it, so I'll drop you there, reader, in northeastern Missouri some eight years ago, where a small-town bright-eyed nineteen year old first fell in love.

I hope you enjoy the story told henceforth. And I know you'll love my Mae.

Yours now and forever,
Dick du Quesne

Chapter Two
How I Came to Love Love

The first time I fell in love my name was David. This was before I realized the importance of a name. I wasn't yet concerned with names—that would come much later. I was only concerned with romance.

She was the younger, being seventeen against my nineteen. We fell in love during one of the coldest winters of my lifetime, everything snow-buried in those first months, constantly shedding clothes or putting them on. That's what I see when I try to recall my first breathless weeks of love; purple-cold and the glassiness of frozen cheeks and hipbones; a young girl in front of me talking exhaustively in a language I'd never heard before, the two of us close beneath bedclothes keeping warm by the heat of our words. I realized I loved her when I first heard her talk about love. She spoke of it as something to be careful with. Something that we were responsible for, something to cherish above all else, something that deserved our undivided devotion. She treated it with a seriousness that I hadn't yet considered at my unlearned boyish age. I naively believed that love would be something that would happen to me, no different than puberty, or death, but she made me understand that love was something that we were privileged to *have happen to us*, like being born, or being forgiven. I was satisfied with every word from her mouth. I knew that she was the answer to my woes, the rickety teenage incertitude that tossed me like waves to and from the empty affairs of adolescent curiosity. I didn't question her, and I didn't seek reprieve elsewhere. For once in my life I didn't feel the need to know everything there was to know, I instead felt I was free to abandon every other adventure that I had started without remorse, only needing to surrender to the one that began with the music of her voice, the sureness of her eyes, the forever of her words. When she called, I answered. Where she commanded, I went. There was nothing more to do.

Yes, we were in love and we knew it and that is a beautiful place to be, not only when you're nineteen, but at any age. What a delight it is to reminisce on those early days of passion! They have so oft been written about that I won't attempt to do it here, though I will say that no other adventure in this life resembles it. No shade of the human condition can compare to the first night a boy realizes he is in love. It is an imposing emotion, hungry and jealous for your full attention. It is the most overbearing, the most penetrating of all loves. Of course, that is not to undermine the love that I have for my Mae—I don't think the severity of one love can be measured against another—but I do believe that the feeling of falling in love for *the first time* is greatly unique in that it usually happens during that gaping, pearl-colored youthtide of one's life, leaving him awestruck and speechless at the marvel of love, the miracle of love, the gift of love. How disorienting it is to live for eighteen or nineteen years—just as one begins to possess a serviceable command of his emotions—only to be blindsided by the all-consuming blow of love! To realize one's morals aren't what one thinks, to suddenly value something more than one's own individuation, once thought invaluable. How it magnifies the role of the soul! It rewrites the rules, shatters the paradigm under which we operate. Man under assault of his first love learns that he isn't in fact only flesh and bone, but instead he is the sum of his impulses. And reader, as I'm musing on it now, I lament greatly over the fact that in this life there are only as many first loves as there are births, for there are few feelings that

I ache to experience once again—even if just out of the vanity of nostalgia—more than that first apprehension of love.

As fate would have it, my first love would not stand the test of time. That novel union forwent us as quickly as it had possessed us for reasons that I feel are necessary to relate here in order to understand the rest of this text. Now, I would be lying if I said our demise wasn't a product of our own hand. It should be noted that this girl was directly responsible for my introduction to the world of written romances. She had bookshelves full of paperbacks and old dusty century-worn editions containing the greatest tales of love ever put to paper just waiting to be read. I found out very soon that it would take a force far greater than the will of man to keep me away from those volumes. See it from my perspective, reader: right as I came to understand just what love was through my devotion to this woman, and just as I came to find all of the treasured fables of love to be true and more alluring than before believed, I suddenly entered a world of a seemingly endless supply of that elixir in the form of the written word! It occurred to me that everything that I loved about love could be found *ad infinitum* inside the pages of these cherished romances! For it was not the superficial warmth of touch or the security of everlasting companionship that I felt was so inspiring about love, it was the dichotomy of its very nature that drew me to its glow. It was the very essence of the stuff, the stuff that love was made of, that I wanted to consume. Love is yearning and nobility pitted against each other; it is virtue and jealousy existing in the same thought. You see it in the way a man in love walks down the street versus the radiating noneness of the man who never had it. These revelations were my real attraction to love—revelations of romance, a door opening to a new life, The Life Romantic.

I can see now in my older and wiser state the magnitude of my early mistake: I was more content to devour the long-tested chronicles of love, than to *be in love*. I regarded those books as a more adequate source of consuming love than love itself! So it was as I began to bury my nose in those books that our finale commenced. I lived out my romance for myself, acting out the stories that I read, hoarding all the great plunder of their depths; their mystery and passion and great poetic tension while completely and utterly ignoring the real love that I had in front of me all along. This caused a season of profound distress between the two of us, to say the least.

By my twenty-first summer we'd set each other free. She would go on to study at a prestigious college far away, and I would spend the next months coping, buried in fiction. Oh, and believe it when I tell you that I so immersed myself in those romances that I spent whole days and nights over those books sleeping so little and reading so much that I once feared that my brain had dried up all together and perhaps I had risked to lose all reason. I withdrew myself from my friends and family, dedicating my whole self and all my talents to understanding my mistake. I yearned to know just what it took to hold on to an authentic romance—just what it took to be a great romantic. I grieved the love that I once knew, laid to waste by my own selfish aspirations, not knowing quite how to handle this immense loss until—like the blinding light of revelation—I realized how I could make it all right. I would have no choice but to write my own romance. I could undo all of my anguish by living out my own book. It would be easy. In my studies, I had become utterly perfect in romance, learning its rules, its emotional borders, its sights and sounds and shapes and colors. There was nobody on earth more acquainted with the trajectory of a romance than me, and for that I elected to absolve myself of my burden by writing a masterpiece of romance, using my own experience as a basework. Oh, how arrogant I was in those days!

After starting and abandoning several manuscripts in vain, I was struck by one more important realization that finally—my patient reader—leads us to the story that I am presently telling. I did not want to write about a love that *failed,* you see, I wanted to write about love as *perfection.* I had no interest in reciting my past story of broken love in all of its turmoil—that was the very thing I was trying to get away from! What I wanted was to write about love in all of its glory! I wanted to write not just about love, but the essence of *romance* as a lifestyle, as divinity. I knew that I—living in my small Midwestern town having only one lover in my life—was not yet equipped to write such a manuscript, regardless of how many classic romances I read. My life was going to have to change, and I wanted to begin as soon as possible.

I chose New York City. I chose it for its romance, which needs little explanation. I chose it for its history. For its color. For its virtue, for its plight. I chose it because a friend of mine went once and told me I'd like it. Now I had never been to New York before but I had read a lot of books about it and decided that there was no better place to begin my search for my new lover than in the heart of Manhattan wherein dwelled the most interesting and beautiful people in the world. Through those books I learned that I could meet somebody just by sitting in a coffee shop or by occupying any given park bench. According to some books, there were even some women who spent the majority of their time in elevators. Others exiting taxi cabs. Even more of them frequenting the subway system. I had an abundance of options, but when I finally did arrive I decided to go with my first instinct, which was to stand and wait on the streetcorners hoping to physically bump into one and strike up a conversation.

I had answered the *when,* the *where,* and the *how;* the only question that remained—and the most exhilarating to answer—was the *who.* Reader, believe me when I tell you, I didn't know her name that first day, but I could see her face. I had always been able to see her in my mind. It wouldn't do any good to describe her now, as I will do plenty of that later on, but let me say that when I first arrived to that city, her image was faint and distant, but as each day came and went, I could see her more clearly. She would come into focus as the woman I was born to love. And through her love, I would write my book. It was written in the stars. It was willed by forces far outside my power. It was unthinkably romantic.

Chapter Three

*How I Arrived in New York City and Struggled Deeply
to Begin My Novel*

I 'll be candid with you now, reader. The genesis of my campaign to find this forever lover of mine was a little disappointing. It became clear to me very quickly that the romance I was looking for was going to be harder to find than I'd thought. Now, I was correct in thinking that the streets of Manhattan were filled with breathstealing women of my approximate age and demographic, though I was completely mistaken about how I might get one into conversation. I stood for hours sometimes watching the women walk by. Just standing. I called this the "stand and wait" method. Having done the math, it seemed to be the most likely way to start a conversation. If I'm stuck in a coffee shop for instance, my will is held hostage by whoever is in that coffee shop at that time. If I'm not pleased with the turnup of that particular hour, the turnover rate would be so slow that I'd likely be asked to leave before I could make a single attempt at conversation. So I decided that the constant traffic of the bustling streets would provide me with a higher rate of success; for that, I stood and waited on the corner of MacDougal Street and West 3rd Street, a corner I deemed the "Holy Waters" of downtown Manhattan due to its role as a junction point between four of the highest trafficked distinct areas in the city: Washington Square Park to the north, world-famous MacDougal Street to the south, New York University's higher campus to the immediate east, and Sixth Avenue and the deeper Village to the west.

There was only one instance during this early period that I actually had success in securing a real conversation with a passing girl. I was on this very corner one late September day, underneath the chill of the blue sky, with the crackings-off of starlings in the air, and the steam pouring out from the pizza place when I saw her walk across the street. I was thinking quickly for the words. She moved with such youthful charm; I could see her speckled cheeks, freckled and patterned as one treebeetle might be. Her amber hair so sweet in the autumn sun, running down her back like honey. I couldn't believe my eyes, and when I saw her gaze shift to mine—help me in my weakness, Lord. My novel would be underway any minute now. What else could I do next but speak?

"Where are you going?" I asked.

"I'm sorry?" she said back to me. She didn't stop walking.

"Where are you going?"

"Hey, get lost."

"I'm just being friendly. Can't a man ask a woman a question anymore?"

"Why should I tell you?"

Shouldn't lovers tell each other everything? I thought it, I dared not say it.

"Just wondering," I said. "I'll tell you where I'm going."

"Where are you going?" she asked. We were walking together now.

"I'm going to the cafe to write. I'm a writer. My name is David Cale, and I'm writing a great romance novel."

"That's really interesting, but I'm going this way. Have a good day."

"And you!" I cried out as I watched her go, disappearing into the tunneling crowd of Sixth Avenue. I took the time then as she fled to contemplate all her mental and bodily perfections, as they were enough to inspire love in a stone statue, let alone the heart and flesh of a man. I ran home in an instant, closed my door, shed my coat, and sat there at my desk writing love-letters to my flower of all flowers. I would dream of her, I hoped. I would go again tomorrow, to stand and to wait for her, praying to talk with her again for some mere moments and discover her name. Surely it would be something gentle and feminine as in the books. How perfect it all became in a flash of an eye; how romantic!

***

Well, reader, you could surely surmise that this woman did not become the love of my life. Through my greatest efforts (standing and waiting) I never did see that darling daffodil again. And in my stubbornness, I refused to talk to even the most feminine looking man during those days that I laid siege to the corner of MacDougal and West 3rd Street looking for her. With weeks behind me and absolutely no prospects of another chance with another girl, I decided I must be doing something wrong.

It was around this same time that I also became considerably worried about my lack of funds. I had moved to New York with some money that I planned to spend sparingly as I aligned the priorities of survival with those of my romantic notions. The order of events was supposed to take place as follows: Firstly, I would find the love of my life. Secondly, through her muse, I would write the greatest romance novel ever written and we would both live comfortably on my earnings in our favorite corner of the city. Unfortunately, I had miscalculated the time in which it would take me to execute the first part of my plan, thus scrambling my life into a state of financial chaos. Ah New York! The great equalizer! I had vastly underestimated the cost I would shoulder in moving to Manhattan without a job. I was made aware very quickly of the discomfort I was to face in the coming months as an unemployed writer. Let me tell you from experience, there is *nothing* romantic about paying $14 for a bacon-lettuce-tomato sandwich. Additionally, there is nothing romantic about paying some $50 a week on a train system that is not completely devoid of human feces. Or about paying $3200 a month to live in a dwelling reminiscent of a Roman prison cell, rats, roaches and all. Now, I've heard all the scolding already, reader. I don't need to hear it from you. I know the crime I committed. I moved to Manhattan without ever having been there. I moved there without even having a job. These are my sins, and I do own up to them. But one reproach I will not stand for is your suggestion to curb some of these costs by doing one unthinkable thing; that thing on your mind so unthinkable that I feel sterile and ashamed just to say it, but say it I will and I will say it loud and clear: There is *absolutely nothing* romantic about living in Brooklyn. So in my stubbornness I stayed, and if it came down to it, there I planned to die. In Manhattan.

Chapter Four

*How I Joined the Working Class All the While Still
Searching for the Impetus of My Novel*

A whole book could be written about the period of time from my arrival to New York City to the fateful events that led to my meeting Mae, but this is not that book. This book is about how I came to write another book, so I'll only convey to the reader the events that directly influenced the subject in question, thus, I will be using this chapter to quickly recount around two years of romantic misadventures and wandering employment.

I'd only been in New York a month when I realized I'd need a job to afford living without any prospect of artistic success at all. It wasn't my favorite decision to make, but it was a necessary one. I was having no luck in my methods of courting, and in all honesty reader, I was beginning to feel that I needed to take a break from my efforts. Frustration was only leading to more fruitless outings.

I would spend two years working a slew of odd jobs, from furniture mover to busboy, to valet driver, to delivery man. I eventually landed as a dishwasher at an Italian restaurant in Midtown. This was my most stable and lasting profession as I navigated the romantic and literary worlds of New York City, albeit to no avail.

The restaurant wasn't anything special, mostly a tourist trap, but it proved vital in my fight to survive the city itself. This was for two reasons: Firstly, I was so poor in those days that my only shot at eating three good meals a day was to work double-shifts at the restaurant. Despite my manager granting me a reasonable discount on menu items, I instead found it more economical—if not completely necessary—to obtain my dinner by way of eating off the dirty plates that came to my dish station in the kitchen. It wasn't romantic, but I was well-fed each and every night without spending a dime.

Secondly, it was through that job that I finally met my first friend in New York, Sam Parasochi, the closest companion I'd ever had. Now, living a life of pure romance is a lonely life for some. It is a sure road to feeling misunderstood, alienated, out in the cold in your undergarments too proud to thumb for a ride. You can't imagine the focus, study, planning, preparation, practice, and prayer that goes into assembling and executing the perfect romance day in and day out; the fleeting chance at finding one's true purpose, in assuring yourself each day when you leave the house that you are equipped with the utmost readiness to act if you should happen upon the love of your life that afternoon. If one is consumed by such strenuous bounds, when is there time for the innocence of same-sex fellowship? It is almost entirely impossible. For years I went without male friends because of my pursuit of the divine. I detested their arrogance, their brutishness towards life. I was embarrassed by their lack of formality, their cardboard sentimentality, their broad and naked disrespect for love and for lovers. Only the great writers who penned the stories under my bedpillow had any idea what was truly happening in this world. They were my friends, and for a long time, that was enough for me. I digress, reader, but my point remains that in the early days of my "standing and waiting," I found no reason for boyish companionship. It wasn't until after I joined the workforce and was so overworked and nervewrackingly poor that I finally found a kinship in the company of my own kind. This certain cretin, Sam, worked as a waiter at the aforementioned restaurant and had the habit of standing at my dish station to pass his breaks. He was a child-eyed, blonde-headed boy a little younger than I. He was red-faced and a little clumsy. He loved to talk, and despite all my initial skepticism, I loved talking with him too. We developed a sort of rapport in our first weeks as workfellows and quickly the conversation turned to the age-old New York City question: "So what do you do outside of this?" It must have surprised him that I was not an actor—the first answer to this question among most dishwashers. I told him that I was a writer, which immediately impressed him.

"What do you write?" he asked. "Like Journalism? Think-pieces?"

"Think-piece? What on earth is that?" I asked.

"You know, like a reader-writer discourse type of thing."

"I don't."

"It's like this, a writer lays out an opinion about something. I don't know, like a topical subject, or just an opinion on something cultural."

"What would be the point of that?"

"To provoke the public to interact with the thought, I guess." He was embarrassed that he'd said anything at all. "Listen, I don't read'em. They're usually sort of one-sided headlines to bait readers."

"I hadn't considered that such people called themselves writers," I said, shaking off what I'd just learned. "I write books. Romances at that."

"Romances? Like dirty books? Erotica?"

"Incorrect again, sir." I was scrubbing alfredo from a saucer pan.

"I don't get it," Sam said.

"I wouldn't expect you to," I started. "The genre of 'romance' goes back some hundreds of years. It is not simply 'erotica' or so-called 'chick-fiction.' It's a beautiful literary tradition that exemplifies not only a fire for love as an emotion, but also love as a lifestyle. A certain romance for life as it were; an idealism, a fate that one knows he is bound for. I write books about being in a passionate love affair with life itself."

"Are they any good?"

"Romances?"

"Yours, I mean."

A great question, and my first clue that he would be a good friend to have around.

"Of course they are good! I wouldn't write anything but the best. In fact, the book I've recently finished is being reviewed by an agent now. He told me that the market is craving a romance of existential proportions as of late, and that mine has real promise to be picked up. If all goes well, I won't be washing these dishes much longer."

"You're kidding," said Sam. "Oh, I'd love to read it sometime! I do read, actually, David. I love classics. If you need an extra set of eyes—"

"That won't be necessary, Sam. I have the best set of eyes in New York on the book now. Perhaps when it's published, I'll get you a copy for free, for your enthusiasm."

Now of course, reader, some of what I told Sam at this time was true, and some of it was not, but as one great book famously declares, *"What is truth?"*

I said I was a writer because I was a writer. Perhaps the manuscript wasn't finished—perhaps it didn't even yet exist—but all I had to do was find *her*, and I could have the book finished in a month—a fortnight! For one, I knew that when I finally met her I wouldn't be able to stop my hand from writing. (And how right I was, my miracle Mae, as you read this, know I love you.) And for two, Sam didn't know how long it took for a publisher to handle a text in the first place—what was the harm in telling him that it was finished? Besides that, I'd long learned that in New York you didn't actually have to do what you claimed to be doing to retain the title of what you claimed to do anyway. That is to say, anyone who wanted to be a writer could just arbitrarily claim to be a writer. The same went for actors, comics, musicians, and performers, but *especially* writers. I had met people who went months or years without touching the pen and wanted to be treated as an authoritative voice on the craft of writing. Such people, I learned, were the devourers of so-called "think-pieces."

Now, I'm sympathetic to circumstances interrupting the creative process, but a profession taken seriously requires some layer of re-sponsibility and accountability. The people that I speak of always had some excuse—too tired, overworked, not inspired enough, or some matter like that. They acted as if it was always someone else's fault that they couldn't write, and yet they demanded that they deserved credit for "doing their best," when their "best" was in fact doing nothing at all on account of their "burnout," or "writer's block." New York is a fairytale land for fairytale people; nobody is required to take responsibility for their own life and I had absolutely no tolerance for being lumped in with charlatans like that. The way I saw it, all the great writers couldn't *help themselves* from writing, even at their saddest, their poorest, their most broken moments, lest they'd go mad and push themselves out a ten-story window, so it was easy to sift the roses from the weeds. In one sense, this was good news for me, for all a writer had to do was actually read and write and they were worlds ahead of the majority of people who claimed to be writers in New York. How much more of a writer is a writing writer than a writer who doesn't write? I didn't feel bad in the slightest about bluffing my numbers a little bit *knowing* that it would only be a matter of time until my manuscript was written, represented, published, and in the hands of Sam Parasochi.

"I'd love to read it, really," Sam said, nodding his shaggy blonde head. "I've never been friends with a writer before. I'd love to help in any way I can."

Chapter Five

How Sam Proved to be a Useful Companion

L ucky for me I'd really struck gold in finding a friend like Sam. He didn't have any opinions, and he didn't care to get any. At his best, he was a sort of sidekick—somebody I could count on no matter what went wrong. At his worst, he was simply a living testament to the axiom of some of the social laws that are impenetrable around us, such as this timeless favorite: *Some men do, and other men get done.* He was a happy fellow. Always content just to be part of whatever it was I dragged him along for. This is not to trivialize what Sam's friendship meant to me. I couldn't write enough words about how dearly I loved him and how much I miss him here in Paris. He was loyal, he was kind, he was as innocent as a cubscout, and funny as a barfly. He was a Midwesterner himself, so we had a common parlance which made it easy for us to relate. His family was just like my family. Our fathers worked labor, our mothers stayed at home. Our uncles sold cars. Our childhoods were filled with bike-riding and skinned knees. Corn on the cob and climbing trees. We got along because we lived on the same planet, which was a lot more than either of us had in common with the creatures from the East Coast.

Sam had lived in New York for two years before we met. He didn't know why he came, he never could tell me. He said he always had pictures of New York City on his bedroom walls growing up. He figured it would be "a fun place to live," so he moved out at eighteen and got a job at the restaurant. After a couple months he met his girlfriend, Katie (who would later come to play a significant role in our story), and moved in with her to curb the rent. She was a New Yorker and studying to become a doctor. She was a dangerously serious girl. It's a miracle she and Sam ever made it work, him being the way he is. Sam liked to read adventure stories. He liked to fish. He liked to watch baseball. He liked to play pool. He liked to drink too, so we spent a lot of time doing that. We went out together after work most nights, drinking and laughing our way through Manhattan, dominating pool tables and spending loads of money we didn't have, but reader, I don't exaggerate when I tell you it was the best money I'd ever spent. I never imagined hanging out with another man could be such a joyous and raucous pastime. We made crude jokes, we looked at beautiful women we had no intention of speaking to, we talked sports, books, and cars. We named off every little town from Ohio to North Dakota that we could think of and then ranked them by the quality of their local cheeses. We talked about the mighty Mississippi and the glorious Great Lakes. And through all of this, I gained not only a best friend, but a person who believed in me. Somebody who was in my corner while I worked on my writing and searched for my one true love.

One particular night, we were crawling through the Lower East Side near where we lived. We had been drinking, snaking our way through those crowded red streets, trash-laden and broken, the homeless screaming foghorn poems from each streetcorner, the psychics smoking Pall Malls in the windows of their parlors. The smell of dumplings and burnt steel knived the winter air. How romantic those days were when I think back on them. To be a young man on the Lower East Side is to have the world's unsightliest pearl in the palm of your hands.

"How about another one here?" Sam mumbled to me. We leaned on each other to walk.

"This place? There aren't any lights on in there."

"Sure. But they sell booze. Come on."

Some rattrap on Essex Street, leather and lace through the window. The warm was what kept us in.

"Two whiskeys?" I asked Sam.

"Get them. I need the john."

"Two whiskeys," I said to the bartender. He lined them up. "Fine place you've got here. Ever think about installing a candle?"

"Fourteen dollars," he said. I handed him the cash.

The bar was full of people standing. Some tables were strewn around in the back where a number of others lingered. The music was offensive, steelcolored and noisy. How do I end up in such places, I thought. I'd begun to sip my whiskey when Sam sat beside me again.

"Whiskeys bad, but cheap," I said.

"That's the key."

"I'm getting toasted."

"Me too," Sam said. "I'm going to need something to eat. You ever been to that cheap dim sum place on this street?"

"I think I know what you're talking about," I said.

"It's a lot of food for the buck."

"Essex and Rivington, right?"

"No, Stanton I think."

"Are you sure?"

"No. It might be between Grand and Hester now that I think about it."

"Isn't that where we are now?" I said. We looked out the window behind us.

"No, we're not past Grand yet," Sam said.

"Yeah we are, we walked right by it."

"You sure?"

"Dead positive."

We both took down the whole glass of whiskey.

"Excuse me," I shouted over the bar. The bartender turned. "Are we on Essex between Grand and Hester?"

"Hester and Canal," the bartender said.

"South of Grand," I said.

"Then I think we passed the place," Sam said.

"We did."

"We should go back. I need something to eat, I'm delirious."

"Hang in there, let's have one more drink and we'll go get dumplings."

"You know what I want?" Sam said smiling. His face was red, his eyes so small in his smiling head they looked closed. "You know what I really want?"

I didn't know.

"A pasty," he said.

"A pasty?"

"What, you never been to Michigan?"

"Yeah, I have."

"You been to the U.P.?"

"Not that far up."

"David…you'd love a pasty. I'm gonna get you a pasty one of these days."

"What is it?"

"It's a meatpie."

"I can get a meatpie anywhere."

"It's more than that though."

"How can a meatpie be anything more than a meatpie?"

"It's a traditional kinda thing. I dunno. It's a Cornish thing up there. Lot of Cornish people up in the U.P. They've got festivals and cookoffs and novelty shops all for the pasty. You wouldn't believe the culture up there around the pasty. Oh man, when you're drinking…you can't imagine how good a pasty is."

"How do you eat it? With your hands?"

"You could. A fork is recommended. Some come covered in gravy, or with gravy on the side, though some folks look down upon us gravy users."

"Why wouldn't you want to put gravy on something?" I asked.

"That's my thinking," Sam said, smiling real big. "Hey, do you ever feel weird eating sushi with chopsticks?"

"You're starving."

"Do you?"

"All the time."

"Like, come on Japanese guy, just cause *you* do it that way, why do I have to?"

"You know just what you're talking about, Sam."

"I *know how* to use the chopsticks. It's not that."

"Of course you do. It's not that hard."

"Two more whiskeys," Sam said to the bartender. "I just don't get stuff like that."

"Say no more my friend."

As we sat in that dungeon of a bar I was doing my survey of the room. With years of practice, I'd gotten very good at it. I can carry on a conversation with two or more people while taking stock of what lies along the furthest outposts of each room completely unbeknownst to my peers. I am subtle, efficient, and deadly in my scoping. Just the underbone of a chin—even in dim light and through a curtain of hair—could alert my senses to the possibility of the beginnings of a new life. I'd always known somewhere inside me that I would know her *firstly by her face*—the ancientness of her young face, deep wellworn eyes, pasture-colored and as marbled as good loinchops—and *secondly by her name*; something musical, tangible, graceful, without being feathery or pretentious or larger than life, just like in all the books. It certainly wouldn't be a jagged name, unstable under its own weight such as Bridget, Meridith, or Matilda. And moreso, it could never be one of these awful academic names you hear in New York circles, the daughters of wealthy Tisch graduates who prance around West Broadway in their careless splendor because they belong to prominent Connecticut families who give them names like Mauve, Calliope, Elora, or Estephanie. No, my lover's name would surely be round and modest, something like Olivia, Emily, Amelia, Ava, Evelyn, or even better; timeless as love itself, as in Mary, Sarah, Anne, or Alice. Now, I don't mean to undermine the importance of such factors as intelligence, or temperament. And of course I value the nature of a woman's interests. These things do hold some level of importance, but all the great romances make it very clear that these matters are negligible in comparison to her face and name. If I'd learned anything from my reading, it was that I would *know her when I saw her*, and that this conviction should be confirmed by the presence of a perfect name. From there, we could then fall deeply in love with each other's person, nameless and faceless if we must be, two souls stirring, breathing as one, indistinguishable from the other in their tormenta of twindom, spread wide like sails in an everwind brought forth by the slow turn of the Earth, moved by movement itself. How unfathomably romantic.

Yes, reader, these are the things that overtook me sitting in the little bar on Essex between Hester and Canal that night beside my companion. He was going on talking while I nodded in compliance and tore through the trashcan of a tavern looking for her face. It wasn't long until I'd found it, tucked between the passing statues of leather jackets, standing at the bar. She was alone, waiting for her drink.

"...and it wasn't even that expensive. I probably paid around nine dollars for each of them, and it was one of the best sandwiches I'd ever had. Even Katie loved it. But of course the next time we go back, it's closed down—out of business. Some Korean corndog place in there now. Haven't tried those yet, but people are crazy about them. Have you?" Sam went on.

She was clueless as to my finding her. One hand brushing through that long black hair let down at her showing shoulder.

"Dave?" Sam said.

"What?"

"Have you tried them?"

"Tried what, sorry?"

"Korean corndogs."

"Sam, do you see what is going on here?"

He stared on.

"Look at what lies in front of us right now, there at the bar between those two homeless-looking people. You want to talk about Korean hotdogs now?"

"They're not really hotdogs—"

"Sam." I hit him.

"That girl?" Sam said, squinting through the dark. "Man, I've got to eat something. Can't we get out of here?"

"Not just *that girl,* Sam. It's *her*! It's the one I'm supposed to love. Look at her. I could love her for a thousand years, I know it by her face."

"Why'ont you go talk to her then? She's alone."

"You don't know anything about this sort of thing, do you? I can't go talk to her just because she's alone at the bar. Chances are *she's not alone.* She's alone now because she's ordering a drink. But you should never approach a girl alone at the bar after only a few moments of observation. Always watch to whom she walks back to. It could be a boyfriend, a brother, someone who is watching you watch her. Someone you don't want to aggravate."

"Getting your ass kicked isn't very romantic," Sam said.

"That is near worst-case scenario."

"What is the worst-case?"

"A group of other women."

Sam looked at me puzzled.

"Are you completely absent from the workings of this world, Sam? It is a wonder you ever got Katie in the first place."

"She asked me, actually."

"And it's not a surprise, I doubt you yourself have ever pursued somebody in your life."

"Will you just tell me why the group of girls is so bad?"

"Because, you idiot, no man in history has ever successfully approached an entire group of girls in public, singled out one, asked for her hand, and made it out unhumiliated. It can't be done. I'm convinced it has never happened. Good men have been shot down all over the world for attempting something like this."

"Really?"

"Entire cultures have instituted the arranged marriage to avoid this exact thing. You can't just approach a group of women as a single man and expect to succeed. You need at least one less man than there are women, and even that is tough to pull off. That is to say, if there are four women, you'd need three men minimum for just one of them to make a move. The exception being for a group of two women, you need to have them matched. You can't do it alone. It can't be done."

"Why is that?"

"I don't know for certain, Sam. I don't know if anybody does. Their solidarity is just stronger than ours. I've seen men get laughed off the face of the planet trying to attempt such a move. Or worse, a man could think he's somehow cracked the code, somehow getting away with a phone number until he tries to get in contact with her. Dead line. No response. Fake number. I've seen it all."

"That's tragic."

"You have no idea. The tragic part is this: that same woman might very well give you the time of day if you'd have gotten her alone. There is something about her being with the others that makes it impossible for her to be interested. Look," I pointed, "watch her go now. She's finished her business at the bar, let's see where she's headed. If it's her boyfriend, we dodged a bullet. If it's her friends, *then* it's a tragedy."

She walked long past the bar and took a seat at a far table.

"Would you look at that," Sam said.

"It's all hitting you now isn't it, buddy?"

"It is."

"The harem dilemma. I could have talked to her there at the bar. It was a perfect opportunity."

"But you couldn't, because you had to wait to see if she was with her boyfriend."

"Bingo."

"And now, you have to wait for her to get through that drink. It could be forty minutes before she gets up for another one."

"Or worse, one of the other girls gets the round. Our chances may be over."

"Do you think you are in love with this woman?" Sam asked.

"I think I might be."

A silence sat between us, even in the noisy bar, as we looked long past the bulky mass of patrons and to the table in the back stacked with the five girls.

"It's like getting the take sign from the manager and watching three fastballs go right down the middle," uttered Sam in disbelief.

"That's exactly what it's like, Sammy. That's exactly what it's like."

We sat without talking in the grievance of this tragedy, drinking our whiskeys and doomed to go home upon finishing them. My head was buried in my hands. Sam, though, had never given up. He sat with his head straight and his eyes wide like a watchdog of the night, unblinking and looking towards what may have been my only chance at love in my lifetime. In the passion of his intensity, he hit my head with his hand and shouted.

"David! David, look. She's getting up. David, she's standing up again."

I looked on to see what he said was true. I couldn't believe my own eyes.

"I don't believe my own eyes," I said.

"Neither do I," said Sam. "It's the one loophole to the harem dilemma. She's getting up again!"

"She's going to the bathroom."

"And there's a line."

We sat still and watched.

"Well, get up and go over there!" cried Sam. "You can wait behind her!"

We smiled at each other with the banner of true friendship shining through our faces. I stood and walked myself—not too urgently—to the cornered cutaway that housed the lone bathroom stall towards the back of the room where the line had formed. It was near the jukebox where our conversation could be clouded by music and well-protected from the other women at their table. I found my place behind her, close enough to nearly drown in the dark crimson of her long hair. It was smooth and clean. She turned her head to look out towards the bar. From this movement I could see her perfect profile; a glowing face, modest chin with long light lips like red ribbon tied tight in just the right place. The line was moving now, I had no choice but to resist my adornment and finally speak.

"I really have to go," I said.

"Oh," she said. "Do you want to go in front of me?"

"No, that's okay," I said. "I can wait."

"I don't mind at all," she said. "I'm only going to touch up my makeup, you might as well go first."

"I don't think your makeup needs any touching up. You look perfect." I was doing great.

"Thanks," she said. "Go ahead and cut me." She passed a hand across my arm and moved me into place. Oh, she touched me! This was going very well. I decided then it was time to set the hook.

"I'm a writer," I said. "My name is David Cale, I'm writing a great romance novel. Well, actually, I've already written it. My agent has it now, he says it will be published."

"Congratulations," she said.

"What do you do? I mean, besides this."

"Besides what?" she asked.

"Besides what we are doing now."

The door ahead of me opened. A burly man pushed his way through the space between the line and the wall, the door coming shut at my shoulder.

"The bathroom is free," she said. "You really have to go, right?"

"Yes," I said. "Would you want to get a coffee sometime?"

I panicked. I don't need to hear it from you, reader. The impending dark of the bathroom had coursed me, and I was afraid of losing her. I'd come so far that night, I couldn't bear the thought. I had no choice but to show my cards once and for all.

"I have a boyfriend," she said. "You should go. It's not healthy to hold it."

I went. I went and stood there in the bathroom, not having to go. Thinking, thinking, thinking, what I could have done wrong, what could have been better. O, Holy Father, is there a sadder place than to be sitting on a closed toilet seat in a Lower East Side bathroom while the woman of your dreams rejects you on the other side of the door? I scoured the walls in my isolation. Heinous, hideous, and hilarious things decorated the bathroom walls. There is nothing more equally repugnant and relatable than the text written in our great American bar bathrooms. The psychosis of the nation is written on our bathroom walls.

After an appropriate length of time, I ran the sink, blowdried my dry hands, and opened the door to see her waning face glance up at me with the politest of all gestures—a half-cocked smile and lift of the eyebrows. She hurried past me and into the bathroom where I heard the door lock.

I walked slowly up the aisle behind the backs of losers, drunks, deadbeats, and punks, to see Sam there, smiling and waiting for me, hardly able to contain his excitement.

"Did you do it?"

"She has a boyfriend, Sam. It's a lost cause."

"What did you say?"

"I don't want to talk about it."

He sighed. "At least you know it's not your fault."

"It still hurts, my friend. To come so close, and to know that she sleeps tonight in the arms of another."

"I'm sorry, David."

"You know what I think, Sammy?"

"What's that?"

"I think I was wrong about my previous statement."

"Which one?"

"How in the history of mankind a single man has never courted a woman in a group." I took a long sip of my whiskey, finishing it and pushing the glass towards the end of the bar where it teetered for a moment under its own weight. "I think perhaps in the history of mankind, a single man has never courted a single woman. It's all one big cosmic joke, and I'm the butt of it."

Sam laid down the tip for the drinks and stood me out of my chair. "Let's go get some dumplings, buddy," he said. "Let's get some dumplings and put you to bed."

Chapter Six

*How I Began to Make Money as a Writer and Some
Other Humorous Tellings of That Winter*

The weeks came and went as I worked double shifts at the Italian restaurant struggling to make my rent. I was sleeping little, never knowing the day of the week, sometimes not even the time of the day, having no ability to recall if something happened yesterday or the previous month in my dissociation. Long bouts of labor were separated by brief and unrestful episodes of dreamless sleep. Only one day began to matter to me. Only one day required lucid action. On the first of each month I met my landlord, Mr. Chong, and handed him a stack of cash. Immediately following this, I checked my bank account to discover once again that I had some $80 to my name.

There was a brief period during my spells of incessant work where I thought the whole racket to be rather enchanting, romantic even. Every great writer must have a great origin story. A broken and exhausted man at the end of his rope, striving each day to make ends meet so he can retire in the spare moments that he has to the solace of his desk and round the edges of that momentous masterpiece that so brewed inside of him. I felt part of a sort of canon, like I was sewing my name into the fabric of the literary lore that had consumed me for so long. However, this feeling wore off by the dead of winter. The cold, the subway creatures, the blistering wind that tore down Broadway in the middle of the night while I walked my way from one closed off subway station to another. There is nothing romantic about being cornered and threatened by the crab-colored, sewer-smelling demonic entities that possess the New York subway system by night. There is nothing romantic about using your last dollars on a pair of poorly knit gloves because your hands are so painfully frozen you can't clamp them enough to pull the handle of a door. Not only this, but despite my ceaseless work, the writing was not going well by any means. I had started several iterations of my novel by this point, none of them catching. I must have written an entire novel's worth of first pages but every word of it belonged in the garbage, for I had no love in my life from which to draw my words.

On one fateful subway ride I spotted, by chance, an ad that read: *Hiring Writers. Consistent work, well-paid, work-from-home.* I felt that this could be the break that I needed. Perhaps it was the opportunity I was waiting for, written in the matrix of my life, destined to propel me to the next level of success wherein I would not only write the world's greatest romance, but also be in the position to live lavishly with the one I truly desired; the pearl of my quarter, my true love.

I called the number listed and explained to the woman who answered that my name was David Cale and I was writing a great romance novel. She seemed uninterested in these personal affairs at first, but I knew that she was only playing hard-to-get. The job she ultimately offered me was a position at a temp firm, staff writing for low-profile clients looking to advertise their businesses. It wasn't exactly what I'd hoped for, but I knew the endgame when the woman slyly remarked that the work was "very steady" with "room to grow." I decoded that she was surely connected with a commercial publishing house and was weeding out the weak links by way of this procedural hackwork. If I could impress her—if I could shine brighter than these other ad-writers for one quarter—I suspected I could have a shot at pitching a finished novel to a legitimate publishing house. I took the job immediately, meeting with her team in person the following day to sign the contract.

I quit the restaurant the same week I took the job, which greatly shocked and excited Sam. The poor boy was unaware of the prison he resided in, his hands on the glass from the inside looking out. He drilled me with questions, remarking how he couldn't fathom what may have occurred in my life to justify my sudden withdrawal from the plebeian workforce.

"Sam, I'm ashamed that you haven't already guessed the catalyst for my sudden stroke of fortune," I told him. "How telling it is of your friendship."

"Did you win the lottery?" he impatiently asked.

"In one way, I have, my friend. I forgive you for not having mustered the answer yourself by now, and I have no problem with briefing you on this precipitate, though not unforeseen, change in circumstances."

He sat wide-eyed and silent, his pupils black as shadows.

"I am being scouted and groomed by a major New York publishing house, my friend. They have shown urgent interest in my novel, and have agreed to pay me a handsome advance in the form of weekly payments while I pass a number of quality control trials for their marketing team to ensure that my writing is the right fit for their brand. It could be a long process, but I am confident that with my skills as a dedicated writer and student of the craft, I could make an impression within the year big enough to have my book published by next winter. What is important is I'll be able to spend all of my time writing and refining my work, and being paid for it, leaving no need for the grisly jobs of lesser artists anymore."

"I don't believe it!" he shouted in glee. "Oh, we have to celebrate! This is amazing news, Dave!"

"Thank you kindly."

"Let me buy you a drink," he said.

"Not so fast," I stopped him. "You, my friend, were my first and forever supporter. I couldn't have gotten to where I am now without your help and friendship. Let *me* buy *you* a drink. After all, you don't have the money to spend working in that horrid restaurant."

We bundled up and marched down East Broadway to the old 169 Bar where I proceeded to spend every last penny to my name in raucous celebration, believing, feeling, knowing that in one short week, I would have the first of many paychecks that would come to support my life as the greatest young novelist in New York City, and perhaps the world.

***

It would be an understatement to say that my life changed immediately upon starting my new job. Within six weeks I felt as though I was living a completely different life, a life one step closer to the one that I knew I was destined to live. I was making money, able to afford to pay my rent, enjoy recreational activities on a regular basis, and treat Sam and Katie to the occasional dinner or round of drinks. I had time to work on my novel which was coming along at a slow but steady pace. By January, it had finally gotten off the ground as a story about a young writer who takes a job as a postal worker and writes love letters to the woman he admires from afar, slipping them into her mail. All the while, I was exploring the untapped corners of New York in search of *her*, and everything all at once.

My job itself was the easiest work I'd ever done. I couldn't believe people go to school for that sort of thing. There was absolutely nothing to it that a literate monkey couldn't do. All you must do is think like a person who is so ghastly brain-empty that they are actually influenced by subway advertisements. The key was to write something simple, cute, inoffensive, and shallow, and the people who hired me ate it up every time. I found very quickly that it was writers who had gone to school to study something called "Ad Design," that had the hardest time with success, trying constantly to over-complicate things, to justify their degree and general level of misery. They became invested in their clients and the *success* of each ad. This is a trap. No, it is more than a trap, it is a waking nightmare. It means that you have nothing outside of your job to live for. For myself, the goal was to get the ad out as soon and as efficiently as possible so as to get paid and move on to the next one, never thinking about the previous one again. This was very lucrative if you followed my four rules for ad writing: simple, cute, inoffensive, and shallow.

For instance, I was picked up to write for a Brooklyn-based bakery. The ad was a photo of a very unnaturally multi-racial group of young people acting like they were having a great time surrounded by pastries and doughy delights. All smiles, all the time. Would you believe it if I told you the client was head-over-heels for my pitch: *Our Bakery Takes the Cake.*

Or how about if I told you that a local electrician posted an ad I wrote to promote his small business. His name was Bill Cousins. The photo was him, smiling, tools out, taking great pride in his work underneath a broken light-socket. He even tipped me an extra $100 for my ever-genius-now-synonymous slogan: *Quit Buzzin' Call Cousins.*

I was coming up with lines like this in my sleep. Because I was doing so well with the ads, clients were recommending me to other clients, and the programmers for my company were shoveling as much work as possible my way. I knew that I was being watched closely and that it was only a matter of time before they requested that I send them a snippet of my fiction for consideration at the publishing house that they were associated with.

At the beginning of February I backed out of my month-by-month lease with Mr. Chong and rented an apartment across the hall from Sam and Katie on 7th and A. Things couldn't have been going better. The only thing missing was true romance.

There was one close call that winter that seemed like it had all the fittings of being the real thing. I really thought in my stomach, in my bones, for just a moment, it was finally happening to me.

It was a beautiful winter day, one of those days where the cold is enjoyable because the sun is out and the city sky is so ardently alive with you, following you, obeying your commands; cracks of nascent blue sky shining through the tall pillars of stone that line the Bowery. Sam, Katie, and I crossed through Cooper Square, our crystalline breath riming the noses of each other as we spoke, and then up to Broadway and finally upon the lively, hiving kingdom we call Union Square. The park was thick with people. The local market flanked each side of the western thoroughfare; tunnels of life between the tents, the vendors barking off meats, vegetables, handmade novelties, and flowers. Sam and Katie were being reeled into each tent by the smells, sights and sounds.

"I've never seen the market this busy," Katie said. "I haven't been here in a long time."

"This is nothing," I said. "You should see it in the fall. It's twice as busy."

"And the summer?"

"Not as busy as you'd think. The fall is the best."

"We need to come out here more, Sam," said Katie.

Sam was bobbing and glaring into each passing tent.

"It's really a beautiful place," I said. "It's good for the soul, these markets. It makes you realize how much fun grocery shopping can be."

"There's so much life to it," Sam said.

"During a better time, this is what life was like," I said. "The market was where all men came to be equal. Everybody had to go to the market; the rich and the poor shopping at the same tent. Passing your neighbor, your enemy, your ex-lover in the plaza. There was no hiding in hideous supermarkets that look like aircraft hangers. No putting on headphones and refusing to greet people. Here is where real-life still happens—in the farmers market. Even just a hundred years ago nearly every street in downtown Manhattan had its own market, they were the lifeblood of the immigrant."

"I think my grandmother used to work in one," Katie said. "In Little Italy. My father has some pictures of her pushing carts around down there."

"It's incredibly romantic, really, being such an ancient profession. Standing in the sun, all your livelihood in front of you. The bartering, the haggling. It's as human as anything. It goes back long past the Romans, the Sumerians even."

"Why do you always have to go there?" Katie said.

"Go where?" I asked. "Sam, did I go somewhere?"

"I didn't see you go anywhere," he said.

"You can't just have a conversation," Katie said. "Everything always has to be related to Romans, or immigrants, or some book, or some lovestory."

"Name me one thing on earth not related to Romans, immigrants, a book, or a lovestory," I countered.

"Go to hell," she fired back.

"Why do you always have to use such language?" I said.

She smiled. "David, I'd love to strangle you, but I'm just too afraid Sam wouldn't know how to go on without his boyfriend."

"Sam, could you go on without me?" I asked him.

"It would be hard, buddy," he said.

We moved through the crowds northward, up towards the mountains of limestone all pale-white and brown in the shivering sunlight, shadows painted across Union Square from easterly buildings and treetops. We were on our way to 22nd Street and Fifth to have lunch at S&P, the only good coffee shop left in New York. I was turned towards Sam when I felt the abrasive blow against my arm. In an instant a tower of books fell down onto the concrete, a girl in panic at the sight of their descent. I couldn't believe it, we'd actually collided, just like in the books!

"Oh!" I shouted. "I am so terribly sorry."

"No, no," she protested. "It was my fault. I wasn't paying attention, I was cloudwatching."

"You oughtn't do that in a park as busy as this," I said. We were on the ground together sweeping up the books.

"I was telling myself that just as we collided," she laughed.

Our hands were gliding between each other as we assembled a stack. When we finished we looked up towards one another. She was celestial. Curly brown hair soft as the clouds she so adored rolled weightless down her head and past her shoulders. She wore peach colored lipstick, and provocative black-rimmed glasses. She smiled big, her perfect white teeth showing through her lips.

"Sorry again. I really should have been paying attention too," I said. I handed her the books. She had a fantastic collection. Henry James, Jane Austen, Shakespeare, and even some compelling philosophy; Aurelius' *Meditations,* and Saint Augustine too. It was very romantic.

"Please, don't apologize. Thanks for the help anyway."

"It's the least I could do," I said. "This is a really great stack of books here. Are you a student?"

"No," she laughed. "I'm well graduated. I was just taking these books over to a friend's place. She has been asking me for recommendations, so I gathered some favorites for her."

"These are your favorites?" I asked.

"Some of them," she said. "Looking at them now, I'm a little embarrassed to admit it. I suppose I'm a romantic at heart."

With that, she smiled again and I was instantly arrested. My blood went cold, my heart unsteady, my tongue as tight and tied as a sailor's knot in a squall. I stood, nodded my head ever so awkwardly and said: "Well, have a good day." And returned to the company of Sam and Katie who stood some ten feet away, patient as cows.

As we walked on I could hear her stand and begin in the opposite direction. At once I was overwhelmed by melancholy.

"I can't believe I just did that," I said.

"I can't believe it either," Katie said. "Did you see her?"

"I know it," I said.

"I mean, I knew you were stupid..."

"Katie, please."

"Don't worry, Dave," Sam said. "Something else will come along."

Something else will come along. The sentence I had been saying to myself everyday since I arrived to the city.

"I am sick of waiting for something else to come along," I said.

"I can't believe you didn't ask her out," Katie said. "That was the cutest thing I've ever seen. If I was that girl, I would have said yes to you regardless of what you looked like."

"I get it, Katie," I said.

"Good," she said. "I just want to make sure you know you blew it."

I blew it. She was right. I'd blown every chance I'd ever had at finding love again, and for once in my life it comes and rams itself right into me, looks me in the eye and tells me that it's there, and I flee the scene like I'd committed a crime. I was sick of it. I wouldn't ever forgive myself. So I made a decision.

"You two go on. I'll meet you at S&P later on. Just go on in and order. I'll see you later," I said. I started off in the other direction.

"What?" they shouted. I could hear the voices fading behind me. "David? Where are you going?" But of course they knew.

I could see her ruby-red wool coat well into the sea of people. I was locked on to her, hoping that she wouldn't make a move between the tents or down the subway before I could get close enough. I trailed her from fifty yards. I dodged and weaved between the masses, bouncing like a bobcat up and off every obstacle in my way. Thirty yards. She was heading straight for 14th Street. Fifteen yards. I knew she could feel me now. I came up close, five yards, reached out my arm, and tapped her once on the right shoulder. She jumped, moved like electricity and almost dropped the books again.

"I'm so sorry!" I shouted. She turned and smiled, happy to see me it seemed.

"Oh, it's you," she said.

We looked on into each other's eyes for some moments, wordless, earthless, only enjoying the warmth.

"It's me," I said.

"I'm glad," she said back.

"Listen, I kind of blew it back there."

"I thought so too."

"I had to catch up with you and see if I was crazy or if this was something."

She laughed, reaching out one hand and grasping my arm with it. "It might have been something. We can't have you walking away like that again or we'll never know."

"You won't believe it," I said, "but some of those books are my favorites too. Particularly the James."

"It's an incredible book. Have you read *The Golden Bowl*?"

"Of course! I've read nearly everything he has written. He's one of my favorites to study. In fact, I'm a writer myself," I choked out. Her eyes widened, her voice softened. She came one half-step closer to me.

"You are?" I thought she might cry.

"I'm writing a great romance now. I'm in talks with a publishing company. I'm their number one prospect for a massive deal. I'm already getting small payments from the advance they will eventually give me."

"Oh, I'd love to read it! You'll have to let me read it!"

"Well then, we'll have to stay in touch won't we?"

"I suppose so," she said. She reached one hand into her coat pocket and produced a pencil. She opened the inside flap of James' *The Tragic Muse,* and wrote her phone number there on the cover page. "Here," she said, "take this."

"Won't your friend want it?"

"She wasn't going to read it anyway," she said.

"That's a pity," I said.

"I'd rather you have it."

We smiled and began to step away from one another. "So, we'll talk," I said.

"I hope so."

We each nodded our heads and turned from one another. I took a few steps away and then it hit me.

"Oh, wait!" I said.

She laughed hardily, putting her head in her one free hand. "How stupid are we?"

I laughed with her. "Apparently very stupid. I'm sorry, I just..." She was standing so gracefully, so womanly there in all the crassness of 14th Street, like a piece of silver in a bed of ashes. "I just haven't done this in a long time," I said. "My name is David Cale."

"Sylvie Adams," she said.

I was devastated.

***

Sam and Katie were sitting at one of the small tables in the back of S&P well into their lunch when I walked in. I nodded towards the man at the counter and, walking slowly, dragging my thoughts behind me across the floor, found my place at the table where they each looked up with only their eyes, their heads parallel to each other and unmoving.

I unbuttoned my jacket, dawdling off each sleeve and cuff, each button and crease, struggling to not tell them in an eruption of baffled disbelief the details of my chance encounter. The sheer odds to run into a woman of such prospect, of such aptitude, and for her name to be such a conundrum as that! It was moments like this reader, that I knew a higher power fully controlled my destiny. It was moments like this that did not disappoint me nor shudder my faith, instead, they made me stronger, more patient, laughing at the humor of God and the signs and signals He showed me.

I sat across from my two companions as they waited for my report.

"Well," I said. "You won't believe it."

"Did you find her?" Katie asked.

"I did more than find her."

"You made love to her there on the cold pavement like in one of your little books?"

"Save it."

"So you went back?" Sam said.

"I went back. I got her number."

"You went back and got her number?" he said. They were both astonished.

"That's what I said."

"But you blew it!" Sam said. "You struck out!"

"I struck out."

"We both saw you strike out. It was hard to watch even. But you're in. Somehow you struck out, and you're in."

"Somehow."

"This is like reaching first on a dropped third strike!"

"That's exactly what it's like!" Katie said.

"You swung at a curveball in the dirt and struck out, but somehow you're standing on first base," Sam said.

"Can he reach home on a dropped third strike is the question," Katie added. She sipped from a milkshake.

"In two years I've never seen him on first base," Sam said.

"Alright, that's enough," I said.

"I'm happy for you," Katie said. "You should get together with her this weekend. If it goes well, maybe we can all do something."

"It would be nice if we could all do something," Sam said.

The three of us sat together in silence for a moment at the linoleum table above the two half-eaten pastrami sandwiches. Not even a clink of tableware pierced our quietude, our reflection on this chain of events. Katie looked at me deeply, sensing something was wrong. She looked to Sam. He smiled, as he usually does, waiting for me to affirm his vicarious joy.

"I don't think I'm going to see her," I said.

Sam's face turned to disbelief. Katie began to laugh. She pointed a finger at Sam saying, "I told you he wouldn't! Didn't I! Tell him, Sam, tell him what I told you."

"What did she say, Sam?" I asked.

"She said even if you got her number, you wouldn't go out with her."

"Is that right, Ms. Cacciatore?" I said.

"David, we go through this every time. Why would this time be any different?"

"No," I shouted. "No, no, no. You're completely off."

"Either you don't like where she lives or you don't like her job—"

"No."

"Or her haircut isn't right, or she doesn't like Chopin or something so mundanely stupid—"

"No, no, it's not that. I just—"

"'*Couldn't be with someone like her!*' Is that what you're about to say?"

"Yeah, Katie, it is. I just couldn't be with someone like her."

"Someone like *her!*" Katie called. "David, all you talk about is *girls like her*! Pretty girls holding a stack of books, prancing through Manhattan without a care in the world. Is this not your type? Is this not the girl you're writing your little stories about? If it isn't, I'd like to know why! What's wrong with her? Tell me right now, what's wrong with her?"

"Nothing is wrong with her. It isn't her fault."

"What isn't her fault?" she said.

Just then a voice came over my shoulder. "What can I get you, sir?"

"Oh, I haven't even looked," I fumbled for a menu on the table. "Just get me what they're having. What are they having?"

"Pastrami on rye," said Sam.

"Make it a pastrami reuben," I said. "Lots of pickles please."

"Pastrami reuben, lots of pickles," said the man.

"And poison it," said Katie.

"Hey, hey, Kate, come on. Give me a break," I said.

"I want to know what it is," she said. "Tell me what it is."

"Alright, just relax. I'll tell you what it is. I don't expect you to get it though. And just because you won't get it doesn't mean you can be mad. You don't understand these types of things. Just don't be mad. Will you just be cool?"

"Just tell me, you idiot."

I sighed. Sam looked on with great curiosity. Katie's arms were folded and she sat far back in her chair.

"It's her name."

"Her name? What's her name?" Katie said.

"It's Sylvie Adams."

"Sylvie. What's wrong with that? It's a gorgeous name. You don't think it's a good name?"

"It's beautiful," I said. "It's a perfect name. I love it."

"Then what's the issue?"

I turned to Sam, who was making the exact face I suspected he'd be making. His mouth so slightly open, his eyes cast low, yellowish with laughter. He wanted to burst but he knew the pain I was feeling.

"I don't believe it," Sam said.

"I know," I said.

"Oh, come on, David, don't let that stop you," Sam said. "She seems amazing."

"She's smart too. We talked about the books after I'd caught up to her again."

Katie was growing angry. "What is the big issue with the name? If you like the name, why is the name the problem?"

"Sam…" I said, gesturing towards him.

"It's just that we know a guy from the restaurant," Sam said. "He's a nightmare."

"First ballot Hall of Fame dunce," I said.

"He's a loser. A slacker. Just one of those guys. He comes in late…leaves early…drinks too much…smokes too much…doesn't have a dime to his name. He's got nothin' going for him at all."

"He's born and raised in New York. He's like, what—fifty? Fifty-one? And lives with his mother in Bayside. Takes the train in to cook at this restaurant five days a week since 1999."

"He's just a nothing-person, a washout, a burnout, a flop."

"A total lemon," I added.

"And his name is Sylvie Adams?" Katie said.

"No," I said.

"Worse," said Sam. "His name is Adam Silvey."

"But we call him 'Silvey.'"

"Everybody does."

"And God if we haven't spent a lifetime making fun of this guy. There have been nights where Sam and I get drinking and rip on Silvey for hours at a time. We've got a ton of inside jokes."

"Making up stories about him, putting him in funny imaginary situations."

"He's the butt of every joke."

"He's the joke of every butt."

"He's totally hilarious. He takes himself really seriously too, like he's some misunderstood genius or something."

"His whole situation is funny," said Sam. "His whole life is very funny."

"In our minds, the whole pastime of loserdom over the course of human history has grown to culminate in the advent of Silvey. Loserdom as a state of existence has been completely and wholly associated with the name Silvey. He's like the messiah of losers."

"And he's really not very attractive."

"He looks like if a mastiff lost a few boxing matches."

"It's not a good situation, Kate," Sam said.

"It's going to be a massive issue," I said.

Katie was bewildered. She sat looking at us, her arms beside each other on the table, her food untouched. She didn't know whether to laugh or to cry. "So," she started slowly, "you won't go out with this girl—this intelligent, romantic, beautiful, book-loving girl, because her name will remind you of a guy that you like to make fun of? Is that what I'm gathering?"

"Essentially, yes," I said. "Put yourself in my shoes. Imagine you spend two years running comedic circles around somebody behind their back and then meet a guy with the same name! You couldn't do it, Katie. Nobody can."

"But they don't have the same name!" she said.

"I can't get past it," I said.

"You belong in an asylum," she said.

"Katie, don't say that," Sam said. "Nobody could do it."

"Thank you, Sam. A name is everything. Look, I know who I'm supposed to be with. I know how she is supposed to be. Her name will be something far preferable to Sylvie Adams. Trust me."

"Supposed to be? How can you say things like this, David? Supposed to be what? You aren't supposed to know anything about the person you're going to be with! Look at Sam and I." She took Sam by the back of the neck like she was his oversized uncle. "We have almost nothing in common, but we love each other! Love goes beyond some romanticized fantasies."

"Katie, will you hear me out on this? I mean, imagine calling out her name in the throes of passion? I couldn't do that."

"I couldn't either," said Sam, laughing. "It would break me. 'Oh, Silvey!'"

"'Oh, Silvey!'" I said.

"'Oh, Silvey!'" Sam said again.

"Might as well be saying, 'Oh, Adam.'"

Sam was laughing. Katie hit him hard in the chest with the back of her hand.

"What's important is Sam is paying for this whole bill," she said. "I knew you wouldn't see her. I just knew it. Do you see what the issue is here, David? It's you. You set these standards for people, you act like everybody understands exactly—"

"Katie!" It was a woman's voice calling out from down the aisle.

The three of us turned and saw a thin, stylish blonde approaching our table. She was smiling and looking right at us.

Katie shouted in that dollish way that women do. She stood up and the two of them hugged. "What are you doing here?"

"Just having lunch with some friends," the stranger said, gesturing to a line of girls sitting at the soda bar. "I heard your voice from over there, I couldn't believe it."

"Oh," Katie blushed. "Yeah, we were having an argument. Long story."

The woman turned to Sam and I and waved.

"Sam, you remember Allison from Shaina's wedding," Katie said. "And David, this is my friend Allison. We went to high school together."

"Hi," I said. "Pleasure to meet you."

"You too, David," Allison said smiling.

"Are you still living in the city?" Katie said.

"Yeah, I am. I'm managing a department at Macy's."

"You work at Macy's?" I chimed in. Katie threw me a look.

"I do," Allison said.

"I always wondered about that big sign out front," I said. "You know the one that says *'The World's Largest Store.'* Is that supposed to be a promotion or a threat?"

Allison laughed.

"No, seriously. The fastest way you could keep me from going into a store is by advertising it as 'the world's largest store.' It might as well say, *'MACY'S: All the Misery of Being in a Regular-Sized Store, Only Unfathomably Worse.'*"

She laughed even more.

"David," Katie threw me a look. "Don't make fun of where she works."

"He's fine," Allison said. "That's a funny way of thinking about it."

"Well," Katie said, "we should grab a drink sometime and catch up."

"We should," said Allison. "I don't mean to interrupt you guys. It's great to see you."

"Oh, it's no problem," Katie said. "It's great to see you too. I'll call you."

"Please do," Allison said. From there her eyes drifted with great purpose from Katie, past Sam, and then to me. "And it was great to meet you, David."

"You as well," I said.

"I'll call you, Al," Katie said.

She turned in all her grace and walked slowly and sensually down the floor of S&P deli. I watched her walk, honest to God, reader, only because she was in my field of view. I had no interest in Allison on that day, having not sensed her flirtatious disposition at all. Besides, I was still riled up from my meeting-gone-wrong with Sylvie Adams. Despite my disinterest, Katie was looking at me when I finally turned my head back to the table.

"Don't even think about it," she said. "I will forgo all forms of murder-for-hire and kill you with my bare hands if you are ever in the same room as her again, you lunatic."

"Settle down, Kate," I said. "She's not my type."

The waiter came with my sandwich. He set it down in front of me, and cleared some of the empty dishes from the table.

"Anything else for you guys?" he asked.

"I'll have an egg cream," I said. "In fact, bring three of them."

"I don't want an egg cream," Katie said.

"Oh, come on, Kate. We're in New York. What's the use of being here if you aren't going to have an egg cream with your pastrami sandwich. Three of them," I said.

The waiter left us. I looked around. I was elated. I had that old feeling I got sometimes that I couldn't believe New York City still existed. I couldn't believe I was a part of it. The old photos on the walls, black and white renditions of the old deli, long before the neighborhood got taken over by Rockefeller's oil money. The yellowish hues from the cigars and pipes that so soiled the new-white interior of the place all the way back in 1928.

"God! I love this place," I said. "This here is a real diner. If only we could light up a few cigarettes, sit back and read the paper as we drank our egg creams. Wouldn't it be so romantic?"

Katie was still staring me down. She had a scowl on her face that I'd never seen before. I hardly recognized her.

"Kate, I get it," I said.

"Just forget her," she said. "Forget her right now."

So I did. I forgot Allison right at that moment. And it was easy. She was the most inconsequential person on the planet to me as I sat in my seat at the S&P anticipating my egg cream. Now, if you would have told me that day just how important this woman would be to the trajectory of my entire life, I would have called you crazy. It would be some months later, reader, before I even thought of her again, but when I did, nothing would ever be the same.

Chapter Seven

On the Incredibly Romantic Story Related to Me on One Winter's Day Outside the Village East Cinema

The baffling situation regarding Sylvie Adams and her cursed name was not the only peculiar eponymic happening that month. There was another incident just some days after the first. How obvious were your signs, Oh Lord! How humorous it is now to look back and see the trail of breadcrumbs you laid for me to follow. Sniffing out your clues as a detective might, following one puzzling bout of synchronicity to the other, of course in the form of names, having known that I would later revolve the whole of my life around the sublimity of two names, slowly awakening my senses to their importance and majesty day by day through your unrivaled hint-riddles of providence.

This other incident I'm referring to occurred on Valentine's Day—one of my favorite days of the year. Now, I had a sort of tradition on Valentine's Day—no, a sacrament. Or perhaps it was more of a ritual, or more yet, a procedure. Whatever it was, I'd done it two years straight for the same reason. I'd spent two consecutive Valentine's Days alone at a day-showing of *Casablanca* at the Village East Cinema on Second Avenue, and I was on my way to a third. Yes, you've read me right, reader, it was Valentine's Day in New York City and I was celebrating my third such year alone seeing one of the world's finest romances.

What can be said about *Casablanca* that hasn't already been said? It is the ultimate romance. It defies our human definition of romance on a surfeit of levels, while simultaneously shaping and reshaping how we think about love and storytelling; informing the very criteria we use to judge whether or not something qualifies as romantic or not. This is why I spent each Valentine's Day alone in a dark theater during midday watching this document of devotion. It is at once a masterclass, a love-letter, a presage, an altar, and a memoriam of what is, what was, and what should be. I worship at its feet, I throw flowers, and I study it, for there is a Rick Blaine in each and every one of us somewhere.

Now, reader, as you may have guessed, my reasons for carrying on such a ludicrous act were not purely devotional. While I do love the film itself, it was my hope, my prayer—my cryptic contour of a pre-monition—that one February 14th as I approached the marquee of the Village East, or perhaps stepped into line for a popcorn, I would feel the winds of love tickle my neck, turn my chin, and force my gaze onto another lone soul, bashless and beautiful waiting for her own Rick Blaine to stir her spirit up and lead her out onto the streets of downtown Manhattan to make her imagine it was Paris in all its sil-ver, smoking, riverness glory. My stratagem was not naive; I bought the day ticket on purpose knowing the night showings were flooded by dinner-dates. During the day, however, there were a variety of lone viewers over a vast range of ages from sixteen to one-hundred. I will confess, even at the day-showing, only about forty percent of the house tended to be single viewers, of which only ten percent were women. Of these women, there were usually somewhere between three and five who looked to be of compatible age. Of these potential prospects, only one had ever struck me as particularly eligible in the ways of courting. She was a slimfaced strawberry-blonde. She was deeply freckled, like a dusting of chestnuts in the golden loom of a wheatbed. She was of my general age, and dressed herself in the much preferred old-style fashion: womanly, understated, and irresistibly alluring. And miraculously enough, she had been present during *all three years* of my attending the event.

I had spoken with her two years before—on my first outing. We smiled at each other as we entered the door that abridged the anteroom of the cinema.

"No date either?" I said, smiling, confident, bold and Blaine-ish.

"No, unfortunately not," she said. There was an air of rue in her voice. She stepped forward to purchase her ticket. "One for *Casablanca,* please." It still rings in my mind to this day. We entered the theater separately after our very brief exchange, and in the chaos of departing the theater after the film, I lost her somewhere in the midst of the crowd.

The following year I saw her again, but not until I had entered the theater, ascending the stairs of the cinema to my designated seat. I smiled and I believe I received a smile in return. *That's the same girl as last year,* I thought. When the film finished I saw her under the coming glow of the post-program lights and leapt from my seat to speak with her, but missed my chance again, stuck behind the rest of the chain-gang beside me in my row as they gathered their many jackets and items of garbage, double-checking, triple-checking their previous positions and stalling in the walkway as I watched the sugar-haired sally exit the theater without even attempting to check upon my whereabouts.

The third year, however, just a mere week after my run-in with the Adams girl, I spotted her again with my hawk-eye before the premier, some blocks down Second Avenue, walking so elegantly across the concrete clouds that paved her road to me. I decided to wait for her under the marquee, feigning a phone call, thus putting the two of us in an identical position as the first year, right beside each other in line. As she opened the doors I followed, positioning myself just behind her, in perfect position to casually offer a word.

"No date either?" I said.

"No. No date." She blushed. She seemed not to recognize me.

"Have you ever seen it before?" I said.

"Sure, plenty of times," she laughed. "Probably more times than you."

"I've seen it a lot of times," I said. "I know every line by heart."

"I could do it backwards," she said. This was incredibly intriguing.

"I'm David Cale." I let my hand fall near her waist.

"Callie David," she chirped. We shook hands.

"Haven't I seen you here before?" I asked.

"Probably. I come on this day every year."

"For how long?"

"Five years now."

"This is my third."

"Rookie numbers."

Our smiles reflected off each other's. For once, for all, it was happening to me. I could feel the line for the box office shrinking. We were only moments away from making that grand decision. Would we change the paradigm on this decisive Day of Saint Valentine and spend the splendor of a new-budding love together? Or would we recoil to our shadows of sorrow, cursed again in contrite and abandonment, staged lonely at our archaic positions in the sorry grotto of the cinema as we had always done and were doomed to do? I decided to act then, with the full confidence and grace of a leading man.

"I don't suppose you are looking for a date, Callie David?" I said. Nothing could stop me now, I felt cold and balanced, ready for anything.

"I'm afraid I'm not, David Cale," she muttered. And then the driving stake: "Thanks though. It's very sweet of you to ask."

I couldn't believe it. There we were, two single people in line for *Casablanca* on Valentine's Day, each of us buying a separate ticket, and she preferred to sit alone. And then to add insult to agony, she thanked me for my efforts! What could I do other than get pushy?

"That surprises me, Callie David. What is a sunflower like your-self doing all alone on this fine holiday seeing *Casablanca* without even the temptation of getting adventurous? Isn't that what this film is all about?"

"I suppose it is."

"So what do you say?"

"I'm sorry, I'm really not interested."

"Is it me?" I was dumbfounded. "You know a lot of people look forward to this day. It's a special day for a lot of people!"

"It's a special day for me too," she said. We were next in line at the booth. She looked at me with her cold, blue eyes and said, "Sorry, David. I can't." And bought one single ticket for herself and walked on past the hall porter and into the theater.

All throughout the movie I couldn't believe what had happened. I could perhaps begin to understand not wanting to go on a date with me, but cold hell, we might as well have sat together! I could hardly concentrate on the film—my favorite film!—because I was working endlessly to wrap my head around the backwards arithmetic that drew Callie David to her fateful decision that afternoon. Reason with this, reader: Why would a beautiful woman whom I'd just met for the third year in a row in line at a historic movie theater to buy tickets to *Casablanca* on Valentine's Day have any opposition whatever to enhance her experience by spending it with me? Add to this that her *name* was even the perfect inverse of my own. I couldn't justify her logic, but as Rick Blaine watched that plane take off under that stormy African sky, I knew that I was bound to find out.

Outside the theater I accosted the poor thing. She was strolling in a lonely fervor, walking south down Second Avenue. I spoke clearly and confidently so as to get the answer I desired.

"Ms. David," I began.

"Hi, David," she said.

"How did you enjoy the film? A bit lonely, wasn't it?"

"I didn't mind."

"You wouldn't have preferred to see it with a partner then?"

"A partner, yes. You, no."

"Ms. David, I can't stand for these head-games any longer," I cried out. I stopped her there on the corner of 10th Street, held her by her wings with great intensity and pleaded. "I could hardly enjoy the film, Callie David. For everything I see in love, I seem to see in you. I can't solve the riddle you present to me. Why, oh why, does one darling dove like yourself choose to see such a film on such a day in solitude, beckoning for a lover, but rejecting the advances of the one I know she craves?"

"I don't crave *you*," she snapped.

"For heaven's sake! What did I ever do wrong?"

"It isn't you. I...I'd really rather not talk about it!"

"I demand an answer!"

"I refuse to give one."

"Oh, Callie, don't you see how romantic this all could be?"

"Is it romance you want? I could tell you a story about romance!"

"Please, do tell!" I said

"Let me warn you," she said. "Love is not the only face of romance. Often it is tragedy that prevails. Are you sure you can stomach it?"

"I was born to stomach it."

And so began her telling of what I believe to be the greatest real-life romance I'd ever heard.

She closed her eyes and breathed deep. The pigeons scattered overhead with the flutter of a thousand winds. "Some years ago I was engaged to be married to the man of my dreams..."

Reader, I will interject here, sparing you the grisly details of what came to follow. It truly wouldn't be appropriate to relate verbatim the tale that I heard from the lips of the beloved widow on that February day. Let it be known, however, that after Callie David's discourse, I fell flat to my knees, shed some several tears at the laces of her shoes, and apologized for my forward behavior. Now, I am not one to write of carnage, butchery, or mortal tragedy, but I will provide a synopsis of her story in my own words so as not to leave you in the dark.

Callie David and her soon-to-be husband (who's name I shall keep confidential for the respect of Ms. David's privacy) took a trip to Paris five years before, on his insistence. His favorite film was *Casablanca* and he had concocted the ever-brilliant idea of marrying there in Paris and honeymooning in the city of Casablanca thereafter. Mere days before they were due to be wed, while dining on the terrace of a well-lighted place called *La Limace Volante* tucked between blissful boughs of blue buildings somewhere in the Latin Quarter just steps from the Seine (not far from where I now relate this tale to you), he was enthusiastically undertaking a plate of the world-famous-Parisian-dish *escargot* when he was suddenly struck with the inability to breathe. One of those slimy bastards had gotten stuck in his windpipe and even with all of his most valiant efforts to cough it up, he was unable to gain traction on the viscid villain. For the oil of the snail was counteracting—in a rapid downward motion—the strenuous hawking of the man attempting to move it upwards. There was relatively no movement on the article, and he was quickly running out of time. One waiter suggested letting the snail slide itself down the whole of the windpipe, allowing it to land amongst the entanglement of the lungshoots, albeit causing pain, but at least freeing the air tube. Another unsavory Frenchman rebutted this stance, saying the spices and oils used on the specimen itself would lead to instant inflammation within the lungs, causing a rapid immune response that was sure to kill the victim before suffocation would. In the midst of their argument, one patron, completely and utterly untrained in the way of manual resuscitation, rose to the occasion of salvation and began to charade a series of apparent abdominal thrusts that in some ways, at some angles, may have slightly resembled the common Heimlich Maneuver to some persons. Now at this point it should be mentioned that the fiancé of Callie David was a small man. He was a small man by weight, by stature, and revealed to me by the woman herself, even his organs were smaller than the common man's. He raised only four feet above the ground and weighed something about one hundred pounds after a good meal. His body was completely unequipped for the onslaught of physical abuse he was taking from the Good Samaritan who attempted to save his life, who in contrast, was described as a portly man. It was discovered later, unbeknownst to the gathering crowd, that during the attempted resuscitations, the obstruction was in fact expelled from the windpipe, shot so far and at such great speeds that no onlooker had even noticed it. As the Good Samaritan carried on with the needless procedure, he managed to break a number of ribs on the victim, all of which wound up puncturing his tiny lungs and playing a significant role in his untimely and tragic death by asphyxiation. Naturally, as life left his eyes, he looked toward his future bride as she howled her hysterical cries: "Please, my love, don't go. Don't leave me now! *What about us?*"

To which he allegedly responded in breathless sublimity: "*We'll always have Paris.*"

When he finally did give up the ghost, he was lying there at the foot of his true love who was maimed; distraught and inconsolable, as the two waiters argued in French over the supposed anatomy of a lung and its immune response to foreign substances such as chili oil.

After Callie had told me this towering epic of romantic ends, I had to ask her the question that had burrowed itself into the earth of my psyche all along. The same question that I'm sure you're asking yourself now, reader.

"With all due respect Ms. David, what was it that made you love so deeply a man of such small stature, such fragile frame and viscera? For you are a maiden of median height and weight, medically conventional, your temperament fair, and your physical person burns with a holy beauty that some certain fellows would wish to encounter only in the world of dreams. I can't, as a common man of superficial desires, understand your reasoning for this bewildering marital arrangement? Was he a rich man? Was it his money?"

"He had not money," she replied.

"Tell me then, poor widow, what was it about him that so harbored your girlish soul?"

She looked past me, far from me towards the bluish clouds of the coming eventide and at once, far from the reality around us, existing only in cages of memory, spoke the devilish truth that would haunt me forever: "The romance," she said softly. "He was so damn romantic."

Chapter Eight

*How I Became Sick of the Lonely Life I was Leading
and Decided to Change*

"*I loved breakfast. The most important meal of the day was breakfast. Even after eating a full steak dinner equipped with hearty sides and a glass of wine I couldn't wait to sleep, looking forward to breakfast, counting down the hours until I could wake up and feast on a plate of pancakes, eggs, bacon, potatoes, yogurt, fruit and orange juice. What made it all the better was that nobody could make breakfast like Mae.*

Each morning, we woke up within moments of one another—as two souls so entangled in an inextricable net of true love do—and rolled around in that little crib of passion of ours, devouring each other's wildest dreams, working up the hardiest and healthiest of all appetites until our hunger heaved us from the sheets and into the kitchen where we danced between the oven, the toaster, the skillet; spreading, cracking, jamming, mixing, and chopping away as the rising sun came through those thin curtains and laid the hands of light across my lover's body so firmly, so suaven, that all occasions were immediately placed on hold so that I may lead her by the pearls of her fingertips back to our disheveled bed where we would lose ourselves in love once more. There we would fall asleep so lightly as if the sleep were a spell, in each other's arms so aware of the other's movements and breaths, unwilling to let go, lest it be the final time that we touch. It wasn't until after our mid-morning sleep, that we arose a second time and finished conducting the masterpiece that was our breakfast.

After breakfast, we cleaned together—the kitchen and ourselves—and I sat down to do my writing as she went out for her walk. I waited by the door to hear her descend down the four flights of stairs of our Manhattan walk-up, then I rushed from the door to the window to watch her exit the building onto the sidewalk. I liked to watch her walk, to study her movements when she left me because it was the only time I ever got to see her alone. She moved north up Avenue A, parkside, between the backdrifts of bodies and crossed the street slantwise without the use of the crosswalk. She stopped in at Ray's, poking her head into the window only to say Good Morning, and sometimes Ray would treat her to an egg cream or fried pie of some sort. She continued walking. Her sunglasses black, her hair high on her head, her pants fitted tight as to see the astonishing muliebrity of her figure. I watched from my window so lively, smirking with joy at her ways, feeling from loin to lips, from brain to bones that she was mine mine mine mine mine mine mine, and when she disappeared down one of those thieving cross-streets I sat to write, and let it be known by God and all who hear me, with what ease and profundity I could write after just a few fair moments of watching that marvel of a maybell walk so unsuspectingly across the city. If I were sentenced to write one hundred thousand books about her love, I would begeth that judge, 'Why not make it one hundred thousand and one?'"

That's another excerpt from my book. I wish I could go on, but that's not what this book is about. This book is about that book, but it isn't that book. If by some droll mishap you are reading this book before you've read that book, let me make it known to you now reader: You've made a mistake! *This* book is the story of how I wrote that book. It is a companion piece to that book. For I know—as do my publishers—that that book will be such a captivating success that an immediate follow-up will be demanded by the literary public. Keeping to my word that I *do not* do so-called "sequels," I decided to offer a more intimate answer to the question of audience capitalization. With *this* book, I can show you just how I came to write *that* book. Now with that in mind, let's continue. In this book, I have not yet begun to write that book. I've been searching for the catalyst for that book, but have so far only encountered a great deal of misfortune and misunderstandings. However, that catalyst will come soon, patient reader. We are arriving someplace, rest assured.

***

With the coming of spring should come hope. That's an old proverb somewhere. Though, in the strangling world I was existing in, hope was specular and intangible, no more real than reflected light coming off the secret world of streetglass. Now, to complain about my position, reader, would have been to overstate my defeats. I was making good money churning out hackwork for the ads company. I lived alone in the East Village—corner of 7th and A—across the hall from my two closest friends. I had the good beginnings of a romance about a writer who falls in love with his mailwoman. But through all of these relative successes, I was failing at the thing that mattered most to me. It had been a long, lonely winter, with one lost cause following another. I failed at my attempts to find love on the street, I'd failed in the subway, I'd failed uptown and downtown. I'd failed at any given bar. I'd failed colliding with it in the park. And then I'd failed again at the cinema, massacred on St. Valentine's Day of all days.

Yes, reader, it is true. On that day, something inside of me died. Here was a woman who even shared my name, let alone my primeval understanding of the unseen, ethereal world of romance. She had shown up in shadows of my mind for three years, coming out in blips to say 'hello,' to tempt me and to cause my curious mind to curse and callous in the face of utter and embittered loneliness. With the loss of her to the greatest romance ever known in our time (God rest his little soul), one can only imagine the hole that was dug for me then! It was well deeper than six feet, and deeper still than a well. I needed only to lay my hands on the soil that sat below me to feel the molten heat of the neverearth beneath and pray one day that I myself could be so content with an eternity of forlorn rage like that which stirs inside the cores of planets for transmillenia rather than need even the slightest taste of love in my life ever again.

In the time that followed I had given up the pursuit all together. The old "stand and wait" had devolved into the miserable "sit and watch." I hardly had the heart to try, reader. I populated the parks pessimistically, unmoved, unshaken, watching one after another as the beautiful beaus crossed the bums of Tompkins Square. Southern belles come up from Savannah, Bostonian stifflips in town to take a semester at NYU, Texas girls, California queens, Midwestern dreamers, and of course the occasional unhinged Canadian. Each one of them passed me by without a fight. I went through the rest of that winter nearly unliving. I must have appeared unapproachable, for so wretched was my loneliness that even the bartenders in the houses I frequented were short with me, seemingly having no ears for my perils. I can't count the nights I spent alone in that little bar on 5th Street east of Cooper Square. Or the times I sat speechless and sordid in the bar of the Roxy Hotel, listening to the ballads go by like the rainy carlights. And each and every one of those little 7th Street bars all began to blend together, nameless and shapeless. I seemed to just drift through the shanty shrines of downtown Manhattan, from one haunt to the next as pale as wind, as if my jacket was blown through the bowels of the Bowery, personless and using the perdurable pinnacle of the Empire State as my northern star. There were even nights I was so gross and drunk, brown bag beer down my chest, asleep in a subway car that I wound up in the tearfields of Sheepshead Bay by accident—oh, how romantic, I thought in my disillusion.

It all came to a head one April afternoon, smelling of yesterday's rain, smelling of trees, so yellow and gray-blue beneath the dying bright. It was the best day of the year so far. You know the one I mean, reader. That first day of spring that feels like summer. It usually comes in early April, accompanied by a rise in temperature, an uncanny closeness of the sun, a great blueness. Birds twirl overhead, bars and restaurants open their shuttered windows and doors, an autumncrossed draft vines at your arms, pulling you to and fro each passing moment. It always happens to come on a Thursday or Friday, and the people poke their heads out of their office buildings and little apartments amused and excited by the emergence of the long hibernating creatures of their neighborhood. Even the bums are smiling.

I spent the day in Tompkins Square Park, "sitting and watching." The main concourse of the park was filled with the exaggerated affection of young couples drawing plans around picnic tapas trysts; floating whispers of lovebirds on every corner exposed and in-heat, indistinguishable from the palpable relique of last spring's phantoms, lovers running out to the greening grass of the park for little bottlettes of white wine and cheeses before uneaten. If it weren't for scenes like this that I had witnessed with my own eyes I would be inclined to think that the passions that I myself dream up are much rarer in real life than in books, but love is a very real gift, holy in character, and, on this particular day, supposedly for everybody besides myself.

I did think this, reader. I was so steeped in self-pity, so downtrodden in the weeks previous to this day, that I was absolutely sure that this display of affection was yet another cosmic joke played on my behalf—an egg of misfortune cracked atop my head. Whichever way I looked, I saw couple after couple pass me by. They held each other with such faith, such true conviction, that even the greatest heretic of love could be converted by the testament of which I was exposed to on that day. I felt awful. I shook my fist in the air, I prayed, I repented, I cried. I wanted to know why of all people, *I* was branded by the burden of romance. Why couldn't I settle for love and love *alone?*

I stood from my bench, passing the droves of lovers; hand-holding, neck-kissing, pocket-swapping heathens of this faithless and perverse generation. Oh! How long shall I be with you? How long shall I bear with you all?

I fled the park to the west, stepping violently and carelessly across the pavement towards Avenue A when suddenly, as the park met the street, a bus pulled in front of my step, the length of my nose separating my body from the beast. I stopped myself just clear of its track, watching my life flash there in the dark of its black windows. One single step would have done it. If I believed before that moment that I'd have benefited by being smothered by the likes of a city bus, I didn't think so then as I saw my young reflection in those passing windows. I thanked God for my life, for my health, and even for my misfortunes. I felt the gravity of that moment in my sinking heart. Then, as it came to a slow stop, I saw the sign from God Himself. It was a large, wide advertisement painted on the hind side of the bus: MACY'S—THE WORLD'S LARGEST STORE. I knew then just what I was meant to do. I had known it from the start. I had tried to deflect the thought since meeting her, but now, with this sign sent down from God placed there at the crossroads of my misery and my mortality, there was no question.

I crossed the street and entered my building, climbing the stairs that led to the fourth floor. I passed by my own door, coming quickly to Sam and Katie's. I knocked hard. Sam came to the door, shirtless and sleepy-eyed.

"Hey, David," he said, pulling the skin from his face for a moment.

"Taking a nap?" I asked.

"Little one."

"You should get outside. It's beautiful out."

"I was thinking about it. What's going on with you? How are you?"

"I'm fine, is Katie home?"

"I was just reading a book by this Spanish guy—"

"Hold your review, my friend. Listen, is Katie home? I need to speak with her."

Her voice came flying from the back bedroom. "I'm here, David. What do you need?"

She walked out, coming free from the concealment of a corner, emotionless and unexcited to see me.

"I have a favor to ask," I said. I stepped in, shutting the door behind me and made my way to the dinner table where Katie had just sat down.

Now reader, let this be an appropriate time for some words to be said about Katelyn Fae Cacciatore.

Chapter Nine

A Brief Chapter on the Nature of One Katelyn Fae Cacciatore

Katie Cacciatore was one of those fine people that keep the world in perfectly working order. Without people like her, we would have no such delights as the corporate call center, district attorneys, the Thanksgiving Day Parade, priority seating on airplanes, or walking tours. She was a pragmatist in every sense of the word. She was a thinker, a doer, and a believer in all things strategy, planning, figure-fueled, and most importantly—a quality we share—human. While she wasn't exactly a pessimist, calling her an optimist would be dishonest as well. She believed that all that must be accomplished can and will be accomplished most efficiently under a hierarchy of power; that is, with the guidance of an organizer to exercise complete control over an army of drones who should be willing to execute whatever orders are laid out for them, whatever the cost. It sounds a bit too German to be trusted, I know, but I can vouch for her heart; she was mostly harmless, and quite compassionate in her person-to-person relations. She had spent the last three years studying medicine at New York University, following in the footsteps of her father's family, all of whom (since their arrival to the state of New York in 1889 from Italy) had done so.

Katie, like her family, was loud, opinionated, fairly unapologetic, and handsome in the Old World sense of that word. She knew exactly what she wanted, and exactly how to get it, which made her perfect for Sam, who, God bless his precious soul, still had a hard time telling east from west, and was liable to get himself mixed up in a bank robbery someday for his inability to say 'no.'

As previously stated, Katie's father, Mark Cacciatore, was a well-off doctor with a popular practice in one of the more conservative, upper-class pockets of Long Island. Katie's mother, Amanda, was a lawyer in the same town, and so the pressure mounted on Katie to carry on the family legacy of administrative grandeur. This is unfathomable to a son of unskilled workers like myself. Never in my life have my parents even considered slipping a hint as to what profession I should pursue—they would feel as though they didn't have the right! For they themselves to spend their entire lives going from job to job to put food on the table, and then to turn around and tell me I had to make something of myself is blasphemy where I come from, but there on the East Coast, with all of these competing colleges and old money feuds between families and communities and ethnicities, a man is not truly born until he has sent his kin to the alma of his own choice, and he cannot die until he sees his successor in his shoes.

I mention these seemingly meaningless aspects of Katie's life, reader, to provide insight to the normal fellow, just how out-of-touch and high strung some of these East Coast folks can be. Undoubtedly at this point in my tale you have been baffled at Katie's lack of faith, absence of imagination, hopeless disposition, and perhaps even sharp tongue. I too was often rendered speechless at some of the downcast, schoolmarm rhetoric that spewed from Katie's mouth, but I'd learned to live with it because she often redeemed herself in unforeseen altruistic moments of tenderness, and the utmost loyalty to those she called friends. Like any good Italian, she'd never cross you as long as you didn't cross her first.

It was for these reasons, reader, that I felt that in this moment, at my all-time-low, it was appropriate to seek out Katie's counsel and ask her the fateful favor that I had been putting off for some months.

I needed Katie in my life. I needed her to look me in the eye and tell me where my marbles were. She was boring, without any imagination, completely oblivious and unconcerned about anything having to do with the so-called *romantic.* She didn't read anything but medical journals, she had no interest in auteurist cinema, she'd never seen a theatre production in her life, she was the utmost definition of a dreamless, practical, hard-headed, matter-of-fact son-of-a-gun; somebody who could build a swingset without even consulting the instructions booklet, but would never stoop to the shameful level of actually *swinging in it.*

Through the years, our two opposite ideologies resulted in some bouts of debate, desperately—though unsuccessfully—trying to frame each of our own cherished perspectives for the other to see in some new light, from some unconsidered angle. Neither of us ever shifted a nugget of a step towards the other. As said, however, our respect for each other, while on faulty ground, never ruptured, and this very respect proved to be the grounds for the decision I made that day in the park: the decision to cast away my pride, to confront myself, to brave the storms of my heart and abandon every instinct I've ever had concerning love, romance, and my own future. I had become sick with myself, reader. I knew that I had to make a change—not just for the sake of my happiness, but for the sake of my survival. Who else to ask for help in such a crisis as this than Katie Cacciatore, half-doctor, half-lawyer. And as I sat down at her table that afternoon, I had a feeling, a premonition, an *intuition,* that this decision of mine would go on to change my life forever.

Chapter Ten

How Katie Arranged a Date for Me With Her Insufferable Friend

"Why should I trust you?"

"Because I don't have another choice, Kate."

"You're that miserable?"

"I got a sign from God, what else am I supposed to do?"

"An ad on the back of a bus isn't a sign from God."

"It can be! That bus almost killed me, Kate. Then clear as day I opened my eyes to this miserable life that I'm leading, and right there in front of me when I came to that realization was that sign. Things like this aren't a coincidence."

Kate tapped her fingers on the table and looked me over skeptically. "I would have to see a dramatic change," she said.

"I need your help, Kate."

"He needs your help, Kate," Sam said. "Look at how earnest he's being."

"Look at me. I don't have enough words to convey my suffering. I'm lonely, Kate. I'm sad. I don't have anything. Anybody. I'll change. I promise I'll change. I won't care any about what she does for a living or what shoes she wears, or her name, her favorite food, nothing of the sort. I just want somebody. I'll stop writing if I have to. Or at least I'll stop reading. I'll burn all my books. I want to be a different man. I want to be cured."

"I don't believe what I'm hearing."

"Believe it now before I change my mind."

"I'm not going to help you if you're going to go in there pretending to be Romeo. Allison is an adult with a career. She exists here on planet Earth with the rest of us."

"You have my word. I'm feeling awful. Not just today, for weeks now. I think—"

"That you need to grow up?"

"Save it, Katie, I'm serious."

"Don't be so hard on him," Sam said. "It's all going to work out for you, Dave. You've got a great heart, and you're talented. Tell her about the book, she'll be impressed by the book."

"My advice is to not tell her about the book," Katie said. "Just try and figure out what *she* likes. She's interesting. She's really smart too, David. You'll like her if you don't go in there with your mind made up about what you're looking for. You need to have an open mind. She's a catch. She's responsible, she's beautiful, and she's artistic too. She paints."

"Wow, a painter," I said. I hadn't considered how romantic a profession a painter was until that moment. "A writer and a painter together! That is—"

"David!" Katie slammed one hand on the table, stunning Sam and I into silence. "She's not a painter! She *paints*. It's called a *hobby*. You're asking me for help, but you've got to hold up your end of this. I mean, I can't stand to see you this way any longer either. You're a great person, David, but if you say you're going to change, you need to change."

"Do you think I'm being crazy?" I asked. "Do you think it's even worth a try?"

"I think you're crazy, but I think it could be worth it too," Katie said. "But you've got to be normal. Besides, she already thinks you're cute."

"She does? What do you mean?"

"Well, I've seen her recently," Katie teetered off.

"And what? You've mentioned me already?"

"She brought you up. She said that day we ran into her at the deli she thought you were cute. She asked me if I'd give her your number."

"And did you?"

"No, I didn't. I told her I didn't have your number and that I didn't know you that well, okay? I couldn't risk it."

"Couldn't risk it? A woman wants my number and you don't give it to her because you *couldn't risk it*? Are you out of your mind? How long ago was this? How long have you been letting me feel like this?"

"I'm sorry."

"What else does she know?"

"I said you've got a great job writing ads, you're very funny, and a loyal and trustworthy person. That's all."

"You told her I wrote ads?" I stood from the seat and began to pace the small kitchen in a circle. "Oh, Katie. You told her I wrote ads? What in the world compelled you to do that?"

"David, *you do write ads!*"

"Hardly! I write books, Katie!"

"Never mind all this," she said. She too stood, putting her hands at her hips and threatening to disappear again around the corner. "You can't do it, David. You're incapable. You almost convinced me you'd be able to do this, but you can't."

"He can do it, Katie!" Sam protested. "David, sit down. Kate, you too. Come on."

The three of us sat together at the table in silence. A shard of sun came through the one window and cast a light on Sam who moved in his seat to avoid it, but as the speechless moments passed it followed him westward as if to give him some inspired decadence as he spoke.

"Dave," he started again, "Kate and I want the best for you. I think you could have any woman that you meet, you've just been going about it the wrong way. Remember the girl from Union Square? You were perfect that day."

"Yeah, but the name."

"Besides the name…you handled the interaction with incredible decency. I've seen other instances where you've come off a little too…"

"Abrasive," Katie added. "Your intensity can be jarring, David. You've got a great heart. It's really very precious that you love love as much as you do, but can't you just get to know somebody first? Look, I love Sam, and we got to know each other slowly. We didn't meet and take off to get married in Venice that night."

"I don't know if I'm built to 'get to know' somebody. I feel like I'll 'know' it when I see it."

"David Cale," Katie started.

"Don't talk to me like that," I said.

"Listen to her," Sam said.

"David Cale, if you are not willing to 'get to know' somebody, then why did you come here? Do you think you're going to sit down with Allison and she's going to fall to her hands and knees and reel off some monologue at your feet? Do you think she's going to quit her job and set aside her life to sit in your little studio apartment and be your muse, hanging on your every word? That's not the kind of girl she is. I don't even know if that kind of girl exists. So why don't you stop wasting your time, make me a promise, and I'll call Allison for you and ask if she'd be interested?"

I was completely disarmed. She was right, and I knew it.

"Okay," I said. "I promise I'll take things slow. Will you call her?"

"Repent," Katie said.

"Excuse me?"

"You know I'm a good Catholic. I'm not letting you off the hook until you repent. Swear off your sins and denounce your religion."

"Katie—"

"Katie nothing."

"Don't be silly, Kate," Sam said. "Just call Allison."

"Silly? I'm being silly? Silly is not going out with a girl because she doesn't know who Babe Ruth is."

"Sam, you told her about that?"

"Silly is refusing to call a girl who was perfect for you because you didn't like her name."

"Katie, that was a one in a million..." I pleaded.

"Silly is spending every day for the last six weeks sitting on that park bench watching couples walk by and being so pathetic that you won't put yourself together and find something real for once! I can see you from the window, David!"

"Katie!" Sam shouted. "He already feels bad enough."

"Repent," she whispered through her teeth. She was visibly upset. It was flattering to see how much she really cared. This is what I mean about Katie being a good person.

"Okay," I said, "I repent. I am sorry for my sins against love. I should not have gone this long treating love like a fairytale. I am the only one to blame. I will not hold women to impossible standards. I will not pretend that I am in a nineteenth century novel. I will try and find love that is respectful and responsible; fair and equal."

"Good," Katie said. "And you will treat Allison like a real person with feelings and goals of her own?"

"I will treat Allison like a person. Yes."

"Good," she said. "Wait here."

Katie wandered off back behind the corner. The sun was setting now and the room grew dark. Sam stood and turned on the light that hung above us at the table. He was uncomfortable with me, bouncing one leg and looking about his kitchen as if he'd never seen it before.

"What's with you?" I asked.

"Nothing. I'm happy for you."

"Thanks, I believe you, but what else?"

"Nothing."

"Sam."

He smiled a little bit and moved his eyes towards me. "You write ads?"

"Oh, don't listen to her!" I moaned. "She doesn't know what she's talking about."

"Do you?"

"I make a little extra money here and there. This publishing deal is really taking a lot of time."

That conniving dame must have poked through my mail and seen the envelopes from my agency.

His half smile became a full smile. "But you're still publishing the book, right?"

"Yes, of course I'm still publishing the book. There have just been some delays. I'm revising the manuscript."

From the other room I could hear Katie's voice valley around between the rush-hour traffic that bled through the half open window of the kitchen.

"I'm with him right now," she said. Words such as *interesting*, *exciting*, *compatible*, and *unique*, came through her muffled discourse. I wondered as I sat if I'd made the right choice. In that moment I couldn't quite comprehend just what I'd sworn off, just what decision I'd made. I thought I was excited, but I couldn't be sure. I thought I was relieved, like forty years of wandering the desert were long behind me, the promised land ahead, given to me under the condition that I stay true to the law handed down. I tried to feel that feeling; that explosive, restless feeling I got when I saw love cross me in the street. I tried and tried, sat there, thinking of Allison—beautiful, delightful Allison—but nothing would come. Fear began to take me, but I refused to let it. I wanted to defeat this disease of mine. I wanted to be better. I wanted to be normal.

Katie came back out to the mellow scene at the kitchen table. "She's in."

"She wants to go out?"

"Here's her number." She handed me a slip of paper. "She said she's free tomorrow night, otherwise not until next weekend."

"I can do tomorrow," I said.

"Then call her."

"I will."

I stood up and gave Katie a hug and held her by the shoulders. "Thanks, Kate."

"Don't be an ass."

***

Lying in bed, flat on my back, I could see the speckled light from the streetbulbs and passing cars, and perhaps even the moon and stars cast across my ceiling and wall like a tapestry. Some of the lights twinkled, and some of them moved, and some came suddenly and stayed and some disappeared and never returned. I watched them for a long time, thinking, chasing down a moment, some conclusion of clarity; some resemblance of myself, lost to me for what seemed like an eternity now. I couldn't believe what I had gotten myself mixed up in. I had felt the full weight of sacrifice for the first time in my life.

Of course I was excited to meet Allison. It wasn't that I regretted my decision. For God's sake, it had been months since I had even talked to a girl, let alone sat across from one all done up in makeup and nightclothes. I was doing my best to not presuppose the cosmic purpose of our meeting, but it was difficult, as even the most un- likely prospect of love ignited an instinct inside of me, no different than that of thirst or hunger. Now, I absolutely intended on keeping my promise to Katie. I would enter with an open mind, I would not impose any unrealistic notions upon poor Allison. I would turn the focus of our encounter to illuminate her instead of myself. I would take things very slowly, and under no circumstances consider it compulsory to know whether she was the love of my life after only one brief meeting. I would be a gentleman, and nothing more.

The date was scheduled for eight o'clock tomorrow, Friday, April 11th. She sounded so animated on the phone, so kindled, so bashful! How long it had been since I'd felt my nerves alight! I decided to sleep so I didn't have to wait to see her. I tried to picture her face as I closed my eyes and sank to sleep. I could hardly remember it. Blonde hair, no, almost brown. Long, shoulder length. She had two round eyes, bluish mascara. Of course she had two eyes. Faithful lips, a long chin. Long chin? Did she have a big chin? Could I be with a woman who had a big chin? Stop it. My books, look at all these books, Austen and James and Bronte and Hawthorne. Even Fitzgerald and Yeats. Shakespeare, oh, my beloved Shakespeare! *Love Sonnets* hangs first and foremost on the shelf nearest my bed, for ease of access when involved with a lover—she allows readings to punctuate even our most intimate moments. Will she? She's too tall, I think. Is she taller than me? Small ears, tucked back between that brown-black hair. A good body, I think. She's a painter, yes. I could live as a writer, and she as a painter, yes. No, it was blonde hair after all. Forget your job, my love, let us sail across an ocean together. That's right, I'll learn to sail, yes. You can be my first mate—and my last! Paint us, love. Writing is painting; no, writing is behind painting. Painting is a purer art. Did you learn from your mother? Oh, your mother always is so funny that way, isn't she? Perfect lips. Yours. Sing those lips, now, yes. My books sing too. I'm a writer now, but for now, not. Only if the books say. Katie says you're a cellar. Underneath, me too. Joy now, peace, my eyes are in such peace. Allison. Allison Adams, the best name, get me a drink! I don't. No, I can't call you that. Don't make Sam laugh. My father neither. It's his problem. I'll ask you for a drink. I'll ask you for a lot. Please don't tell me you live in Brooklyn, I can't go there, I not allowed. Only the books say. Katie says you're love. I don't want love, I promised her. Do you? Do you want me? I'll fill the space, that is what is in me; only the books say…

Chapter Eleven

How Went the Date With Katie's Insufferable Friend

It was five minutes to eight and I was seated at a table at the little French bistro that I had suggested over the phone the night before. It was on the corner of Spring and Thompson. I checked my watch, checked the window, checked my hair, and nearly asked for the check. I couldn't stand the anticipation. I thought about getting out while I still could. Waiting there alone for Allison under the looming eye of the wading chandelier, it was all nearly too much to handle. The waiter came to me, asking if I wanted to order a drink.

"No, I'll wait for her. She'll be here. The reservation is for eight."

"Okay, sir."

"It's only 7:58, she's not late."

"Of course not, sir."

"Listen, what's your name?"

"Ricardo, sir."

"Ricardo, this is our first date, so be nice, would you? Be really polite to her?"

"Sir, of course I plan to be polite. Whether it's your first date or your last, my job is to be polite."

"Our last? Why would you think it's our last?"

"I don't think it's your last, sir. I only mean to say that I don't need to be reminded to be polite. Take comfort that she will not receive better service anywhere in the entire city."

"Don't tell me that. If she has a great time I'll think it's because of you and I won't be able to take her anywhere else."

"I think she will find our service as satisfactory as any of the top restaurants in Manhattan sir, and I don't think it will be your last date, but the first of many thousands of dates that the two of you will go on until the ends of your lives. Now sir, just to confirm, you don't want a glass of water? Maybe to calm your nerves?"

"Do I look nervous? You think I need water?"

The door came open. It was her. I recognized her blonde-brown hair, indiscriminate height, and suspiciously sized chin. She had two eyes.

"Ricardo, get out of here, it's her! It's her! Come back after she sits down! Be nice!"

The waiter scurried from the scene. I stood and gave a light greeting to the fair damsel; a friendly embrace and kiss on one cheek. I pulled her chair out for her, which she greatly appreciated. Ricardo returned and asked the madam if he could take her coat. He was very nice. She was very grateful for his service.

"Any trouble getting in?" I asked.

"No, not at all. The trains were on time for once."

"I don't even bother with them," I said. "I get everywhere by greyhound."

"Oh, I didn't realize they ran regular stops in the city."

"Oh, the dogs will stop anywhere you tell them to."

She laughed. "Its nice to finally meet you like this. Katie has told me so much."

Blasted, Katie! *So much?* What does that mean? What does *"so much"* mean? Why did she have to tell her so much? Why couldn't she have told her almost nothing? Let me speak for myself. I can tell you so much about me. Katie doesn't know the first thing about me!

"Oh really?" I smiled back. "Like what? What sort of things?"

"Well, she told me you're from Missouri, which I thought was very cool. I was in Missouri once for a summer camp when I was a teenager. It was near one of the big lakes."

"The big lakes?"

"Yeah, you couldn't even see the other side. It was really majestic."

"Do you mean the Great Lakes?"

"Yes! One of the Great Lakes."

"I think you mean Michigan, not Missouri."

"That's right, it was Michigan. Sorry."

"It's a common mistake. You can't imagine how often people mix them up. Which lake was it, anyway?"

"Well, I can't remember which one of the lakes it was, but it was really amazing. I guess I haven't been to Missouri."

Off to a bad start. Doesn't know Michigan from Missouri? Can't discern the Great Lakes? Could I be with somebody who doesn't know the Great Lakes? How blessed are the Great Lakes! No, David, don't. You made a promise. She isn't a poor lover just because she doesn't know the Great Lakes.

"How interesting," I said. "Well, my town is on the northeast side of the state, near the Mississippi River. It's called Complutum. There are a lot of great summer camps around there too. Beautiful land, good clean air, and the river is really something to see."

"I'd love to see it."

"The whole Midwest is worth seeing really. Every state has its treasures."

"What counts as the Midwest?" she asked. "Is North Dakota in the Midwest? Ohio?"

"That is actually a point of fierce debate," I said. "I won't get into the whole of it now, but if you ask me, the Midwest can be divided into two smaller subregions."

"Really?"

"You have the Great Lakes, and you have the Plains. The Great Lakes region has a more independent culture of its own, while sharing some small similarities with the East Coast solely because of the existence of giant industrial cities like Cleveland, Chicago, and Detroit, that were built sort of in the same spirit as New York, Philadelphia and Baltimore. And a town like Buffalo can be very liberally included into the 'Midwest' due to its cultural proximity to, say, Milwaukee. It is a lot more similar to Milwaukee than to New York City. But don't tell someone from Buffalo that."

Oh, *what am I doing*? She doesn't want to hear all this!

"Now on the other side, places like Iowa and Indiana have much more in common with, say, Nebraska, because of their distance from the coasts and their shared conglomerate of alike ancestors—Germans. So those states tend to bond together in cultural solidarity to form the Plains region. Still, a lot of so-called 'Midwestern Values' can be found all the way from east Ohio to west Nebraska."

"Wow, I never realized that," she said. "You're very passionate about geography."

"Well, I wouldn't say that."

"You're very passionate about the Midwest then."

Ricardo greeted us very kindly and asked if we were ready to order a round of drinks. I ordered the red, she the white.

"What a lot of people don't realize," I began again, to null the impending silence, "is that so many of the coolest people ever came from the Midwest. If you think of any prototypical mid-century superstar, odds are they're from my neck of the woods."

"Really? Like who?"

"Okay, look: James Dean, Indiana."

"Wow, I would have thought California!"

"Of course, everybody does. But he's just a farm boy at heart."

"Who else?"

"F. Scott Fitzgerald. Guess where."

"Michigan?"

"No, close though. Minnesota."

"He's from way up there?"

"Way up there. Another; Dean Martin, Ohio. Wait, another; Steve McQueen, Indiana. Clark Gable, Ohio. See what I mean? You think famous stars used to be born in New York City back then? The place was just one big slum. There were just factories. The talent was grown where real life happens—in towns and on farms, and shipped around the country like corn. Eventually the cities found it cheaper just to manufacture their own rather than import them, but that didn't come till about the 60s."

"That's so fascinating."

"Raquel Welch, Chicago girl."

"Really?"

"Another; Paul Newman—"

"Ohio?"

"Bingo."

She smiled big and laughed.

"Oh, you won't believe this one. This one is a true mind-bender. Montgomery Clift, Nebraska! Can you believe that? In those days there were only like a hundred people living in Nebraska and one of them turned out to be Monty Clift!"

"Who?"

Perhaps she misheard me.

"Montgomery Clift."

"I don't know that one. What's he in?"

"What's he in?" I shouted. Ricardo and some of our fellow dinnerfolk turned to look at me. Allison was alarmed, but equally amused. "You don't know Montgomery Clift? *A Place in the Sun? The Misfits? Red River?*"

"No."

"*From Here to Eternity? I Confess?* That's Hitchcock. You know Hitchcock right?"

"Hitchcock is from the Midwest? I thought he was English."

"He *is* English! I mean he directed *I Confess.* Monty Clift stars in it. You've never seen it?"

"No, never seen it."

"You've never heard of Montgomery Clift?"

"Well, don't make me feel stupid!" She blushed.

She was right. I needed to drop it. I made a promise to Katie and myself. What did it matter that she didn't know Montgomery Clift? What did it matter? Besides, I could have the pleasure of introducing her to Monty myself, we could hold a weekly film-night, a formal education of sorts. We could watch his filmography together. I needed to settle down. It didn't matter. It didn't have to matter.

"Well, you'd really like him," I muttered. "He was in a lot of great films."

Ricardo came back with our drinks. He smiled very wide, his black hair gelled so neatly to one side, looking with eager discipleship towards my fair flower of the eve. She ordered some dish relating to a small French chicken. I ordered the duck.

We batted eyes for a moment behind our respective glasses of wine. The restaurant was filling up now, conversations floating and intercepting our words; the occasional business conversation, other lovers casting spells of devotion upon one another, a brew of languages being tossed up and around the wafting air of the little bistro, Russian, Spanish, Chinese, all as one muddle of sound, exciting and at once demanding that the two of us join in on the effort to populate the space with our timid lovesounds. In the falling yellow light that came from the lantern on the wall I could see that Allison was very beautiful. Her chin was of proportionate size. Her eyes were gray-green with brown webbing so delicately spun between the pall of the colors that surrounded the purple fountain of a pupil, so wide and throbbing in the dark of the room. Her hair was longer than I remember and very clean, almost reflecting off the light that hung near. She had straight, white, American teeth that poked out reluctantly from a set of rose-red lips. It was a wonder she was there across from me at all. I watched her closely to see if she watched me. Her eyes fell upon me every so often, retreating down towards her lap, and back up again to see if mine had stayed. She drank quickly, nervously.

"So what is it that you do exactly?" I asked.

"I'm in sales," she said.

"I don't really know what that means to tell you the truth," I said.

"I lead a sales department at Macy's. Skincare and makeup."

"So, department stores have other departments?" I asked.

"More than you'd believe," she said.

"I guess it'd never struck me that that's why they call them department stores. See, I always thought the whole place was a department, but I suppose it's a department store because it's made up of departments. Am I right?"

"You've got it."

"So, sales."

"You know all those Christmas movies where the main character is trudging through Macy's with all of those fragrance girls puffing perfume in their face?"

"Vaguely."

"Well, I am sort of involved with that. Though less perfumes, more lotions, mascaras, lipstick, things like that."

"And you lead that team?"

"Well, I lead *a* team. There are a lot of moving parts."

A lotion pusher? How did I ever get fixed up with somebody with such low aspirations as that? I swear I was trying, reader, I was trying to hold up my end of the deal so hard, but the everyday affairs of the pedestrian population are far outside my vocabulary.

"Is that what you went to school for?" I asked.

"Business administration," she said.

"Is that what that is?"

"Well—"

"Was this what you had in mind when you went through college?"

"Somewhat. It's a related field, what I'm doing now. I do enjoy it, though. And there's a lot of room to grow as well."

"Well, that's all that counts, right?"

She laughed. "And what did you go to school for?"

"I didn't," I said.

She was surprised. "I hadn't realized that. Was that a choice?"

"Well, I wanted to be sure that I had time in my early twenties to obtain an education so I decided not to go to college."

"So people who go to college are uneducated then?" she laughed.

"Well, I didn't mean that."

"Well, I'd like to see you run a sales team."

"I'd probably find a pretty good way to do it," I said. "Selling lotion to women who love lotion can't be that hard."

We both sat quietly under the pressure of the discussion. It wasn't quite an argument—nobody became angry, but there was a mutual fear festering that our fundamental view of reality may be vastly different. We smiled as we exchanged quips, treating it as an exercise of diplomacy; flirtatious negotiation.

"You're feisty," she finally said.

"I don't mean to be," I said. "I just don't like when things don't make sense."

"And I wasn't making sense?"

"Oh, just drop it. Look, here comes the food."

Ricardo came tiptoeing behind her, balancing the food like a circus star, coming down to the table with bent knees so perfectly in sync that it was as if the food was just floating there above our appetites and then set ever so gently in front of us. Ricardo looked square at the lady with full and unmatched humility. "Is there *any-thing else* I can get for you, miss?"

"I don't think so. Everything looks perfect."

"*Bon appétit*," he said.

He walked from us, disappearing far behind a curtain and into the kitchen.

"He is *so nice,*" Allison said.

My fine Ricardo, how I wish I could take you with me everywhere.

"So you're a writer?" she asked. We both moved lightly towards the food, keeping our mouths intermittently free.

"I am. I'm working on a book now."

"I've always admired writers. I could never do it, but I love to talk to them, to hear what's on their mind—their process. A friend of mine is a travel writer. Last summer she was doing a piece about Spain. I went with her for two weeks. It was the most amazing place I've ever been. Have you been?"

"I have actually, some years ago."

"I was in Barcelona. What an incredible city. We have nothing like that here, nothing on this side of the world that feels that old, that delicate. It was like stepping into the past. Not in a way that you can do here in New York or in Boston, but like being a part of a fairytale."

"I think it's a shame they made the most beautiful part of the city a shopping mall."

"What do you mean?"

"There's absolutely nothing to do in the Gothic Quarter unless you want to go into a *Sketchers.*"

"Ah, right, stores."

"It's not even about the stores, it's about the principle matter of turning eight-hundred year old buildings into sex shops and jewelry outlets and places to buy sweatpants and exercise equipment."

"Well, you've gotta stay with the times, right? Do you think they would still allow them to be dungeons and blacksmiths?"

"They wouldn't have to do that...it isn't about staying with the times, it's about the city having some self-respect instead of being a whore for American brands. It's sacrilegious to have corporations in these precious buildings. It's like the Pharisees selling doves in the temple. Those corridors in Barcelona are a temple of history, it's Holy ground that's been turned into a den of thieves. It's a shame, that's all I mean to say."

She was silent.

"I liked *La Barceloneta*," I said. "That little area by the sea."

"I didn't go out that far. We read the farther out you go from the city center the less people speak English."

"Well, I'm sure the whole city was a lot better before the *Burger King* moved in and they started speaking English."

"Oh, how can you say that, *you* speak English!" she said.

"Yeah, but I don't want the place I'm traveling to to speak English. That defeats the whole purpose of traveling. If I wanted to be around a bunch of Hispanics speaking English I'd just walk over to Avenue C."

"This date is going really well. It's important to be aware of what we disagree on," she said. She was still smiling of course, now eating faster, waving down Ricardo for another wine. He filled the glass ever so pleasantly and flashed me a wink. Thanks Ricardo. You're doing great. If only you could be the one sitting here instead of me. I was beginning to feel lifeless, uninterested. I knew I'd made the promise, but how was I supposed to keep it now, talking about how I felt about things, how I saw the world. If she wasn't able to understand me, then why should I change? Let's call a spade and spade and get this over with.

"So, where are you from?" I said, hoping I hadn't asked that question already.

"Rhode Island, originally. Have any strong opinions on Rhode Island? Anything I need to be aware of?"

"Hey now," I said. "Look, I'm sorry. I don't mean to offend you."

"You didn't offend me. I'm not hurt by your opinions, but I do think you're wrong."

"Fair. Go ahead, think that I'm wrong. Just don't be mad at me."

"I'm not mad at you."

She was mad at me.

"And you moved to New York when?" I asked.

"My dad moved us to Long Island when I was in middle school. He got a job."

"Very cool."

She finished her wine and called Ricardo once again. He filled her glass. She took a hardy swig from the glass and went back to her plate. I could see what she was trying to do. It was a sabotage. She was trying to run up the bill. She knew darn well I was going to pay for all of this, and we both knew—as well as everybody for the next ten blocks—that we would never speak again once we left this building. She was going to stick me with a goliath of a bill, tell Katie I'm a jerk, and go off and get married to some asshole who roots for the Dodgers. She thinks she's so smart because she runs the henpen at Macy's makeup station. Well you've got another thing coming, Allison from Rhode Island. You don't know who you're playing games with. And truth be told, you aren't the most rewarding date yourself. You wouldn't know the first thing about romance if it hit you square in your big chin. I can drink too. Oh, can I ever drink. I can put them back. In fact, I think I'll switch over to whiskey.

"Ricardo!" I called. "Oh, Ricardo, would you bring me your best bourbon on the rocks please?"

"You're a whiskey man?" she smiled, and sank her glass of wine, waving to Ricardo to bring the bottle once more.

"Only when I'm in the mood to talk," I said.

"You like to talk?" she asked.

"As much as you do."

"Let's talk."

Ricardo brought the drinks, took our discarded plates and begged that we use his service for something more.

"Dessert," she said. "Pie, ice cream, however it comes, whatever you have."

"As you wish," Ricardo said.

We stared at each other long and hard. Our guns were cocked, we waited for the signal.

"What else can we disagree on?" she said.

"You like baseball?" I asked.

"Boring."

"Next."

"You like movies?" she asked.

"Of course I do."

"Like what?"

"You first."

"Hard to say," she started. She sat back deep in her chair and talked slowly. "I really like thrillers, or just odd-ball stuff."

"Do you like Westerns?"

"Weird Westerns. I like when someone can totally turn a Western on its head or make a Crime movie more than just a Crime movie."

"Do you actually like Westerns and Noirs just as they are, or do you only like it when they're deconstructed?"

"I'm not sure, I haven't seen a lot of regular Westerns or Noirs. I can't watch old movies, they're a little drawn out."

"So what directors do you like?"

"I like the Coen Brothers."

"Oh, God, the Coen Brothers."

"What a miracle, you hate them."

"You don't think they're preachy? They're almost insufferable."

"What do you mean? They don't seem preachy to me."

"Well, that's just it. There's just so much loaded emotion in those films. Like they're annoyed that they have to make them. Every Coen Brothers film has the exact same tone, like they're inconvenienced that they have to teach me about nihilism or something. I can't stand things like that. I can't stand people who are only interested in deconstructing beauty instead of actually experiencing it. It's such a forced attitude."

"Well everybody's definition of beauty is different."

"Everybody's *opinion* of beauty might be different, but that doesn't mean beautiful things aren't objective."

"Speaking of preachy."

"I'm not trying to preach. Let's stick to movies."

"Okay, who's good then? If you know films so well, you and your friend Milton Cliff or whoever he is."

"Montgomery Clift."

"Come on, then. What do you like?"

"My favorite is Howard Hawks. He's consistent, crafty. He can do anything. Howard tells a great story and he can be funny when he needs to be, epic when the time calls for it. 'Three good scenes and no bad ones,' is the best advice for filmmaking I can think of."

"What did he make?"

"*Red River* for one. With Clift. *Bringing Up Baby*, with Cary Grant."

"I've actually seen that one. A little dry."

"Are you kidding me? You think *Bringing Up Baby* is dry?"

"Bo-ring," she smiled. She sipped her drink with smug delight.

"Your whole life is boring!" I shouted.

"Excuse me?"

"Not everything has to be ironic, you know. Some things can just be beautiful."

"You should hear yourself. Is this what your books are like? Is this what you write about? You're a walking-talking male gaze."

"I'm very interested in the male gaze, actually. I'm trying to bring it back, in fact, it seems to me it was the best gaze."

"What in the hell is wrong with you?" she yelled out. The whole restaurant looked on now. "Sir, would you get my coat?" she called to Ricardo.

"Good, take your coat and go," I said back. "And don't forget to finish your wine."

"I don't know what Katie sees in you. You're sick in the head."

With that, she drank the last of her white, let Ricardo adorn her with her pompous fur dinner jacket, and walked with a strange, sexy conviction towards the door. From the sidewalk through the window she made a most discourteous gesture in my general direction and fled into the darkened April of the city.

"I've never seen somebody that angry in my life," said Ricardo, astonished. "Was it something I said?"

Chapter Twelve

How My Entire Life Would Come to Change as a Direct Result of This Date With Katie's Insufferable Friend

It was a long walk back to Avenue A. I bought a pack of cigarettes for the walk. I was feeling the wine and whiskey and it felt great to breathe in the smoke with the cool evening air. The city was full, parties pouring out of bar windows, taxis up in arms trying to outsmart one another in the race downtown. I crossed Houston at West Broadway and could see a garden of bright red lights to the distant east, all piling up in a long line as far as I could see. There were gold lights too, all along Houston like slivers of candy and then the dimmer, darker lights attached to the horrible high rise buildings between Broadway and Ludlow. It's a shame they put all those ugly buildings on Ludlow, I thought.

There was music and dancing, even in the darkness of some of the poorly lit Village streets. Up through Washington Square I saw the ghosts of a thousand years between the passing bodies of the college kids taking over the park after dark, a tradition as old as time. You could smell the floating clouds of pot and halal through the masses, the round blooming of trumpets from the shaded dark, and the laughter from teenagers in the grass experimenting with heaven for all the world to see. I went up through Cooper Square and then up the Bowery. McSorley's was still there and Ray's was flooded. All was as it should be. On St. Mark's the pushers stood in front of the smokeshops chirping, gawking at the cheap leather skirts that strolled up and down. Nestled between those shops were the skinny

Asian girls brooding from the parlor windowlights, pink as camellias in the cold. Some things never change.

I thought about what had happened back at the restaurant. I thought about facing Katie and Sam and what they would say once they heard Allison's side of the story. Oh, Sam, the poor blockhead. My heart couldn't handle thinking of how he might feel upon receiving such news. I knew it wasn't his problem to bear, but what on earth does that sorry bugger really have to live for if not for me finally meeting the one and true love of my life?

As I turned onto Avenue A, I saw my building across the park. I dreaded walking up those stairs. Maybe my night wasn't yet over. Maybe I had one more date to keep. A date with an old reliable barstool at the center of the universe: the corner of St. Mark's and Avenue A. I stood on the corner, victim to the plush red rain of the light above the door that so faithfully and perpetually read *BAR*. I could hear dimly the evermoaning words of George Jones through the doors and out onto the street:

Step right up,
Come on in.

The place was lively, the tables about the room all full of glass and secrets. I found a place at the bar rail, and sat down.

"What'll it be, Dave?" asked the bartender. I never could remember his name.

"Whiskey, rocks."

He brought it back to me. It was tall, stiff. It would do the trick. I took a few sips and settled back into the stool, looking all over the crowded room. Happy people doing happy things, just as the day before in the park. Well-shaven boys in hundred dollar sweaters all crowded around two or three short-skirted girls with wide, white smiles.

If I looked out the window that was to my back I could see my apartment building—my bedroom window—across the park and through the slated treelimbs all dark like bones in the blackened sky. Seeing that window put a wrench in my gut. I trembled in anger when I saw it, thinking of the moment that I'd have to sit down alone on that unmade bed and wiggle off my shoes, drunken and sad. The moment I'd have to turn out that lamp and spin with the freefalling universe into dreamless sleep, unheld even by the darkness, forever forlorn and never loved by anybody anywhere. What I knew I'd have to face in the sight of that window was too much for me to handle. So I ordered another whiskey. And so came the words of Merle just after George:

Drink up and be somebody, I'll have another round.

I took a long slug of the whiskey and set it down.

I hadn't heard the door open, but I felt the cool air rush in from the street and twirl around the room. I turned my head to the door and that's when I first saw her. Oh, reader, if I had known just what this moment meant! I was so ignorant of it on that night! She weaved between bodies, her arms up and over the frozen silhouettes where humans once stood. She came to the bar, standing bright as Venus and perfectly perfect up and down, from the peculiar suggestions of her tidal smile—as far erotic as it was familiar—to the grace of her body, well-loved and unhidden in the scheme of herself. She exuded all great things from the many hundreds of books I had read. She exuded *words*, reader, the only woman I'd ever seen who looked like *words!* Her perfection was impossible, it was as if I'd dreamed her! It was like she had come from one of the books themselves. In fact, she had all the impossible and chimerical attributes of beauty that great poets assign to their ladies: that her hair was gold, her forehead the Elysian fields, her eyebrows rainbows, her eyes suns, her cheeks roses, her lips corals, pearls her teeth, alabaster her neck, marble her bosom, ivory her hands, and her complexion snow, and those parts that modesty had veiled from human sight were such—I think and trust—that discretion could praise them, but make no comparison.

I was in love just then, in the morrow of moments that it took her to walk from the door to the bar.

"A beer please," she said. I watched. "This one here," pointing to one of the drafthandles. She stood with her faultless elbows on the bar, waiting for something. She looked about, her chin up, her smile not so much a reaction as it was a reverence for what was occurring around her. She shed a coat revealing a sea-colored turtleneck. Her sinless face so young looking, though so ancient, so human a face, the face of love itself, shining behind a pair of eyeglasses through which she thought.

She took a sip of the beer and tried to settle into her standing room at the bar, but couldn't keep still for more than a few moments. She draped her coat over each of her arms, back and forth, and looked sometimes at the door, sometimes behind her at the patrons so happy and foolishly drunk behind her. In her gazing, reader, I believe she even noticed me for a snippet of a second. Me! Helplessly ogling, working as my trusty machine works to try and understand just what it was that I saw in front of me. I cannot overstate my claim, reader, *it was as if I dreamed her.*

I knew then that if I hoped to live another day I needed to say something. The thought of how unbearably cruel, how helplessly harrowing those aforementioned moments in the bedroom would be *now;* now that I'd seen the future of my soul flash before me, there was no alternative but to tell her then how madly and how deeply I'd fallen. The Lord as my witness, if it were all true—the stories, the proverbs, the romances—then she would take me in her arms there and we'd begin a journey like a newly constructed ship set out onto the Mediterranean headed for the straits, knowing that what lies ahead is a vast adventure of unknowing.

I finished my drink, I stepped up out of my seat, and immediately sat right back down. A man had approached her from behind.

"Sarah, sorry I'm late," he said. She smiled, they embraced, he ordered a drink and they walked together through the crowd to one of the newly opened tables in the center of the room. There they sat across from one another speaking excitedly and tenderly. Yes, I'll say it was so, reader, it was her date. And yes, I sat there and drank all night and watched them. I watched them, cursing God for not making me him. She was loving him, everything he said; every wave of his hand made her laugh. Oh! What a laugh she had, like morningbirds sewing ribbons of song through perfect air. He must have been funny because she laughed, and laughed, and laughed. As they drank more, they touched. He assumed a position closer to her, getting comfortable, getting cocky, his confident aura moving her to do things that such women don't usually do on a date as early as this. Oh, yes, reader, let it be known that it was surely an early date. The second, I presumed. They were familiar, but had yet to have been intimate. Not even a kiss was laid in my presence, though I presume by the looks of their mutual jubilation that many such kisses resounded later in the night, long after I'd left them. Why did you have to do it, Sarah? Oh, Sarah! My sweet Sarah, what a name as that! The perfect name, really; strong though porous, musical and pleasant to the ear. Unpretentious and yet stable and old as time; the first true daughter of the Lord was called Sarah! Why, all women of virtue have inside of them some veiled Sarah, waiting to be shown to the world, but so specifically female is the unconscious form of *Sarah;* Sarah the mother, Sarah the keeper, Sarah the partner, for we all know that nothing accomplished by Abraham was accomplished alone, no, he first prayed to the Lord, and then with what little power he had left he gave to Sarah—prayer offerings and worship, thanks and blessings. She has ruled our hearts and minds since her death. Now it was I who had her, the very Sarah written into the lines of my life by the same God who gave unto Abraham that barren woman who bore children that so blessed him! And suddenly, as soon as she had come, she was taken from me? Swept up by a man unknown? Who was this man, the devil himself? I could not take the curses any longer. I was no Abraham that night, reader, surely I was called Job in the bleachers of heaven.

I prayed in that bar as I watched the two of them touch. I prayed that I be given something. I prayed it all in vain. I prayed out of jealousy, rage, cowardice. I prayed so that I would be blessed out of my desire for riches, not my poverty. And I prayed and I watched them, reader, and I watched them and I drank. And as the young man approached the bar in the late hours of the night to reckon their bill, I was only getting started. For I saw them out the door, sure to watch every precious step she took behind him, laughing, moving in divine vision, an enchantress of our times, gone now, onto the black sidewalk of Avenue A forever. Where they would go next, I did not want to know. I only wanted to sit in that bar and drink. And I drank, and I drank, and I drank.

Chapter Thirteen

On the Aftermath of the Horrific Date With Allison and Some Other Curious Happenings That Followed

It wasn't any later than a mere few hours after I watched Sarah leave with that pondtoad of a date that Katie woke me up from a drunken half-sleep at seven in the morning by pounding on my door, having spoken to Allison late into the night. I was blinded by the dawn bleeding in through the open curtains and assembled what I believed were clothes to meet her at the door. She was already dressed for the day when I answered the door, allowing me no grace whatsoever in my hard-luck state.

"You told her she was boring?" Katie yelled. She punched me with her small fists in the center of my chest. "You called her boring and said she should leave?"

"No," I began, "no, no, no, no, that isn't what happened."

"I don't believe you."

"I said the things that she liked were boring."

"You said the things that she liked were boring? What is wrong with you?"

"Or maybe I said her life is boring. And she left all by herself. I didn't tell her to go. I simply affirmed her going. I didn't tell her to leave. And I certainly didn't say the words 'You are boring.'"

"You didn't tell her to stay either!"

"She was being awful, Katie!"

"That's very funny, because she says that *you were being awful.* She told me that you were doing things on purpose to bother her. Do you know that there is something seriously wrong with you? I go out of my way to fix you up with a good friend of mine—Allison *is my friend, David*—I had to apologize to her! Do you know how embarrassing that is? I'm going to have to apologize again. You made a promise to me! You're sick! You made a promise to me!" There were tears in her voice, but she tried to not let it show. "I don't know what's wrong with you but you need to see a doctor or somebody, David. Sam agrees."

"Sam said that?"

"Yes."

"Sam said I need to see a doctor?"

"I asked him if he thought you needed to see a doctor and he said yes."

"But he didn't say the words 'David needs to see a doctor?'"

"That's not the point, David. You really hurt me."

"Sam does not think I need to go to a doctor. I'm sure he doesn't. I tell him everything, he knows how hard this is."

"How hard what is? Being a certifiable basketcase?"

"Being like this. He knows how hard it is for me. I can't just fall in love with anyone, Katie, I'm not like you two."

"Excuse me?" She punched me again. "You better stop talking. What is wrong with you? It smells like booze in here. You smell. Did you get drunk after the date? How classy of you, David. Just like a real writer, you went and got bombed because you couldn't get the girl. Montgomery Clift? Who the hell knows who Montgomery Clift is anymore? He's been dead longer than my dad has been alive."

"You do. You know who he is. I know who he is. Sam knows. A lot of people know. Go to Union Square right now and start asking people who Montgomery Clift is, I guarantee—"

"Don't ask me for anything ever again. I'm done with you. And don't be surprised if Sam is done with you too." She turned and started to march down the stairs between my front door and hers.

"Sam isn't done with me!" I yelled down the stairwell. She disappeared. The patter of her steps were two flights down. "Sam loves me, unlike you! You don't love me! Sam won't turn his back on me, he knows how hard it is. You have no sympathy, Kate—none!"

And from there I heard the door of the building slam, and I didn't see Katie for nearly six weeks. When I finally did see her, she was different. She was calm, amicable, though unforgiving. She told me that she would be polite to me, but unwilling to befriend me in any way. We were to function merely as neighbors; half-crooked smiles while passing in the hall, occasionally asking to borrow some eggs or butter, but there were no more favors, no more dinners, no more drinks, no more laughter, no more dates. No more Katie.

I tried to see Sam as much as I could but Katie would hardly permit it. He tried to please both of us—bless his sorry heart—by only seeing me when he knew Katie was occupied. When Katie was out with friends, Sam and I played pool like old times. When Katie was away at school or work, Sam and I sat in the park. We still had our friendship, and damnit if Sam wasn't the best friend I'd ever had in those months. He encouraged me, listened to me, and attempted to ease my mind in regards to Sarah, which proved to be an impossible task as I shall relate now.

Even in my estrangement from Katie I had ample reason to be happy, for I had seen the unfiltered face of love and I was sure I was meant to see it again. No matter how hard I tried I couldn't shake off what I had experienced that night in that little corner bar, beholding that piece of perfection that called herself Sarah. I spent night after night at that same barstool waiting on her to come blowing in with the wind again. She never came. By June I became even more desperate, so I put out a subway ad to assist me in my search for her. I had made enough connections through my agency to get a good rate on some monthly ad space, and this seemed like the only real measure I could take to solve this urgent problem of mine.

Yes, reader. I wasn't giving up this time. Perhaps Katie was right, perhaps I was crazy. Maybe I needed to see a doctor. I was happy to concede that it was my fault alone in ruining the date with Allison and virtually any other date I had been on in the last three years of my life, but this, reader, this was different. Sarah was like nothing I'd ever come across before. It wasn't just love, it was rebirth. It was like dancing with a dream. It was that chance that each person gets only once in a lifetime to be truly, everlastingly happy. Sarah was my answer, she was exactly what I had craved since my first taste of love as an adolescent. And I knew in my heart, she would be my last. So even while depressed, exhausted, and apathetic, I pressed on. I would find this Sarah, and I would love her.

My aforementioned advertisement read as such:

Sarah, so sweet on St. Mark's and A,
I saw you that night, but he took you away.
It is me that you want, you must trust me on this
I can show you true love, made real with a kiss.
Yours truly, David

Included at the end was my phone number.

I got a call almost immediately, the day the ad was placed if I remember correctly. Her voice was soft as feathers across the phone.

"David?"

"Yes?"

"This is Sarah. I saw your ad."

"You're kidding."

"I can't believe I saw it. I've been thinking of you for weeks."

"It's really you?"

"From the bar on St. Mark's and A, right?"

"Mhm."

"Can we meet?"

Reader, if you could only have seen how quickly I melted at these words. For once in my sorry life, fortune was willing to swing in my direction. After years of hardship and wretched misunderstandings, the woman I was meant to love was finally here, seeking me with the same grappling intensity that I had sought her with for so long.

"Of course we can," I said. "You're sure I'm the one you're looking for? I saw you on the corner of A and St. Mark's in early April. It was a Friday night. You were with a guy, but I'm sure our eyes met for just a second and I loved you instantly."

"I swear it's me," she said. "You're the one I'm looking for. I saw you, and I wished that I was going to meet you that night instead of that horrible date I went on."

"You mean you didn't like that guy?"

"I left him on the doorstep. I couldn't stand another moment with him after I saw you. I can't believe I saw your ad."

"Oh, Sarah, this is marvelous. You have no idea how great this makes me feel. When can we meet?"

"Tonight?"

"Tonight! Sure, of course! Tonight!"

"Same place, eight o'clock?"

"I'll see you there."

"Don't be late."

At 7:55 I was sat at that same barstool waiting. I watched the door. I was fully prepared for our meeting. Earlier that day I had cut my hair, cleaned my clothes, gone to the dentist, shaved my face, bought a new watch, and memorized several verses of poetry by heart. There was no chance of her getting by me this time. I waited and waited, the bartender refilling my glass of seltzer instinctively.

By eight-thirty I had grown nervous, by nine outright suspicious, and by nine-thirty I'd given up. Unless she suffered some cosmically impossible ill-timed accident on the way to the bar, it was all a hoax. Somebody got me good. And thus began the stream of prank, crank, and wank callers that so consumed my phone line over the next few weeks. One day it was the deep, porous voice of an overweight man,

"Hello my sweet David, this is Sarah," and the next day the sensual velvety tones of some cold-hearted bimbo with nothing better to do, "Looking for a good time, Daveyboy?"

Only once over the course of three months did the caller on the other side expose herself in complete humility and transparency.

"I'm sorry to disturb you," she said over the line.

"Look, I'm not in the mood for games. I'm working on getting this ad taken down and—"

"It's not a game," she said. "My name is Amelia and I saw your poem on the subway wall. I know I'm not Sarah, but I thought maybe we could..."

"We could what?"

"I don't know. Get together. I really loved the poem. It's really truly romantic."

We agreed to meet that night, unenthusiastically, and solely because the name Amelia was so amorously enchanting.

At the St. Mark's bar at nine o'clock, she came in. She wore a leather pilot's cap, flying goggles, a bomber jacket and thick leather gloves. Her hair was cut short and she walked with a sort of limp. You couldn't miss her if you were blind.

"I always wanted to be a pilot, but I wound up a stewardess," I recall her saying. "So now when I'm not working, I live out my greatest dream."

"To take down the Red Baron once and for all?" I asked.

"You're very funny," she said, batting her eyes. She had a long distant stare, like she'd seen unspeakable evil done by the hands of mortal men. She was at once very present with me and completely nonexistent. She didn't drink—only lemonade—while I was sucking down whiskeys faster than I could order them to try and make sense of whatever world it was I had stepped into. Ironically, reader, I don't think that this was a prank at all, I think this woman was totally serious and wholly convinced she was Amelia Earhart, which is not only a testament to New York City, but a testament to what sort of insanity I had gotten myself mixed up in by putting my name and phone number on the subway wall. After this instance I decided it was necessary to remove my ad.

***

An uneventful fall would pass us by and I came to understand the possibility that I would never see Sarah again. I had not *accepted* that possibility just yet, but I did understand that it existed. I had thought for sure that the winds of fate would blow her my way, that the passion that I felt was too divine to be of human origin. I thought that I'd really struck something special this time, but as the days passed and I became lonelier and lonelier, I worked to move my attention further from my obsession with love and towards my manuscript about the mailman who steals the mail of the woman he loves. It wasn't coming along very well at all.

Suddenly without warning it was winter again, and so came the time for my Valentine's Day date with myself, and by proxy, Callie David. I was hoping that in the days leading up to February 14th I would again see my beloved Sarah, finding her newly available and asking her to see *Casablanca* with me, not only to finally celebrate that holiday with the company of another, but also to selfishly boast in the general direction of Callie David, proving in the span of one year that I too am a great romantic in the vein of Byron, Yeats, Emerson, and Ms. David's late fiancée whom I did in fact pay tribute to on the morning of that Valentinus holiday.

Alas, I wound up alone at the theater again, catching but a faint glimpse of Callie David on the way in, and sitting just some rows behind her during the premier. She laughed, she cried, she clapped, and she looked as sorrowful and as precious as ever under those dim theater lights. After the picture, I caught up to her in the lobby to say hello and give my regards.

"Happy Valentine's Day, Callie," I offered.

"Thanks David. That's really sweet of you."

"It is really admirable that you can keep this tradition up. I know it must be painful."

"It is, but it's what he would have wanted. How are you? How was your year?"

"Me?"

Reader, I hadn't considered *how I was* in some time. There, standing before Callie David, I was forced to consider *how I was* and at once, how to describe it. I quickly concluded I wasn't good and didn't want to talk about it, so I lied. "I'm fantastic, Callie. I'm in love, in fact."

"Oh, how wonderful! I'm so glad to hear that."

It was that ancient case of man lying for no other reason than to hear himself speak. A miserable condition.

"Yes, she's everything I've always wanted. My twin soul, my mirrored image, the Alkaid to my Mizar; together we are a constellation."

"I knew you would find somebody, David. It was only a matter of time. How I wish I could find it all over again. Just to feel that rush of blood one more time. But I'm so afraid to try. Losing it once was all too painful the first time."

"Well, sometimes it strikes us but once, I suppose."

"And I suppose you're right. So what's her name?"

"Who?"

"Your lover. What's her name?"

"Oh, right. It's Sarah."

"You can't go wrong with Sarah. It's eternally romantic."

"That's what I always tell her."

"And if you don't mind my asking, where is she?"

"Who?"

"Sarah."

"Where?"

"Well, yes. It is Valentine's Day, and you're at *Casablanca* alone. Where is she? I'd have thought you'd have brought her."

"Brought her?"

"Well, why not?"

"Why not!" I laughed. "Why not bring her! I mean, it is Valentine's Day."

"That is exactly what I've just said. Where is she?"

I hadn't a clue what to say next.

"Working," I choked out.

"Well, the film is showing all day, you know. They show it all weekend in fact. Why wouldn't you come together tonight or tomorrow instead of coming alone like you always do?"

Callie David was frustrating me now. I raised my voice and spoke sternly at her. "We *are* coming together tonight, Callie. We're going to catch the nine o'clock showing. I came alone today because it's what I've always done. That's called tradition. You know how far a romantic will go to keep tradition, don't you? I mean look at you. What a sheer sucker you are for tradition yourself. I'd rather keep it and appear as a fool than to break from its precious bounds. After all, 'Tradition is a guide, not a jailer.' That's Maugham."

"Oh, David, you're so romantic! Your Sarah is a very lucky girl, and I wish the two of you the best."

With that, we parted, and I watched her go, long down that silver corridor of East 12th Street against the brick of the brownstones. As I watched her I wondered if Callie David was the one all along. There was something peculiar about that girl, I thought. Something I couldn't put my finger on that I had felt from the start. No matter how many times she walked away from me, I always knew it wouldn't be the last.

Chapter Fourteen

On a Humorous Occurrence Regarding a Party I Attended, and the Jarring Conversation Had Between Sam and I on That Very Same Night

One night that April, Sam and I were attending a party on the 43rd floor of a Midtown apartment building overlooking the city. We were guests of guests of guests of some Mexican millionaire who owned the place. It was an awful looking place, all white and silver, windowish and devoid of soul or craftsmanship. We weaved between the dark bodies, lit only by small strategically placed lights, deepcolored like whalebelly and pointed upwards so only the mists of the lights rained down on the room leaving faces as indistinguishable as names. There were plenty of beautiful girls there, some of which I would have normally approached had it not been for one peculiarity in the party format. Audaciously, the master of the house—whoever that might have been—implemented a "no shoes policy" within the apartment. Muse with me for a moment, reader: The nerve you've got to have to invite a good lot of strangers over to your house and tell them to walk around *in their socks*! People were dressed to the gills for this thing! Blazers, vests, dresses, tights, makeup, and...*socks*? Reader, have you ever tried to charm a woman you have never met before *in your socks*? It is next to impossible. So there I was, wandering about this dark room striking up unbalanced conversations with beautiful women with absolutely no ground support. My entire posture was affected by my lack of shoes. I had no authority, no fortitude. I felt like a toddler going around the room asking for candy.

After some indiscernible period of time I wound up sitting on an ottoman with a girl whose name I think was Margo. She was from Arizona, in for school at one of those artsy colleges that I can never remember the name of. We were shouting over the bass of the god-awful music.

"So it's not that I was criticizing her for not knowing Montgomery Clift," I went on. "I was just so surprised."

"Of course," said my unlucky lassie. "I think she overreacted."

"Thank you. And quite frankly so did my friend Katie. She won't even talk to me because she was the one who set me up on the date."

"Sounds like a big misunderstanding."

"Welcome to my world."

"I'm sorry it didn't work out with her," she said.

"That doesn't bother me at all," I said. "The first thing wrong with this whole situation is that there are people in this world that don't know who Montgomery Clift is!"

"Absolutely," she said. "I remember the first time I saw *I Confess*, one of my moms took me to the theater. They were doing a Hitchcock marathon one October. It was so amazing, we watched like five films that weekend. This other one we saw, I can't remember the name of, but it had this scene—"

"I'm sorry," I said hesitantly. "I don't mean to interrupt, but did you say 'one of my moms?'"

"Yes," she said, laughing.

"You mean your step-mom or something?"

"No," she said, "I have two moms."

"A medical miracle," I said.

"Excuse me?"

"It was a joke."

"You should work on your material."

"I'm sorry, I don't mean to be insensitive. I've just never met a person who—well, you know."

"Was raised by lesbians?"

"Well, if you choose to put it that way."

"It really isn't that strange. Anyway, this other film that we saw, I remember a particular moment—"

"Did you have to come out to them as straight?"

"What?"

"When you were a teenager, did you sit them down and say, 'Moms, I have to talk to you about something—'"

"What in the hell is wrong with you?"

"Why do people keep asking me that?"

"Maybe you should take the hint."

"You know," I said, "it's actually pretty surprising—if not impressive—that you're *not* a lesbian. Think about it—"

And with that she smacked me across the face and walked into the ramble of drunks and dorks that filled such an atrocious apartment party as that. I downed my drink, weaved through the crowd, plucked Sam by his shirt collar, and made towards the shoe rack. I made out with a great pair of slick black Louboutins, while Sam—drunken and cursed by his own humility—searched endlessly for his matching sneakers. We made our way into the elevator and then out onto the street.

"You're kidding," Sam said. He was laughing hard. We were walking down Broadway, stumbling and slurring our way to the pizza shop. "You told her it was surprising that she wasn't a lesbian?"

"Quite frankly it was a heinous folly," I admitted.

"He blows it again."

"Oh, as if I was going to pursue something with her anyway. I didn't blow anything. I'm bound to Sarah, my friend. No woman who comes along could ever take her place in my heart, in my dreams, in my..."

"In your what?"

"I don't know. I'm blank."

Sam lit a cigarette, walking as a newborn would through the northbound crowd of Broadway's Saturday night. He collided in a baffling display of impudence with every other person he crossed. One shoelace untied, coughing and saying something unworthy of being said to the unlistening night.

"What are you going on about?" I said.

"I'm drunk as a fiddler's bitch," he exclaimed.

"Thanks for telling us all your great secret."

"I must'a had ten drinks walking around that place in circles waiting for you to say something stupid and get us kicked out."

"I'm sorry I couldn't have done it sooner."

"What a laborin that place was. Shoot, I never did find the bathroom in there. I really need to go. Do you think the pizza place will have one?"

"A laborin?"

"No, a pisser."

"No, I mean, what the hell is a laborin?"

"Like a maze."

"What? A labyrinth, you mean?"

"Do you think the pizza place will let me piss?"

"I don't think the pizza place will let you eat. Come on, let's just get on the train and go home."

"I gotta eat, Dave. I need something."

"Why do I feel like we have this conversation once a week?"

"Dave—"

"Let's get on the train and we'll get something downtown."

"I can't get on the train right now, can I get us a cab?"

"Sure," I said. "Get us a cab."

So there we were, back on Avenue A, outside the pizza place between St. Mark's and 9th, well fed, well pissed, and starving for another drink. Sam dreaded the thought of being back in the apartment with Katie; he knew that she knew he'd spent the evening with me. And I— having nothing better to do than to prompt Sam for his thoughts on my hopelessness— suggested we have a nightcap at that old bar, on St. Mark's and A. We were sitting at the bar rail, staring deep into the two glasses of beer bubbling in front of us.

"She absolutely hates me doesn't she, Sam?"

"She doesn't hate you. She just needs a break from you."

We were both resting our heads on one arm. Sam's one open eye wandered about the little bar to stay balanced. I slammed my hand on the bar.

"Don't give me that, Sam, she hates me! I know she does. I blew it. It's been a year and I've barely even seen her. She avoids me. And it doesn't feel right to me. Does it feel right to you?"

"No. It doesn't feel right."

"Let's fix it."

"She doesn't hate you though, Dave. She asks about you."

"She asks about me?"

"Sure, all the time. She asks if I've seen you, how you are, if you're seeing anybody."

"If I'm seeing anybody?"

"She's curious. Believe it or not, she wants to see you happy. So do I."

"I'm going to talk to her," I decided. "Tomorrow, I'm coming over and I'm going to talk to her."

"You can't just come over and act like nothin' happened. You hafta apologize."

"I didn't do anything!" I shouted. "Her floozie of a friend is the one who started it."

"I don't care if you did anything or not, you still hafta apologize, that's how it works. She wasn't there, and you really embarrassed her. Just say you're sorry. It's so long ago anyway, just do it."

"Won't matter anyway, she hates me. She's always hated me, in fact. I can feel it."

"Oh shut up, woe is you, isn't it." You knew Sam was drunk when he started giving it back to me.

"Yes, woe is me, boo-hoo, me," I said.

"You know she's always loved you, Dave. We're a team, the three of us. We always have been. Who did she call when something in the apartment was broken? God knows it wasn't me."

"Me, I guess."

"Who's her favorite person to go to ballgames with?"

I looked on.

"And when the three of us were walking down the street together, didn't you notice she always walked next to you? She loved your conversation, she loved your opinions on things."

"Oh, that's not true."

"Yes, it is. If the three of us were walking down the street together she always left me in the dust to talk to you."

"So what—"

"And who did she always make a Christmas card for even though we lived across the hall?"

"Me, but—"

"You just have to apologize and we'll clear all this up. We'll go back to how things used to be."

"She's not going to be able to stand me like this, Sam. I'm too pitiful now."

"Like what?"

"Stuck on Sarah like this. If she couldn't handle me before I fell in love, how is she going to take me now?"

Sam took a long slug of beer. He set the empty glass down on the bar with force and it made a sort of unsatisfactory dull sound. The bartender came and set two more beers before us. "You've gotta snap out of this, David," Sam said.

"You could never know what it's like to love this woman. I'm in bondage. I'm a slave to her. To a ghost that haunts this bar."

"You're talking crazy! You don't even know her! Chances are you never will."

"Take it back," I said.

"Tell me the honest truth. Do you really think you're going to see this woman again?"

"I do. I really do. You don't know it, Sam, but I put up ads in the subway for her."

"I've seen them."

"You have?"

"I didn't want to bring it up. It's pathetic, man."

"I'm not crazy. I took them down. But I know I'll see her. I can feel it this time, it's destiny. Do you remember that big fat guy I saw on Jersey Transit that one day a few years ago? Coming into the city from Secaucus?"

"Yes, and you both got off at Port Authority at noon and saw each other again that night on the Upper West Side."

"Not noon, Sam, but ten in the morning. We saw each other at ten. I went home. Presumably he went home too. I showered, wrote, read, worked, napped, ate, and then at nine that night found myself on the Upper West Side and walked right by him on Columbus Avenue."

"So what, that happens—"

"How about the time I sat across from the same girl on the train two days in a row? What are the odds of that?"

"Not as bleak as you'd think!" Sam shouted. "New York is a small town."

"*Exactly*," I reasoned, "so why can't I run into Sarah again? Tell me that. Here, or on the train, or anywhere. If I could just have one word with her."

A silence fell between us. We both stared forward, speechless.

"You really think it's going to happen don't you?" he asked me.

"Sam, everything, or almost everything that happens to me exceeds the ordinary limits of what happens to other people. It has been this way since the day I was born, and I presume it will be this way until the day I die. I have a feeling about this. It is all too romantic to give up on."

"Alright, Davey," he said. He took another big slug, laughing into his beer. "The worst that could happen is you make a bigger fool out of yourself than you already have."

"Exactly, buddy. Exactly."

We finished our beers and I waved over for the bartender to ring us up. He brought the bill and set it in front of me. "Last round is on me fellas," he said.

"Thanks, Kenny," Sam said.

"You're a gentleman, Kenny," I said.

"She didn't show tonight either, huh, Dave?" he said.

"No. You haven't seen her, have you?"

"Haven't seen her."

Sam and I threw a couple of fivers on the billbook and took our jackets from the hooks and fell out the door onto the cold April street. We walked south down Avenue A, the glow of our bedroom windows in sight through the coming fog.

"So you think I should talk to Kate?" I asked.

"You have to," Sam said. He stopped walking and looked at me deep and soberly. "Listen, Dave. I gotta tell you something."

"Hit me," I said.

"We haven't told you yet because, well, Katie feels bad telling you without making things better. But, we're moving. Next month, we're out."

"You're moving out of the building?"

"We have to. Katie's pregnant."

"What?"

"She's graduating this year and she's going to get a job at Lennox. Her dad is going to get her in. We found a place on the West Side, we're moving in on the first."

"On the first? In three weeks?"

"Yes."

"And you're just telling me?"

"Dave, it's been hard lately, we've been wanting—"

"You're moving to the Village?"

"Yes."

"That's a coldcut betrayal, Sam! You're Judas, you're Claudius, you're Arnold!"

"Dave, we have to. We need a bigger place."

"But the *West Side?* You can't go play on that team, Sam. We play for this team! We have Tompkins and Avenue B. We have Mona's! What will happen to Mona's if we aren't there paying their electricity bill? We have Ray's and Veselka. The West Side?"

"It's going to be a good thing. You can help us move. It would really mean a lot to Katie. Come over on the first, give us a hand, talk to Kate, make things better with her. We need the help, and she wants you to be in her life again. You're going to be the uncle to our baby, Dave. She wants you to be."

We approached 7th Street and looked up at the building to be sure the window wasn't open. We stood outside the door, talking low, being sure to finish all that must be said before stepping into the booming concrete stairwell.

"The first?"

"May 1st."

"Alright," I whispered. "I'll help you out. And I'll talk to Kate."

"It'll be good for us. Besides, you'll like the place. It's a beautiful place, right on Jackson Square. West 13th Street."

"Right by the hospital," I admitted.

"Right by the hospital."

"I guess it was going to have to be one of us," I said laughing. I put my hand on Sam's shoulder and propped the door open with my foot. "I'm glad I'm not the one who's going down as the traitor."

We walked up the stairs to the fourth floor and saw each other off, whispering a drunken goodnight to one other across the hallway. As I shimmied my door open, I turned once again to Sam and signaled with my hand for his attention.

"Sam," I said.

"Shh. What?"

"Congratulations," I said. "On the baby."

"Goodnight, David."

Chapter Fifteen

*Of What Happened on May 1st While Helping Sam
and Katie Move Into Their New Apartment, Being
Perhaps the Most Unbelievable Occurrence Thus Far
in This Already Curious Tale*

I let myself into Sam and Katie's place about nine o'clock the morning of May 1st, stepping so lightly, as balanced as an albatross on a buoy through the thin crevices between the boxpiles. They were stacked high, taped and labeled with mundane epitaphs like "Silverware," "Closet Stuff," and "Winter Clothes." The morning slashed in through the window, half-eclipsed by the door frame—its own ration of light blocked by some boxes.

How strange it always is to see a dying home. One's life turned upside down, floating scraps of memories strewn all across the space intertwined with other memories where they never should be; decorative ceramics from some forgettable vacation mingling with the most personal of love-letters; straggling cleaning utensils hurriedly rushed into boxes containing lingerie and makeup. The space is unrecognizable, already a memory, long forgotten as all eyes look forward.

I could hear a frantic busyness around the corner in the master bedroom. Not the deliberate, organized business of a woman, but the frustrated half-assedness of a man, working to finish something quickly before the woman returns and asks him why he's doing it that way.

"Sam," I called out.

"In here," he called back. "Come help me out for a second." He was disassembling a bedframe. "Come down here and hold this."

He tilted one end of a large piece of wood in my direction. I held it steady and he pulled off a brass bracket of some sort and went at it with a drill for a few moments. We turned what was left of the frame on its side without speaking, and repeated the process on its opposite end, before laying all the long assemblies flush against each other, tucked against the headboard and other miscellaneous ends.

"Where's Kate?" I asked.

Sam wiped his head of sweat. "Downstairs with the truck. There's already some boxes down there, she's 'distributing the space.'"

"Well let's start bringing some of this stuff down there, there's a lot of stuff here."

"Not yet. Just let her finish what she's doing. It'll mess with her rhythm."

"She really is the *ducessa* around here, isn't she?"

"Judge and jury."

We worked a little more, brushing some of the newly discovered minutia that leaked from closets and loose drawers into bags and boxes. After some time we moved what remained in the bedroom out into the main space where Katie finally met us, crawling up the stairs, sweating and breathless. She wore her hair up high, a gray sleepshirt under tight overalls which held tape, markers, and a pack of stickers in the joey pocket.

"Hi," she said to me.

"Hey, Kate."

"Grab this box here, or as many as you can carry and follow me down. I'll show you how I have the space distributed."

Down at the truck we worked together—the three of us—stacking each and every box by length and by height. Katie ordered us around, unwilling to look me in the eyes, not because she was angry with me, but because now was not the time for repentance and forgiveness. She needed my help, and I supposed the best way I could show that I cared was to just do what she said.

We had everything loaded by noon and Sam drove us across town to the West Side. As we crossed Broadway I could feel the sights and sounds were different. I thought about how much time I would have to spend now on this side of town, trying to convince Sam to make his way back to the old trusty East Side. The West Side was academic, it was procured, it was gated, it was sterile. How was I supposed to find any life out there in those parts, I thought. I couldn't believe they'd done it. They'd really gone and ruined a perfect thing for me.

We pulled up to the building, a red brownstone three stories high, the kernelpoint of a triplicate of identical red homes on the northern corner of 13th and Greenwich. Sun melted off of it like a candystick. It stood out from all the other buildings around it, much more beautiful than the building we were coming from. They'd done it. Sam and Katie got pregnant and moved to the West Side. Was this what life was supposed to come to?

Sam got out first and lept towards the back of the vehicle to bring up the hatch to begin the unloading. Katie and I sat together on the bench seat. I knew with just the two of us there I had to say something. I couldn't step out of the van leaving her alone without clearing the air.

"Congratulations on the baby, Kate," I said. "I'm really proud of you guys."

"Thanks," she said. We smiled at one another. I wanted to talk again but as I opened my mouth, she spoke. "That's all you need to say for now, David. Let's move this stuff in."

We spent most of the day moving in the boxes and furniture and organizing them all into their temporary places. Boxes lay open, tipped over, cavernous along the redwood floors of the brownstone. Tall chamberous ceilings with floral binding tracked along its heights. The doorways were wide, the windows were tall, and there was even the luxury of two grand fireplaces, regal with brick faces and dancing ladies in distant charcoal-colored pastures engraved onto the shields that covered their stovefronts. It was by all means a beautiful home, worlds above the home they were coming from.

In the early evening Katie and I sat on the floor of the salon attributing loose trinkets to boxes and then boxes to other rooms.

"How's your book going?" she asked me.

"Fine," I said. "The publisher should be calling me any day now. They've loved everything I've sent them thus far."

"And when you get famous you're going to move to the West Side right?"

"I wouldn't be caught dead," I said. "You're lucky I'm here now."

"I *am lucky*," she said. "There's no way me and Sam could have done this ourselves."

"I'm happy to help, Kate. And I hope you can forgive me for what I did to Allison."

"Forget it," she said.

"Only if you will."

"I will. However, I'll never introduce you to another living person again, and I'll deny knowing you in public for the rest of my life. We'll call it even."

"Good. As long as we can do this and go to ballgames."

"I'm going to make a Mets fan out of you," she said.

"I'm going to make a Cards fan out of your kid."

"I'd rather not have one than that."

We both laughed.

"I missed you, Kate."

"I missed you too. Even if you are crazy."

Sam walked through the doorway jollily. "He's not crazy, but foolhardy," he said.

"Thanks, pal," I said.

"I think he can be both," Katie said. "Sam told me you've been going to that bar to stake out some girl you saw there over a year ago. That isn't foolhardy. That's asinine."

"Must you tell her everything?" I asked Sam.

He took what he needed from one of the open boxes and scurried out of the room.

"Katie, your problem is you have no imagination," I said. "You have no knack for romance, for miracles, for the unknown."

"You're right! And I don't believe in ghosts, dragons, fairies, or magic either. Only children do."

"I pray to heaven that you come to see how beneficial and necessary the great romantics were to the world in past ages and how useful they would be today if they were in fashion."

"And I pray to heaven that the world never loses its mind the way you have."

It was precisely between the words "you" and "have" that the knock on the door broke through the room. It was the front door. It was a loud, confident knock. Katie turned her head towards the door as she finished speaking. I'll never forget this moment, reader, the moment—the flicker of a finite trice!—between the knock and Sam answering the door where the world truly did stand still. It was as if it all moved in half-time.

When he answered it, I could not see her. From where I was sitting, the frame of the door was hidden by a further inlet so that when the door came open, it was only her voice that entered. The lovewarm sound of her perfect voice through my ear and quickly down my spine, finding some breach in the network of nerves through which it could illuminate my longdarkened soul. She needn't say too much, lest I'd have died. They were talking but I couldn't hear them, reader. The three of them going on, and myself lost to ecstasy. It seemed that after hearing just her initial greeting, I'd gone deaf so as to protect myself from an excess, a defense of the senses; a soundless euphoria of the seraphic. Sarahfic she was, reader! *It was her*, walking in behind Sam, my world still soundless, though I could see them talking; only blood beating at my eardrums, my head underwater for a synapse of a second until it all rushed back to me: the sound, the cold, the air that I breathed awkwardly filling my lungs and raising the scales of my skin at once.

"—and I'd really appreciate it if you could. I'm sure you're really busy," she said, smiling the same smile as the year before. Her hair was up, not lazily, but provokingly, two long pins keeping it in place; long ribbons of sparrowcolored hair falling from their cradle, floating and weightless as the gardens of Babylon.

"It shouldn't be a problem at all," Katie said. "I'm glad you came over to let us know."

"It feels strange to be here," she laughed. "It doesn't look anything like home now."

"For us either," Katie said. "We're working on that. How is your move going?"

"It's been fine," she said. "Luckily I didn't move far, just to the other side of the neighborhood."

"Where to?" asked Sam.

"I'm on Jones now."

"Oh, that's not far at all," Katie said. "If I'm ever walking that way I could always drop off the mail there so you don't have to come here. I don't mind at all."

I must have still looked as if I was in a state of comatose. Staring from my crosslegged sanctuary there on the floor.

"That would be so nice," she said. "Hopefully it isn't more than a week or two, but you know how it is."

"Of course," Katie said. "Give me your number and new address and I'll let you know if we get anything." Katie sourced a piece of paper and a pen from the collective of junk and gave it to my love. She began to write. I wished I could talk, I wished I could stand, but I could only look. I looked on as her pupils swelled towards the paper, her faultless cheeks coming round as hills, as serious as stone as she worked to remember her new address to write it down. Loose strings of hair fell in front of her face. I could see, as I had seen in so many dreams that year, the subtitles of her soul shining through that easy face; the bite of a lip, the twirl of a tongue, the ducts of her youth coming carved through her cheeks when she smiled, a certain womanly gesture of the eye, turning up towards the heavens from where she came when she contemplated these things. Oh, I could see her so clearly there at that bar, that little look she had given me, my Sarah, my sweetest promise of passion, how I prayed for you! I prayed that you would see my ad, or that you'd remember my distraught disposition that night and return to the scene of the crime to wait for me, or better yet, that you yourself would dream of me and spend your life searching for that nameless face in your nocturnal visions as I have spent the whole of my life's ardor devoted to you, evangelizing for you, missioning for you my sweetest secret! I worked hard to speak, but when? And what? If I should try and speak, I feared I would bark. So I looked, I looked on until I had no choice...

"I hadn't even thought of doing that for our old place actually," Katie said.

"Neither had I," Sam said.

"David," Katie called over to me, "when your new neighbors move in, can you let them know you'll take any mail that comes for us? That's probably the easiest way to do it, if you don't mind."

"I don't mind," I must have choked out.

"That's David, by the way," Sam said, pointing. "He's our good friend, and old neighbor."

She looked at me and smiled like lightning. "Hi, David, it's nice to meet you."

Lord, I hope I smiled. My brain gave the command, but to this day I fear that what came across my face was merely a widened mouth, gnashed teeth, and hopeless, absent unflinching eyeballs. "Hi," I said. "It's nice to meet you too." And as I saw her nod and turn away, I knew I wouldn't allow myself to live another day—another minute!—if I didn't make some sort of further inquiry, if only just to hear the marvelous music of her voice once more. "I'm sorry, but I didn't catch your name."

Rolling from her lips like thunder came the beginning of the greatest conundrum of my life. "Mae," she said. "My name is Mae."

Chapter Sixteen

*Of My Initial Reactions to This Meeting, and the Plan
I Formulated Therein Related*

*M**ae!* The sweetest word I'd ever heard!

Reader, in all truth, I did not even consider the obvious dilemma regarding the names at that time. I was so arrested by seeing her—by the word that slipped through the sleight of her teeth—that to even think about the problem at hand was to betray her. Mae! It was the brightest of all names, the most elegant and fundamentally attractive of natal titles I could possibly conjure up. It is sunshine, yellows and oranges, soft horns and harps; nature's most benevolent creatures nesting in the many ledges of the heavens, blessed by birds and butterflies; bars of light streaming in through her roundness, all springolden and sunsmothered. All I'd heard for the remainder of that evening was "Mae," ringing in my head like bells, knowing I'd never heard a better name in my life. I must have appeared as though I'd spilled my very soul out onto the floor when she told me. I said nothing more after that, reader. My hearing left me again in the rush of elatedness that followed her decree. When she departed, I let myself imagine her, there in her former house as she had been when she lived there. I watched those ghosts of Mae twirl across the hardwood floors, watching her laugh, watching her cry, watching her sing as if it were just the two of us there, relishing in those metadimensional specters that she left for me; seeing each and every miracle and misstep she took within those walls through love's eyes. It would quickly become my new hobby. I surprised not only Katie and Sam, but myself in those coming days when I spent every petty portion of my free time in that room, in the master bedroom with my nose to the ground working like a good pointer, flushing like a spaniel, to decipher which ground was holy and which was still virgin and useless to me. I must have felt every moment of her life in that building through my many meditations. I could see her so completely that I—during some rather poignant moments of sensation—felt I could not only smell her, hear her, and taste her, but also communicate with her, sending her all of the famed scriptures of love ranging from the antiquated Hebrew verses of our well-known theological ancestry to the patient and visceral poetry of Keats by the transcendence of telepathy.

This is all to say that it was via this sudden occupation of elation that I was able to temporarily distract myself from the problem at hand. I cared not to think about any other cursed names; not Sarah, not Callie, not Amelia, but only of Mae. I hadn't thought even once to consider the contradiction before me. I was willing to completely ignore the necessity of uncovering this enigma in exchange for the gluttonous revelry of *finding her*, just seeing her again, and reaffirming her existence. Afterall, there was surely some good reason why she had gone by two different names, what did it matter if I knew that reason or not? There was probably a simple explanation that I was missing, or even an impossibly complex set of circumstances I would fail to understand. Whatever it was, I just wasn't concerned with it, reader. What was important was that I was sure it was her, and she was in my life again! Now the only thing to do was to find a way to keep her there.

My plan was simple: To obtain her address from Katie, and to pay her a visit. The trouble with that of course being that Katie vouched to never take part in any act that would directly assist me in romance ever again. I couldn't ask her, she'd tell me no. She might have been my friend once more, but on the field of battle she was my sworn enemy. I had to gain access another way, and I needed not look any farther than the loyal companion I'd called my best friend. For nobody, perhaps even myself, would be happier to see me find the love I deserved more than Samuel Chester Parasochi of Eau Claire, Wisconsin.

***

"Where am I supposed to put all of it?" Sam asked, waving his hands in the air. "The place is still a mess, there's no telling what drawers or boxes or closets she's going to be digging through. You know I can't get caught with them."

"Well don't *hide them*," I said. "You could put them in a place too obvious for her to find, like within the pages of a notebook or under the mattress or something."

"I couldn't do that, I'd be worrying about it constantly."

"What's there to worry about?"

"She's going to ask about it, or say something about it eventually. A week or two will go by and she'll say, 'It's pretty strange no mail ended up coming for Mae afterall.' I mean, there's no way she'll buy it. Not even a credit card company or a wedding invitation? I wouldn't be able to keep it straight, you know me."

"What's the worst she's going to do? Think about it, Sam. So what if she finds out you're doing me a favor, why does it bother her any?"

"I don't know the answer to that, but I do know that I'm not supposed to lie to her or trick her or keep things from her or be involved with you falling in love with anybody that she knows. She's made that very clear to me, and unfortunately she knows Mae now."

"Sam—"

"That's what she told me."

"Well how about this," I started. Sam's face was a desperate, dog-gish mix of sad and anxious. The poor chap hardly had his freedom anymore, and this move was killing him. I knew it was. He wasn't ready for a baby. How could a guy who worked as a line cook in an Italian-American restaurant on 48th Street be ready for a baby? He needed a drink. "How about this: I'll come by everyday and pick them up. Katie's gone most days till evening and during the week you don't go in until four, right? So if you've got any mail, let me know and I'll come by and pick them up that day, before you leave for work. If you need to leave the house, hoard them under the sofa and I swear I'll get to them before she gets back. Give me a spare key, she can't object to that. That way they'll never be in the house and it'll be off your conscience. I'll take care of everything. Just collect them and put them under the sofa. You don't understand, Sam. I need that mail."

"What the hell are you even going to do with her mail?" he cried out. "So what if you have a couple of phony insurance bills and a coupon ad, you don't know where she lives."

"But Katie does. That's why you've got to help me, Sam."

"You think I know where she put that little piece of paper?" he scoffed. "I don't know where that thing is, you'll have to ask her yourself."

"I don't expect you to know, I'm asking you to find out. Think, Sam, you know Katie. Where does she keep things like that? A drawer? Her wallet? Maybe in the mail slot?"

"In the state our house is in, it could be anywhere."

"It could be in a purse or handbag. Check there first."

"I can't be digging through her things."

"I need this address, Sam, I don't think you quite understand how dire this is. This is perhaps the pivotal moment of my entire life, and I don't have another option but to go through with this plan."

"She said she lived on Jones Street. It's a small street, can't you just hangout on the block for a couple days? I'm sure you'll see her."

"And tell her what? That I've just been hanging around waiting for her? That's no way to nurture love, Sammyboy. These things have an *order and a nature* to them. To stand around and wait for her to pass me by and then to lie about my intentions is not a great start to a relationship that I plan to have for the rest of my life."

"Well there aren't any better ideas!"

"A better idea is for you to give me a couple week's worth of mail and her new address and I can take it to her one evening, telling her that I was walking from your place to mine and thought it would be nice to drop off her mail on my way home. That's the plan, Sam, that's the perfect plan, and right now you're the only thing standing in the way of that plan, so I suggest, if you have any concern for my happiness whatsoever—which seems incredibly unlikely in this moment—that you take a quick dig through Katie's purse while she's in the shower tonight, take a picture of that address for me, and let destiny do the rest." I took Sam by his trembling shoulders. He looked as if he'd had a cold, like he'd been standing out in the elements, wet and malweathered listening to me talk. "Look at you, kid. You're a mess right now. This move, this baby, it's all taking a toll on you. I can see it."

"You can see it?"

"Of course I can see it. Everybody can see it, but not everybody is going to tell you the truth. You're a mess. I want to help you, Sam. I want you to be a great husband and a great father."

"I want to be a great father," he said, the words falling from his mouth like spilled milk.

"You will be, but you need to find the man inside of you first. You need to put your foot down, access that primal male that lives and rages in all of us. Don't be afraid of Katie, she shouldn't hold the power."

"She shouldn't?"

"Don't you know it was Eve who ate from the tree first, my friend? I'm not saying don't love her, but you shouldn't always trust her."

"I shouldn't?"

"Why should you? You have to at least make her prove it."

"I do?"

"If a couple can't share property and space, what can they share? Certainly not a child. To trust Katie, you must know she trusts you. For her to trust you, she must respect you. You think she respects you, Sammy? Look at you, you're terrified of the next nine months. You can't even say the word 'baby,' you just keep saying that 'Katie's pregnant,' like it's a condition she has. You're going to be a father! Stand up for yourself, do something bold! I want to help you! This could be a way for you to gain your confidence back. Don't be afraid of her, just do it!"

"Do what again?"

"Go into her purse and find the paper with the address written on it! It's for the sake of your baby, Sam."

"You think this will make me a better father? If I get caught going through her purse there is no telling what sort of punishment I'll get."

I sighed. He was a lost cause. There was only one thing I could think to do. It was the only thing that Sam loved more than hockey, duck-hunting, and Katie telling him he's doing a great job: Getting drunk on Wisconsin beer.

"Do you want to get out of the house, Sam?" I asked him. "You look like you haven't slept in days."

"I haven't."

"You're stressed out, man."

"I am. I don't know what to do. Everything is happening so fast and I have so much responsibility and I feel like I have no time." He was getting choked up now, talking through a frayed voice. "And money is tight, and I don't know what to do. I'm terrified, David. You have no idea."

"Could I suggest something?"

"What do you have in mind?"

It wasn't pretty, reader, and it cost me $56 worth of Miller High Life and another $10 in street tacos, but there in the backseat of a taxi cab, with the world spinning and the poor cabbie cursing at us, Sam promised to get that address for me. He might have been a coward, but he always kept his promises.

Chapter Seventeen

*How I Took the Mail to Mae's Apartment and the
Improbable Instance that Occurred at Fanelli Cafe
Some Weeks After*

2 0 Jones Street, Apt. 2B

That's what the paper read. It took almost three weeks before anything came, but when it did, Sam did exactly as instructed. I found a phone bill, a renewal request from Yellowstone National Park, and a clothing catalogue all bound together by a rubber band and tucked beneath the sofa at Sam's place. I left there at about three-thirty and walked south down Seventh Avenue to Bleecker and then to Jones. I stood at the mouth of the small halfstreet and looked down its throat. I had no idea what I was going to say.

It had been almost a month since the day I'd seen her at Sam and Katie's apartment. A month of replaying that meeting in my head once and again, mixing it up, letting it mingle with not only the first meeting, but with a thousand fictional meetings, and future meetings, constructing what the concourse of our love might look like. Would it resemble the slow and steady congeniality of the romances of old? Or would it be an outbreak; a sudden and immediate consummation there at her doorstep as if she had been waiting one long month for me to appear and wrap herself around me?

I stepped down the street feeling the good spring breeze move past me as it does on those small funneling streets in Manhattan. The sky was pure blue, bluer than my eyes could handle. Up above me I noticed the tops of the buildings closing inward like cave walls, like I was down at the bottom of some ravine alone and doomed and the walls would begin to crumble down and enclose me in that horrid place forever. I didn't know what to say. I stepped up to the door and studied the buzzer box. I didn't know what to say. There I stood, just one finger's motion away from being face to face with the woman I'd so longed for, and yet, I couldn't get myself to press it. There were no thoughts. Not only did I not know what to say, but my own monologue suddenly ceased, my mind was blank; sheet white and empty. I couldn't remember my name. There alone on the step of the building, tiny as tiny could be against the facade of those canyon walls, I couldn't speak aloud. My blood went cold. The only pestering thing that kept my mind moving ever so slowly in that moment was the coming and going of the romantic scenes I'd studied in the books I'd read over all my years. The stories I had consumed all blended together at once and I was assaulted by the greatest heroes of their pages and their ever-famous efforts, lines, words, and poems of courtship. Remembering them there on her stoop, I began to wonder: If this romance was to take the same course as those ones, how could I ever begin it? How could I ever compete with the sublimity of those masterful stories? How could I find the poetry, how could I not feel shameful over my own efforts? How would I ever live with myself if my attempts came up short in that very critical moment? How was I supposed to recite love's greatest words when I couldn't even speak a simple *hello*? I knew at once I couldn't.

I regret to inform the reader, as it shivers me with shame each time I think of it, that I fled. I dropped those letters and I raced up Jones Street to Sixth Avenue as quickly as I could and I didn't stop running until I was back on Avenue A safe and sound in my darkened room surrounded by those very books that made such a coward out of me.

***

That feeling stuck like tar for days. I was left wondering what I could possibly do to redeem myself now. My self-pity had gotten so bad that I considered leaving New York—the grandest heresy of them all—and I'm sure I would have in the following weeks had I not been saved. Yes, reader, *saved.* What would you say if I tried to convince you that yet another miracle occurred at this point in my story? A miracle so vastly unlikely that I still to this day burst out in tears and laughter when I think of it. I would call it the most miraculous event of my entire tale if it weren't for the previous miracle of Mae entering through that door of her once home to subsequently reenter the door of my soul forever.

Nineteen days after my failed attempt at delivering the mail I was strolling on Mercer Street, north towards Prince, when I passed by the forever famed Fanelli Cafe there on the corner as it has stood for nearly two hundred years. Fanelli Cafe is a staple location of downtown Manhattan; an Old World-style cafe with all of the great romantic offerings that one like myself may want when dining, such as coffee, pastries, small plates, cocktails and vermouth, beer, light music, well-mannered waitstaff, and otherwise bygone sensibilities. It is at once wooden and brass, gilded and worn, old and new, and for that, I always treated myself to looking in its long, mooncolored windows as I walked by to see what kind of life or death lurked inside. Well wouldn't I be a liar if I said I didn't see Mae with an apron around her Venetian body waiting tables in the famed cafe on this day. I saw her in all of her light, her brightness, her perfection. She spoke soft (I could tell even through the glass) towards the patrons sat below her; she chuckled, smiled, graced them with a tonguish phrase that so exhibited the dexterity of that magnificent muscle, and then she twirled off towards the backroom and out of sight. I knew then, reader, that this wasn't at all a game of dice. This wasn't a mere stack of coinciding events for the sake of God's amusement (or worse—God's wrath on me for sins unknown), but instead it was He Himself loaning me the playbook, the script, the cheatcards. I'd been let in on the secret: *This woman is your destiny, David. Stop your moping and take her now.*

I watched her there for over two hours. I stood, kittycorner at Prince and Mercer, buildingside and out of sight, her figure moving from table to table. I felt it was not appropriate nor advantageous to disturb her as she worked—though as romantic as it might have been—for Fanelli is a relatively small place and I didn't want to make any trouble with management, and I knew when Mae saw me she would drop her duties and declare her love for me there at the scene. For that reason, I was waiting. I was waiting for her to exit the place and see me across the way.

It must have been about six o'clock when it happened. She exited the building. I could see her in the natural light of the sun once and for all! How I'd forgotten how glorious each crest of her figure was! As I stepped out from behind my facade, she disappeared behind a car that had slowed and rolled up to the entrance of Fanelli. I saw the top of her angel head—just the halo—descend deep into the black vehicle. I tried to shout for her but found myself stunned and silent. Within ten seconds of her coming out into my world, she was lost to another. The car door shut, and it drove off. It was anger that I felt this time, reader. It was the rage of all the world boiling inside me.

I stomped myself into the cafe. This saga will end now, I determined. Enough waiting on mail, enough thinking of what to say, enough blowing it in the bottom of the ninth. I entered that cafe, I approached that empty ghost-lighted bar and summoned the aging bartender with the fair wave of a hand like one might hail a taxi. He stepped from his leisure and met me there at the black bar, sensing that I had a loaded question for him.

"What is it?" he asked. He knew I wasn't ordering a drink.

"I hate to bother you," I said. "But I'm a good friend of Mae's and I was supposed to meet her here and I just saw her leave in a car as

I walked up. Did she happen to mention where she was headed?" That would be my plan. I would figure out where she was going and I would go there. I would go in my own cab. I'd be just a few minutes behind her. I would meet her there and I would love her there.

"Mae?" he said back to me.

I smiled. "Mae, the waitress here."

"We don't have a Mae here. Could be the wrong place?"

"No, no," I pondered for a moment. "The very pretty girl who was working here...she just left not two minutes ago. You saw her didn't you? Is she a phantom or a woman? The waitress who just walked out this same door I've entered from."

"There was a waitress here, yes." He looked at me cock-eyed and leaned in on the bar as if to study me. We fell deep into a faceoff that seemed to last minutes, though it likely failed to withstand the whole of a long second. "What's your name?"

"Arthur," I said.

"Arthur what?"

"Bandini."

"Mr. Bandini, I can't give you the name of somebody who works here if you don't know them. I'm sorry, but I think you've got the wrong place."

"*I do know her,*" I pleaded. "We are good friends, I—"

"Why don't you call her then?"

"I would," I started. "But, listen...maybe it is a mixup. Can't you just tell me the name of that waitress who just left? I'm sure it's just a misunderstanding."

"It doesn't sound like a misunderstanding to me, it sounds like something much worse."

"What could be worse than a misunderstanding?" I said. "If I want you to understand something and you don't understand it, that's about as bad as it gets."

"I think you should leave."

"But I haven't done anything."

"I'm going to give you the chance to leave peacefully," he said loudly.

The patrons in the room began to peak over their teacups and salad bowls at us. A hush fell upon that once chatter-laden dinner crowd. I could feel their eyes swimming upon the back of my neck and I watched as the bartender's anxious eyes moved from me to the distance of the room and then back to me. "If you don't leave on your own," he said, "I'd be happy to show you out." I took a step backwards, looking now at the interested patrons. Those desperate wolves, pathetic and thirsty for some excitement in their sorry lives; their trivial days of cafe dining and corporate brouhaha. I could only hope to disrupt what they perceived to be a "normal" "day." They and their boring little lives. They didn't know truth, love, beauty, or any of the golden virtues of romance. No! They were sorry impressions of sadness laid like thumbprints on the film of time. I loathed them like vermin.

"How dare you threaten me!" I shouted as loudly as my own ears could stand. "I could have you arrested for threatening a city official like that!" The heads turned sweepingly to my announcement. "If this place doesn't meet the city's health code by this time next week, we're going to have to shut you down! And I surmise that will be the case after seeing the irreparable state of your kitchen today. You should be ashamed to serve food here."

"You little shit!" the man shouted.

It was at this moment that a woman appeared from the backroom of the cafe and came upon the bar where our misunderstanding was taking place. She possessed all the superficial qualities of a so-called "manager." The tucked in shirt, the ravish lipstick, the unspecified radio device attached to her belt.

"What the hell is going on here?" she shouted between us.

"This creep is stalking Sarah."

Our eyes met—the three of us. He cursed to himself and began to babble in explanation to the woman who had joined us. I would record what he said to her here in this document, but before he'd finished his first sentence, I was on Houston Street running east for home.

Chapter Eighteen

Of the Subsequent Period That Would Bring About
the Most Romantic Adventure To Be Lived By Your
Author Up Until That Point in His Life and Other
Superfluous Details Concerning This Curious Case of
Star-Crossed Love

Now, reader, I want to make it clear as day to your skeptical mind that I was absolutely sure that the woman I saw in Fanelli Cafe was the same woman that I saw in Sam and Katie's new apartment, and that that was the very same woman—down to the eyelash—that I saw at the corner bar of St. Mark's and A on that long-winded April night. I not only knew it by my rational, provably stable human senses, but also by my intuitive instincts aforementioned in this document. The voice, the smile, the light that shone from her person, the warming of my spirit just by being in proximity to her perfection is testament enough to my sureness. I was overcome by identical cognitive and spiritual responses by the many complex material systems of my body by *laying mere eyes* on this woman on three very different and unrelated occasions. It was her. Mae was Sarah and Sarah was Mae, and somehow I didn't mind, but now, I knew I had to. I had to because it had happened again. For something like this to happen once is a fluke, it requires no attention, but twice, it is a conspiracy, and I knew that it would hang over my head like a willow if I never did get to the bottom of that mystery. And if it hung over my head, then it would hang over our love. Contrarily, I suspected I could use this mystery as fodder to nurture our blossoming love. After all, how could she not appreciate the romance, the bookworthiness of what lay between us!

A struggling writer sweeping the city for his muse happening upon a woman bearing a double identity is about as romantic as it gets. And this was all without taking into consideration that the problem very well might naturally *resolve itself* in some early, mundane, though satisfying, way upon our meeting each other once or twice more. It could come out that she sometimes went by a middle-name, or perhaps for some unimaginably complex set of circumstances, she was bound to call herself Mae on that specific night.

So there it stood. I had been given the name Sarah once more, not by her own lips, but again, by the word of another. With the circular trajectory of my journey, I was enthralled to get to the bottom of this case. I was completely intrigued by the circumstances that defined these weeks, and now, awakened to how purely romantic it all was, it was easy to see what must come next. It was my conviction that this part of the adventure needed to be done according to the books. It was a very delicate case that would require the utmost finesse by the world's finest romantic or else it would be at risk of falling apart at the hands of the cold ignorance of an incompetent world. That is to say, to handle a situation so inherently romantic without consulting the courtesy of a textbook romance, might implode the situation on itself all together, costing one the satisfaction of seeing its sovereign conclusion. That meant I could not go about this situation in any sterile or municipal way. The words of one wise boy who lived inside a great novel rang through my ears: *"I've seen it in the books, so that's what we've got to do. Do you want to go to doing things different from what's in the books and get things all muddled up?"*

My plan was to play detective. I would follow her and learn all there was to know about her life, gathering clues that could help me in discovering her true identity, all the while loving her more and more. Learning, loving, and *living* her. In my observing of her life, I could live her life. Only through this immersive process could I put the pieces together and know how to proceed. It was clear to me that she was doing it on purpose; I knew she was. She was leaving clues for me to follow, unrolling a riddle at my feet, and I knew that if I could only find the key to the chest I would have full access to what may lie within her holy heart. It was better than any book I'd ever read. It was more complete and complex than any plot I could conjure up. It was definitively and explicitly romantic. And it was at this point, reader, that I began to write my book. This is the all-definite moment of this text—the moment the idea hatched to scrap all other manuscripts that collected space on my desk, to abandon any idea of a lovestruck postman, all in favor of writing now about my Mae. From this day forward I began writing verses about Mae which eventually, as you will soon read, evolved into relations, and then chapters, and then the corpus that would become my book. And I knew it from the start that it would be a perfect book. After all, what reader of modern romances could resist the mystery and the tension that populated my true story? It already had everything that they were looking for, and now, as I was to shadow her each and every day, I was going to know her better than she even knew herself. I would live in disguises and survive by fake names. I would reach parts of the city I never before dared to go. I would use strategy, creative tact, and cunning to be exactly where I needed to be when I needed to be there. I would be with her at all times, and she would never even have a clue. Then once I came to solve the mystery of her identity, I would pounce; making my love known and showing my face, just as she wanted; oh, how romantic it all was!

***

I began each day at the corner of Jones and Bleecker, watching her door. I would arrive very early before the sun so as to catch her on her way out. The first day was a Tuesday and she left only once to go to the bank, and then to a bodega on Sixth Avenue on her way home. The following day she left very early to an apartment in Soho where she remained inside for nearly six hours. I stood by a coffee cart and drank strong cups of black coffee very slowly so as not to need to relieve myself too frequently. In the early afternoon she emerged from the apartment with a friend. They both took the subway uptown to 33rd Street where they dined with another three friends, after which, she took the subway back downtown to her house where she remained for the night. The third day, Thursday, was where the real action began. I followed her in the morning to a diner where she had breakfast. It was otherwise empty so I couldn't chance going in. I found a bench across the street and ate a bagel and watched the door. She ate quickly, coming back out after only thirty minutes, shining like the sun with two sandy ropes of hair pigtailed to either side, and a sunyellow shirt tucked behind a denim jacket well-buttoned and tight fitting. She smiled—the lovely thing—bouncing with excitement to the art supplies store where she came out with a plastic bag bulging with product. From there we took the subway together—in the very same car. I looked down the long tubular center of the car watching her watch people, hoping that she didn't watch me watch her. It was the A train. We stopped at Canal, she shifted in her seat but remained there, and we carried on. I thought surely she would get off at Fulton, not considering the possibility that we would be going to Brooklyn, but she didn't. As we were underwater, she looked in the black of the windows, checking out her hair. She was the sweetest thing I'd ever seen. I couldn't believe she had me going to Brooklyn, but there I was, following her all the way to High Street. It was only the first stop in Brooklyn, but enough for me to be amused at my commitment to this game we played with each other, chasing each other like minks of love all around this city.

We walked a few blocks away from the perfect blue bridge that towered through the gashes of sky between the buildings. It seemed to follow us everywhere we went. She was walking quickly, and I was hoping she wasn't suspicious of my trailing her. I was absolutely sure she hadn't gotten a deliberate look at me, though still I fell back a few extra feet and stayed small behind the bodies as I watched her bob up and down through the column of heads long ahead of me. Finally, she entered a building. It took me about twenty seconds to approach it after she entered it, but I could tell by its shape just what it was. It was an art gallery. That was the day I learned that my love was a painter.

The next few days mirrored this Thursday almost to a T.

I met her early on Jones Street, and then she had breakfast in the neighborhood while I waited on the bench outside. Some days she skipped the art store, and others she emerged from it with canvases the size of small tables. We took the train into Brooklyn, she worked some hours at the gallery and then walked about fifteen minutes to a building full of studios where she painted late into the evening. From this studio, she often emerged covered in all the colors of the rainforest, having the blood of parrots, insects, sunsets, frogthings all smeared and carved into her clothes and skin. While she was captive inside, I waited in the park imagining what it was she was painting; how beautiful must be her creations if she herself were the epitome of all beauty. I thought of our future: me, a great renowned writer, and her, a successful painter. We would grow to be a well-known and powerful socialite couple like the Fitzgeralds. We could get a table at any restaurant in the world at the snap of a finger. We could have seats to any world premier with only a phone call. I knew there was no stopping us now. I'd found exactly what I'd been looking for my entire life; a painter! The most tragic and lonely of all the creative professions, how well-versed she must be in the art of romance!

Each evening when we returned from Brooklyn, I followed her from the train at West 4th Street down Jones Street by some distance, and could usually watch her enter her apartment. Some days I waited at the corner to see if she would come out for the night, perhaps to meet some friends or to go for a walk, but she never did. Occasionally she had visitors—always female—and after her guests departed I watched the window carefully until I saw her bedroom light go dark. Then I would rush home and write my novel, immortalizing forever so carefully all those things I had mused on that day.

This routine was all good and fine, and I valued my time with my mysterious Mae, my secret Sarah, getting to know her by immersing myself in her exciting life, but I was not getting any closer to discovering her true identity, nor was I getting any more confident in my ability to finally approach her. What I was looking for was a clue, any evidence that would tie her to either of the previous identities I'd come to know her by. I was searching for absolutely anything that could distinguish Mae from Sarah, or even the corner bar on Avenue A from Sam and Katie's apartment. After two weeks of this routine, and all of these moments and images from past and future being mixed up in my head, I wasn't even sure that the girl I was following existed at all. I began to question my mission all together. Each day was leading to the same dead-ends, each question spawning only more questions. I was desperate, and asking myself if my methods were at fault. That was, until the day I watched her walk into Fanelli Cafe.

In two weeks I hadn't once seen her go to Fanelli Cafe, the place where I knew that she worked. She only seemed to go between home and the gallery and her studio, and never to her place of work. This of course struck me as peculiar and I began to wonder if I'd even seen her at Fanelli at all. I began to distrust my own senses—the greatest mistake a romantic can make—which sent me into a spiral of distress. When she finally did go there, one Friday afternoon, I felt a great deal of relief. I stood at my usual corner place, watching through the window. I could see her waiting tables in the glass, her hair tightly pulled back and her lipstick as red as the balm of a rosebud.

Around five o'clock the bartender whom I had once scuffled with left the place. I watched him as he relinquished his shift, left the building, and was replaced by a brutish woman with less hair than he. I knew this would be my chance to finally make my move. My lover moved about the tables. I could see her well from across the street, rocking from one set of customers to the other. I decided then that this would be the day of reckoning. No time seemed more fitting than this. I would take a seat at one of the empty tables in the cafe and strike up a conversation by reminding her of our meeting at Sam and Katie's apartment all those weeks ago. Having gathered some foreknowledge about her personal life would be the difference maker; it would provide me the courage to finally execute my plan as it deserved, something that seemed impossible on that day I had attempted to deliver the mail. Now I could work some favorable material into the conversation and gain an early edge, leaving her no choice but to be as irrevocably in love with me as I was with her. I took three deep breaths at my corner place, watched as she glided across the cafe floor into the backroom, and took my first step toward the rest of my life. There were no books to compete with now. I was living the real thing.

Inside the restaurant I sat down, making myself cozy in a corner towards the south side of the front room. The place was nearly full and a great afternoon haze fell in from the windows and made the place mellow and nostalgic like every old cafe in New York should feel. The waitstaff moved back and forth through the room and the backroom as well where another set of small tables lived. I had sat for about two minutes when a male waiter finally came and attended to me.

"Something to drink, sir?" he asked.

"No thanks, I'm fine."

"Glass of water?"

"No thanks."

He cocked his head.

"Something to eat, sir?"

"No thanks."

Behind him she moved slowly and towards one of the tables at the front of the dining room near the street. She looked wonderful, so unaware of our blossoming love.

"Well, you have to order something," he said. I forgot he was there.

"I will," I said. "Can I have a minute?"

He was ruining everything. I supposed if I sat there without a drink for long enough she would feel like she needed to come over. If I could only lock eyes with her for a moment, I would have her.

"Sure, take your time," he said. He was a little bothered and walked to the bar where he and the balding woman began to talk quietly. My lover joined them for a moment and then walked back towards me and through the hole in the wall that led to the back-room. Missed her. I pretended to study the menu deeply to buy time, waiting for her to come back through the door and into the main dining room.

The cafe was the perfect setting for what I had planned. It was old, rustic, well-lit and romantic. I shivered thinking of how many lovers had made it their home over the years, and still, it hadn't seen its greatest love story yet. The people sitting around me had no idea that they would be present to witness the coming of one of the world's greatest romances, just a few moments away, any second now, when she enters back...through...that...door...

"Excuse me!" I shouted.

She stopped right away and turned her head, her hair waterfalling behind her.

"Could you come here for just a moment?" I asked.

She came.

"I have a question about the menu."

"What is it?"

Oh, that voice. So much richer than in my head. She put her hands flat on the end of the table and leaned down towards me to see the menu. A few strands of hair fell between us, dangling there at my brow. I could smell her now; sweet and humid like passion. She smelled like a woman, she smelled like Athens, like ripeness, like springtime. She smelled like love, and nothing more.

"I was just wondering about this here—" I looked up towards her and our eyes met.

"About what?" she said, staring back at me.

"I'm sorry," I said, "but we've met before, I'm sure of it."

"Have we?" she laughed. She stood up straight, so as not to intensify the moment.

"Yes, we have. I'm David. I met you at Sam and Katie's apartment. That is, your old apartment. Last month."

"Sam and Katie?"

"Yes, Sam and Katie. They moved into your old place on 13th Street. I'm sorry, I know it's strange. But you came to give Katie your new address to forward your mail. I was sitting there on the ground when you came in, I remember it well."

"Oh, I'm so sorry, but that wasn't me," she said.

I squinted.

"You must have met my sister, Mae."

"Oh, your sister!" I said. "I hadn't considered that perhaps you had a sister!"

"Of course not, why would you?" she laughed.

"Why would I!" I laughed along.

Oh, reader, they were twins! How romantic!

"I'm Sarah," she said. "It happens all the time, don't feel bad."

Feel bad? How could I feel anything at all, sitting there beneath her breath, learning that my little Suzhou mermaid wasn't a mermaid at all, but instead a girl; a twin, a sister! It was as joyous as it was tragic—a rush of panic overtaking me to consider the innate complications that had begun flooding my brain at once. I lost her for a moment there at the table, gone deep into thought. It was all of the previous years' events—the entire dossier of what had been collected—crumbling down before me like the walls of Jericho. For the slow reader who has not yet reasoned just what crises this implicated, I will summarize: This revelation exposed two *real problems.* The first, and more immediate, was how could I be talking with Sarah, if the one I had followed into the cafe was surely Mae? I had heard Mae introduce herself at Sam and Katie's place, and obtained her address directly from Sam who stole it from Katie who had it written down by Mae herself. I staked out that address and followed Mae for some days all around the city until she eventually came into Fanelli, where I found Sarah.

The second problem was the more serious of the two, provoking the very foundation my entire mission was built upon with epistemological fury. Although it was Mae that I had been following for the last several weeks (and had been inserting into all my farthest fantasies) it was in fact *Sarah,* the woman who stood before me now, whom I first saw the previous year at the corner bar on Avenue A. It was for Sarah I had placed the subway ad, and in a way, it was Sarah, who I believed Mae was all along, starting when I saw her at the 13th Street apartment. It was Sarah who I was in love with, not her sister Mae. Which led to the inevitable question: Did it matter which one I loved? Of course it mattered. But I couldn't understand how. It must have been Sarah, for it was by the force of her divine beauty that began this whole marathon in the first place. It was her hair, it was her smile, it was her voice, it was her walk into that bar that set off the initial fuse that lit this fire that has turned into a smoldering inferno of love. And there she was before me, talking with me, laughing that laugh and smiling that smile, and I couldn't take it anymore, I had to say *something! Anything!* These were the things I was considering as she stood in front of me, my mind under the merciless onslaught of my deepest fears. Lord, help me, I'm burning now, I'm at the stake, I can feel the flames...mayday...mayday...mayday...

"The funny thing is," I blurted out, "I've seen *you* before as well. I've seen both of you."

"You have?" she blushed. "And how do you know it was me and not my sister?"

"Because I remember your name."

"Where did we meet?"

"Well, we didn't meet. We...well..." I had to come out with it. I knew to hold it in any longer would kill me, it would kill me in my sleep. "It was about a year ago. I saw you at the bar on the corner of Avenue A and St. Mark's. You know it?"

"I know it."

"I saw you there. I was drinking there alone. I saw you and I thought you were extraordinary. I thought you were the most beautiful girl I'd ever seen. I was going to talk to you then, but suddenly your date came in, and the two of you sat down together."

She blushed even more, so much so it may have had a reverse effect, returning the color to her face.

"Oh," she said. "I remember that night."

"And it was about a year after that I saw your sister, Mae, while helping my friends move into their new place. So you can see where I'm going with this."

"Where are you going?"

"It's just that I thought it was strange that I had seen you twice—well, I thought it was you—in two unrelated situations, and then again just now."

"New York is a small town."

"I agree, it is, but given the circumstances around how I felt about you the first time I saw you—"

"You think that we are supposed to meet or something?" she laughed. She knew what she said was ridiculous.

"Just that!" I smiled.

"How romantic," she said.

"It is quite romantic isn't it?"

"And how do you know it isn't Mae that you're supposed to meet?"

"Well, I'm not sure. But I think it has to be you."

We were talking rather loudly at first, but as we spoke more our voices fell quieter. She came down again, closer to me so that we could speak very softly and not be heard.

"It is a little tricky," I said, "you know, with the twin thing."

"I suppose it is."

"I reckon I'd be happy to love either of you," I said. I felt stupid saying it. "But not both of you."

"I'd hope not."

"Whichever one of you is the original."

"The original?"

"I don't know."

"We aren't a pair of watches," she said.

"I know. I didn't mean it like that. It's just, I know I feel something for one of you, so whichever one that is, is the one I want."

"How bad do you want us?" she said, smiling.

Oh, Lord. She was playing with me now, I could tell. I felt horrible. I felt like a sick animal that she'd found on the side of the road and was caring for.

"I'll let you in on something that might help your decision, David," she said. "I'm going to marry that man that you saw me with that night on Avenue A. I love him very much."

"That's bad news."

"For you, I'm afraid it is."

"Do you have any good news?"

She knew just what I was referring to.

"I have *great news.* Better than you could imagine."

"Don't play games with me, please. I can't handle it."

"No games. The great news is, Mae isn't seeing anybody right now, and she happens to be in this building."

"You're kidding."

"She's there, in the backroom alone. She's having dinner and doing some sketching. She's an artist."

"An artist?"

"Yes. It's much more interesting than what I do. It seems more your speed, from what I can tell about you."

"What do you do?"

"I'm in school to be a veterinarian."

"That's nice too," I offered absently.

"But you'd love to love a painter wouldn't you? You're so romantic, I can tell."

"I suppose I am…"

"Listen, here's what we'll do. I'll take you back there and introduce you. I'll tell her that you thought that I was her and that you remembered her from your friend's apartment. She'll think it's amazing that you remembered her, and even more so that she happens to be here now. It's an amazing coincidence. She loves these sorts of things."

"She does?"

"She'll think it's so romantic. Come on, follow me."

I followed Sarah to the backroom. There, sitting alone at the picnic-plaid table was my Mae. They looked exactly alike. There were as identical as raindrops, smiling just the same way, moving about mirrorwise and having a sort of marvelous telepathy so that when I had entered with Sarah, Mae was already smiling, looking at me with fireworks bleating out from the teeth that came uncovered from her lips.

Sarah pulled out a chair for me. "Mae, this is—"

"David," Mae said. "From my old apartment. I remember him."

"This is amazing," Sarah said. "He thought that I was you."

"A lot of people do," Mae laughed.

"You really remember me?" I said.

"I do," Mae said. "I absolutely do."

"Do you mind if I sit?" I said.

"Of course not," she said.

"I'll bring you two some drinks?" Sarah said.

"A beer please," I said.

"You know what I want," Mae said.

"In fact, get me what Mae's having," I said. We both smiled big.

"This really is amazing," Mae said. "You know, I don't know why, but I was hoping I would see you again."

Chapter Nineteen

How I Spent the Rest of That Fateful Night With Mae, and the Dismaying Finale to the First Part of This Book

She was the most incredible person I'd ever met. She was the center of the universe. I'll refrain from calling her much more beyond that because doing so would only be to stretch the bounds of poetry and language to lengths exceedingly and embarrassingly beyond my own means. Not to mention how all known appropriate descriptions of her have already been written—wasted on some lesser, unworthy soul, incomparable and shriveled when measured up against my Mae.

We talked close and slow in the darksetting backroom of the restaurant, allowing space for love to bloom. We spoke of nearly everything; of writing, of painting, of God and death, of New York and Paris, of swimming, of solar flares, of wine, of dance, of dogs, of skin, of ghosts, of snails, of rain, of love, of loss, of sisters, of twins, of mothers, of fathers, of Jung, of Freud, of Milton, of Bach, of baseball, of war, of her and of I. We talked until we couldn't talk any longer and were forced to touch or do nothing at all. When we touched it was like feeling the coils of a fuming sun. I was blind to all but her face, her glorious and saintly face. We said our goodbyes to Sarah, and slipped out the door onto Mercer Street. I had no time or strength to speak before she took my hand. She took it deliberately and she took it tightly.

"I want to show you something," she said.

She dragged me south on Mercer through a few winding city blocks. It was the blue hour now, and the brightest lights came from the windows above us, acting as sort of second moons, though far more silver and blue than the moon of the sky. Some funny shadows followed us, limping behind as we moved quickly under such lights. Her hand was tight around mine and we were falling recklessly towards love.

"I adore this part of the city," she said. "The *feeling* of this part of town."

"It feels like being young, doesn't it?" It was a bad line, but I said it, and this is a true document.

"It does," she said.

A silence passed.

"What are you going to do when you aren't young anymore?" she said. "Are you going to leave New York?"

"I haven't thought about that much."

"Leaving New York?"

"Not being young."

"I think when I'm old I'll move uptown where it's more appropriate."

"How old are you talking?" I said.

"I guess when I start to feel old. When does that happen?"

"I think at thirty."

"Then I'll move up there at thirty. I'll have a townhouse to myself and have servants for everything. I'll be too old to have any fun down here. I'll get cranky and shout at schoolboys and turn the heat up to a hundred."

"I think I'd rather die than be thirty," I said.

"Look at these windows here," she pointed. Some virgin-white curtains wailed from the edges of the windows. "And those doors! It's so romantic! I just want to put on a long gown and open up those French doors in the evening. Have a glass of wine and a cigarette."

"It sounds lovely," I said.

"Imagine the writing you could get done on that balcony, sitting there with a glass of wine and a cigarette. I always paint better with a cigarette. Don't you write better when you smoke?"

"I'm not sure, but I do love a cigarette."

"I've always said it's a shame people don't smoke anymore."

"They still do in the East Village."

"Yeah, but not because they have to," she said.

"That's true."

"I'd kill to paint on that balcony. I could paint something incredible on that balcony."

"I could write the greatest romance you've ever read on that balcony."

"I want to read something you've written," she said. She smiled at me. Her lips were red and I could hardly talk when I saw them.

"Sure, anything," I said. "I'm working on a novel, actually."

"What about?"

"This."

"What do you mean?"

"Well, I'll let you read it sometime. Another time. Okay?"

"Sure," she said softly. She looked so perfect. We were walking on Canal Street now and turned east towards the bridge, but still far from it. "Whenever you want."

We came to a red door. It was an old door, actually wooden like they used to make doors, and hanging on its hinges just enough to be called a door. The latch wasn't engaged on the lock. It wasn't quite cracked, but you could tell it wasn't locked.

"This door is always open," she said. "I discovered it a few years ago and I'm not sure if anybody else knows about it. It goes straight to the roof. I go when I want to be alone, or want to feel like the only person in the city. Even with the streetnoise you feel alone. You can't see anybody else. I want to take you."

We entered the door into a grayish foyer with a gray and black checkered floor. There were mailboxes with Chinese names written on them and a staircase that winded almost directly upwards at no slant. We climbed it quickly, passing an array of doors where Chinese sounds and smells came poking out from underneath wooden doors. At the top we propped open another door and the dark of the night fell on us like a wave. It was chilly and felt good to be back in the thin air after only a few moments in the humid Chinese stairwell.

"How about this?" she laughed. "How amazing is this?"

It was amazing. The rooftop was barren and long. We could walk all the way to the edge and lean over and see down seven or eight stories; thousands of people walking up and down Canal Street, and even Mulberry Street too. It was as if the tenants of the building didn't know the rooftop existed. There was no furniture. It was clean and empty, and we sat at the lip of the building very closely, our knees almost touching, and looked together without words at the bustling night across Canal Street and down into the throat of Chinatown.

It could have been ten minutes or it could have been an hour, but at some point while we sat, Mae began to hum. She was humming like an organ. Her pipes glowed as she hummed and it made me feel great, the humming. I was glowing as she was now and I began to hum too, even though I wasn't sure what song we hummed. I was a writer, and Mae was a painter and there we were, humming together on a vacant Chinese rooftop, underneath the blue dark and fading constellations of New York City. Forever we'd be there and I knew it. Forever.

Kissing her was to love her. Kissing her was to love the moon. I knew it then as it happened. As we touched our humming lips, I knew that I loved her and I knew she loved me. We kissed for a long time, even shivering under the spring night, kissing, and talking into those kisses without care for what was said. We said foolish, funny, beautiful things into each other's mouths that night, kissing and shivering and humming and being in love. I never wanted it to end, and oh God, how I prayed.

"Oh Lord of all things help me endure. I'll say a hundred Our Fathers and a hundred Hail Marys, but I can't say them now, just please, consider them said. I'll say them later, if only you let me go home with this girl tonight. I don't want anything but to sleep close with her. If you could just give me that, to hold her and to love her, I'll be the greatest disciple you've ever known. I'll say two hundred prayers first thing in the morning, oh, sweet Lord."

We came down onto Canal Street and she waved for a cab. She looked like a statue out on the side of the street with one hand in the air, her earrings melting in light, her mouth just a crescent of a light too. When one taxi finally came, we fell into the backseat, kissing horribly, across the leather seat. "The Final Countdown" was playing on the radio, getting me excited for sex. She pulled away from me for a moment, breathing heavily and looking very deeply.

"I feel like I've known you forever," she said. "As if we've been everywhere together. Do you feel that? Have you ever felt this way?"

"I never have," I said.

"I'm not kidding," she said. "I know it sounds crazy, but it's real. Do you think things can be like this?"

"What do you mean by things?"

"Like, love."

"Do I think love can be like this?"

"I don't know what I'm saying," she laughed. "I don't know if I know what love is. But I wonder if this is it."

"The books say that love is the grandest and most tragic of all human emotions. Does this feel grand and tragic to you?"

"I can't say. I don't know how I feel. This was just so unexpected. I don't know how I feel about love. I almost feel as if love isn't an emotion at all," she said.

"What is it then?"

"It feels more as if it's...as if it's a location. Or a state. Like it can't exist unless two people reach a certain place. It's a state of things. I can say that I'm in love with somebody, but unless they're in love with me too, it's just semantics, don't you think?"

"I think whatever you think."

"No, seriously!" she said. "This is important."

"I know it is. I'm listening, tell me."

"We say 'I love you,' all the time. I can say, 'I love something,' and we know just what I mean, but it's different than *Love. L-O-V-E.* Love is a facility between two people, it's a state of transmutation, a state of sanctification."

"Love is patient, love is kind, yeah, yeah," I kissed her again.

"David! I'm serious."

"I'm sorry."

"You can call love anything you want, but you're not really defining it, you're just talking about what goes into making it. Ingredients for a recipe. Love is patient, sure. Love is sacrificial, maybe. But perhaps it's more like how God is not the sum of his parts, but everything in God is identical with his being. He is not merely merciful and truthful and good, He is Mercy, and Truth, and Goodness. Love is not patient, it is Patience. It isn't sacrificial, it is Sacrifice. I don't know—"

"I don't know either, but you're incredible."

"But what I mean to say is, love can be all of these things, or these things can be a part of love if you wish, but love in its truthfulness is a *position*, not an attribute, not an emotion. It is what you feel when two people are there together."

"And what about when somebody loves another and it's unreciprocated?"

"Maybe it's impossible for one person to love someone and the other person not. I think we try and call it love, but it's a betrayal of words. I think love is outside of us. It's a certain homeostasis, and if one person is in love and the other person out of love, then there is no homeostasis. I don't know, I'm only thinking about all of this now."

"Love," I said, looking off into the passing night. "What can I say about love that hasn't been said by you already?"

We both laughed. I saw that she was serious now. Her eyes very dark, nearly black, as there was no light anywhere between us.

"Love," I started again. "Love is when two people find themselves within each other. When looking in their eyes feels like looking in a mirror. When you can be close to them even when you are far, because when you close your eyes you remember that you were born from the same star, twins in constellation, making love and mixing electrons since before there was an Earth."

"That I agree with," she said.

"Maybe that's too intense," I said. "Nobody needs to hear that right now."

"No, go on. Tell me more."

I kissed her and held her head with one hand at the chin. "Love is safety, Mae. Your heart, your thoughts, your words, your body, your freedom; they're all safe with me. I have loved you forever. My spring, my rain, my sun, my Maest of them all. Can you feel it?"

"This is the place?" the cabbie asked. It was the corner of Bleecker and Jones, where Mae had told him.

"This is it," she said, startled. "This is the place."

"Okay, eighteen-fifty," he said. Mae already had the cash in hand and stuck it through the hole in the glass.

"Keep it all," she said.

I was already stepping out of the car and standing on the sidewalk as she made her way out. She fell into my arms and we kissed again. We walked a few steps down Jones Street, closely, with her holding my arm.

How perfect it had all been up until this moment. I should have known it wasn't going to last.

Reader, I've relived the shame of this mistake time and time again since that night, for it was here on Jones Street that I made my first of many crucial errors.

In my elated delirium I motioned towards her building, pulling her onto the first step of her own stoop. I hadn't realized it yet.

"How do you know I live here?" she asked. She was smiling, and wasn't so serious.

"Sorry?" I said.

"We were walking together, and you moved to my stoop. I hadn't moved yet."

"You moved."

"I didn't. I was about to, but you were closer and you moved."

"How would I have moved? How would I know which place is yours?"

"That's what I just asked you. You moved, David. I felt you move. Look, you're standing on the first step of my stoop. You moved."

"Well—" I had no words. She could see it in my eyes.

"David!" she laughed and grabbed both my arms. "What is going on?"

I felt just as I did that day on her doorstep with her mail in my hands. I was not only speechless, but empty.

"It's funny," I started.

"What's funny?"

"You won't be mad?"

"I don't know."

"It's nothing bad. It's funny."

"I'm waiting."

"Well, you remember how you left Katie your address? For your mail?"

"Yes."

"Well, I brought some mail over here one day. I had felt something, even then when I saw you. I asked Katie if I could have the address so I could bring your mail over. But I got nervous and left it here."

"That's where that mail came from!" she smiled.

"I'm glad you found it. I was going to talk to you, but I got nervous and left. That's it. That's all."

She started to wail with laughter. We both laughed. She hugged me laughing and then kissed me twice on the chin and then on the lips.

"You're a sweetheart!" she said. "I absolutely love this. I can't believe you."

"You can't?" I said. We were both still laughing. We were laughing so hard we were falling into each other. She loved it. She didn't mind at all. She thought that my cowardice was winsome; my insistence, romantic. I should have left it at that. I should have taken the rest of the truth with me to my grave, but I didn't. Reader, I don't know what came over me next, but in the midst of my laughter and my fervor I made yet another bad decision. This one, far worse than the last.

"You want to know something else funny?" I said, laughing, gently kissing her cheek. We stood now at her door. Our own reflections laughing with us in the windowglass of the door.

"What? What? Tell me," she said.

"Well, after that day. I had your address, you know?"

"Yeah?"

"And I came back."

"You did? For what?"

"Just to see you."

"What do you mean, 'see me?'"

It all came pouring out. I told her everything. I laughed as I told her. I waited and waited for her to laugh, to see how romantic it all was, but she just stared on. I told her how I watched her. I told her about going with her to the diners, to the train, to the gallery. I told her I'd seen her friends and I'd seen her paintings. I told her I'd seen her job and her clothes and her favorite foods. She was speechless. I didn't understand her at all. What was so romantic about delivering the mail that following her through the city didn't have? It was essentially the same act, only full of even more passion! She didn't laugh. I told her about her sister. I couldn't stop talking. I told her about my book. I was waiting for her to laugh, so I kept on speaking hoping I'd get her back, but I felt her move farther and farther away as I babbled. The less she laughed the more I spoke. I told her about the subway ad. I told her about the daydreams. I told her about Fanelli Cafe and the ill-tempered bartender. I told her about Sam stealing the address. I told her about Katie's insufferable friend. I told her about Montgomery Clift and the delightful waiter from the French bistro. I told her about Avenue A and St. Mark's. I told her everything.

She hit me very, very hard.

"You creep!" she shouted. "You lunatic!" She hit me again.

My nose was bleeding. I stepped down off the stoop.

"Mae, it's because I love you!" I shouted.

"What in the hell is wrong with you?"

"What about all of those amazing things we just said in the cab? You don't love me now?"

"You're a freak! You should be in prison."

"It's romantic, Mae! Why can't you see that it's romantic? It's just like the books!"

"It would be romantic to see you in a guillotine, you worm! If I ever, *ever* see you anywhere near me or my sister I will call the police. I will tell them everything." She pointed towards Bleecker Street. "GO! LEAVE!"

I stepped backwards into the middle of the street, holding my nose. I felt that I was looking up a hundred feet at her now. She hurried to turn her key in the door and then disappeared just as quickly behind the black of it. The door shut with a devilish conviction. I could still hear her voice in my head telling me to go. I still can to this day. All in a matter of minutes, I'd gone from having it all to having less than I'd ever had before. I walked home slowly, occasionally looking back to see if maybe she'd come back for me out of remorse. I was thinking of what I'd done wrong; what I could have done right.

Mayday. Mayday. Mayday.

Reader, I suppose only one thing kept me from killing myself that awful night. It was the thought that perhaps hope is always twinborn with love, and for that night, for the first time in a long time, I'd really felt love so I had to keep hope.

Chapter Twenty

How I Coped With My Most Recent Tragedy

S adness is sickness and sickness has symptoms. I saw her everywhere; hoping her everywhere, dreaming her everywhere. In ghosts, cannonfire, I saw her with long eyes—eyes that reached two or three city blocks, stalking me, putting me to sleep there on the sidewalk, deadcold and away as wind. I could hear things too. Her voice woven between rustling bus horns or dog games—the city rolling soft beneath her words when I went, and I went often. It's all still there when I think about it, her face reshapen as light reflected off a hubcap, bodies who moved like her but looked like mercury—her Venus ablaze, even the arrangement of faces in the trees, eyes cut out in brown, and all that long summertime green around her hair, swerving circles and headshapes, arboreal like her, and incredibly alive. I saw her everywhere. Not a night passed for months that I didn't think of being entangled in Mae's arms in the back of that taxi cab, speaking of love, speaking of us. I could lie in my bed alone listening to the nightbugs sing, feeling my lips move against the surface of that snowsoft skin again, haunted by the smell of her. I was besieged, entrenched. I was distraught. Many times I considered going back to Jones Street and lying, telling her it was all a joke; a farce intended to test her limits. Or to arrange a spontaneous meeting on the street near her studio where I could apologize and plead for a second chance back into her life, but every time I worked up the courage to leave my apartment the sunken stone of the truth sat deep in my stomach like hell in a ball. I would never see her again, and it hurt a lot.

Hardly sleeping a wink, I had plenty of time to write. I wrote up to five or six thousand words a day that summer, and edited and reedited my manuscript several times a week without seeing the sun. I had quit my job so that I could spend all the day writing. I wrote of our love. Oh, how much more verse-inspiring she was, *My Mae,* than all the previous lovers I'd encountered in my life! In Mae I had my ticket to greatness! Anything I wrote would surely prevail now, as she served as the perfect centerpiece of my story. It was so easy to write of her, to sit with eyes closed and remember those touches, those kisses, those golden breaths atop my skin.

Sam would come to visit me that summer, usually just to check that I was breathing, and to talk me out of my mania. He tried to convince me that what I had done to Mae was wrong, and that she had every right to leave me as she did. He couldn't see the truth.

"I really think you should see a professional, Dave," he said.

I could tell that Katie was getting to him and I told him so.

"Katie doesn't even know about any of this!" he claimed. He was lying to me. Everybody was lying to me. "She's been asking about you. I just want to tell her you're doing well. Can't we go for a walk? Or go for a beer? You've got to get out of this apartment."

"I can't leave right now, Sam," I said. "I'm working really well. You're going to love this book. You're going to understand every-thing when you read this book. This book is going to change my life. It could change your life too, Sammy."

"What about the other book?"

"What other book?"

"The book you were writing before, you told me it's going to be published soon."

"Yes, yes, that book. I've recalled it, Sam. It isn't worthy of being published. Not in comparison to this book, at least. This book, this will be the one to put me on the map. There's no chance for it to fail. I wish you could have met Mae. You would have loved her. She was everything I told you she'd be."

"I'm worried about you," he said. He came down to where I was sitting, cross-legged on a rug, hunched over a smoking ashtray. "I think this is all hitting you too hard. I'm sure the book is great, but you can't just live in this room like this. You need to make money, you need to breathe fresh air."

"I have the window cracked when I smoke."

"It smells like a V.F.W. hall in here. How much have you been smoking?"

"Whatever it takes."

"Come outside, please, let's take a walk."

I could see exactly what he was trying to do. He wanted to lure me outside where Katie was and they were going to find some way to embarrass me. Maybe they were going to take me to Mae's house. Or perhaps Kaite was going to scold me and tell me, 'I told you so, I told you so,' about all that had happened. I didn't feel safe going outside. I didn't feel safe with Sam. I didn't need Sam. I didn't need Katie. I didn't need anybody. All I needed was Mae and my old Underwood typewriter and my ten packs of Pall Malls and my Johnny Carson reruns. If I ever felt discouraged, all I had to do was remember. If I remembered, I could be happy. Sam didn't want me to be happy, he wanted me to think about other things. He wanted to take Mae away from me. He wanted to change me.

"If you want to sit in here and rot and die with your fantasies, go ahead," he said. "You could be so great, Dave. You really could be the best writer in this city. You're so smart, so passionate, so ambitious, but you're sick, and you let yourself be. You could even be in love too, if you'd let yourself get better."

"You sound like Katie," I said. "All you want is to bring me down."

"I'm trying to help you and you can't even see it. There's a giant glass wall between your world and ours."

"Who's?"

"Everybody's! The real world! A real world with real women, one of whom—God bless her heart—might *actually* love you! But look at you! You're never going to meet her, you're hung up on all the ones that hate you, while there is some poor woman out there as crazy and as stupid as you who you're missing out on by locking yourself up in this smokehouse and pretending to be a writer. It's insanity, Dave. Katie's right and she's always been right. You're crazy, and you won't let anybody help you." Sam took a few steps towards the door and swung it open. "I'm sorry but I can't do it anymore. I've gotta go. If you want to reach out, do it, but don't expect me to come back over here."

So there it happened, the greatest betrayal of man since Judas kissed his master. That is just the way of the world, reader; an enemy can partly ruin a man, but it takes a good-natured and judicious friend to complete the thing and make it perfect.

It's surely one of the most emotional episodes in this tale, something that I'm bothered talking about even now, but I swore I would inscribe in this document nothing but the whole truth. It all piled on so high that day in my apartment as I watched Sam walk out my door having been so twisted and rotted by the world that he couldn't see the truth before him.

As he stepped out the door, I turned in my misery to face him, taking a draw from my cigarette. "Sam," I called, "you really think there's somebody else out there for me?"

He stood looking at me through the crack of the door. I can see him now, thinking about my question. "I do, Dave. But she'd have to be the looniest woman who's ever lived."

Chapter Twenty-One
*How I Came to Meet the Looniest Woman Who's Ever
Lived*

New York was suffering from August. It happens every year. The sun rose each day with such intense heat that it would have been enough to dissolve my brains if I'd had any. The skin was peeling from the walls in my apartment, lifted and bubbling from a foul concoction of heat, cigarette smoke, and the indiscernible radiation that came off of me in rays.

I was transfigured in that room, reader. There's no other explanation for what happened to me. I was glowing and melting all at once, maddened by the heat, maddened more by Mae still, bearded and somewhere lost between cursed and holy. Time didn't exist in that room. I sat and slept cross-legged in the same place I was when Sam left me that day in June. I can't remember moving from it, though logic says I must have. I must have done a lot of things I don't remember. I must have written two-hundred thousand words that summer, smoked another twenty-thousand cigarettes, and spent two-thousand hours in the presence of myself, writing myself, righting wrongs all wrung out in rites and rings that I'd wrought. When the heat got unbearable I shut the curtains, sometimes having them shut for days or weeks at a time. There was no day or night, just blue. Blue-hanging smoke heavy and flat in the center of the room lit by lamplight, moving, but only as the ocean might; seasmoke-steady, with horizon and all. One column of chrysus-colored light from beneath a lampshade slicing across the smoke, avoiding it for fear of being cut wide-open and killed there on my workshop floor. I'd forgotten Sam and Katie all together. I'd forgotten my job. There had been some letters and calls but I hadn't attended to them.

Towards the end of August, nearing what I decided must surely have been death, I had written all that providence would allow about Mae, and I wasn't sure how to write anymore. I could hardly remember how my story with Mae ended, for I'd written and rewritten it so many times that I couldn't tell what had happened and what I'd imagined. I spent days in anguish over the manuscript, completing some few dozen drafts but none of them leaving me with a feeling of resolve. None of them felt like home, like love, like breathing. They felt like drowning. I found myself confronted with a problem that I mentioned long at the beginning of this document: I did not want to write about a love that *failed*. I wanted to write about love as perfection. And while Mae provided me the basis for the face and voice—*the center*—of my story, I still had no idea what it felt like to recline at love's table, to soak in its bath. I was starting to fear that love was not all that I'd dreamed that it was. I was starting to fear I'd never really find it. And what I had written about it wasn't good enough. I needed something more.

***

When the harrowing of hell passed and September came born from its ashes, I made the decision one day—by instincts of survival alone—to clean myself up and open the windows letting the apartment breathe for the first time since Mae left me. The sun was beginning to make its descent beneath the skyline. I loved to watch the sun move slowly, even with the aching of my eyes at its fullness I liked it.

I took to cleaning the place. I put on a Chet Baker record and let the evening breeze fill the room. I swept and mopped. I took a shower and shaved, and put on fresh clothes. I was organizing the things at my work desk—paper, pencil, and Pall Malls—when I noticed something peculiar through the open window. The street beneath my building was empty. It was a Thursday evening, a temperate September night fine for merrymaking, and there was not a soul on either Avenue A nor East 7th Street, perhaps for the first time since the Dutch had landed on the island in 1624. My initial reaction was fear, reader, as you could imagine. For I'd spent three months hibernating, becoming wholly numb to the bustle and noise outside the window, wrestling with the demons that overtook me in that cell of a room. I truly began to fear that I had missed a public evacuation of some sort, or worse, a mass extinction event. My mind raced, looking frantically into the park and atop the powerlines for so much as a bird, but nothing moved—nothing chirped. My fear grew until I saw one lone figure bobbing down Avenue A seemingly coming born from a netherworld, crossing a threshold from her far reality into mine, just far enough out of my field of view so that I could never know from where she entered my life. She appeared, ignorant of my watching her, and walked the long block parallel to the park in blissful silence, the single moving thing in New York City that moment, strutting like sunlight across the imperceptible skin of a river. She was beautiful. Dressed all in black—though shining somehow. I felt a great weakness as I watched her, almost hypnotized, like I had been only once before. She turned west onto 7th Street and went out and away from my vision, and just as I lost her down that outstretched avenue block, a flood of people repopulated the streets and music rang and cars purred and horns boomed as they fought their little wars in the streets. The world had come back to life. I knew at once it was a sign. O, my everloving Lord, how rich you are with your signs! How your humor shakes me! You with your clever riddles leading me with clue after clue, allowing me for mere moments at a time to glance into another world, just enough to know what may lie upstream. I opened my curtains to allow the evening air to overtake my room, and you graciously allowed love to overtake my heart once again. I dared not waste this gesture of mercy, and so I gathered my things, put on my shoes, and started down the stairs so as to follow this angel of the eve, hoping to catch her before her dreaded recoiling into the world of which she belonged.

Running down the street that night is something I will never forget. I was weaving myself between the dense crowd of shoppers and drinkers and commuters, feeling the setting sun cool the city. I'll remember feeling the passing of moments so slowly, letting my skin and lungs and eyes remember what it was like to live on Earth again. After about two frantic blocks, I saw her. She was sitting at a cafe that I liked on the outskirts of the neighborhood, reading at an umbrelled table on the sidewalk, as lonely as ever. I found my own table and ordered a cappuccino and laid my manuscript there in front of me. She hadn't heard me sit down. How I treasure this memory—these last moments as strangers! She was in black. Her hair was black and long, falling below the shoulders both beside and behind. Her long dress was black, consuming her full, bended body. She looked like a woman. Her shoes were black. She could tell I was looking at her now. She turned and smiled at me and I smiled back at her. I wanted her to know that I knew. She wasn't beating me. She wasn't catching me. I was letting her look. She was hidden behind black sunglasses. I wished I could see her eyes, wanting to catch them wandering to and from me in all their delight, but all I could see when I looked in their place was a faint reflection of myself loving her, backlit by the final vapors of light on that fateful day. She smiled again when I noticed myself in that reflection. Her lips were pitifully perfectly red. She set her chin upon her fist and looked back at me. Now we were in it. One of us would have to speak. I thought hard, but she drew first.

"Writing letters?" she asked.

"Yeah, I've got one here for you actually," I replied.

She laughed and sipped her coffee. I pushed out the seat in front of me with one foot, just like the books and gestured for her to sit with me.

"I can see you just fine from here," she said. She had an accent. I couldn't tell where from, but it was delectable.

"I'd love to see you a little better," I said.

"I don't let just any stranger do that," she said. "What's your name?"

"David Cale. I'm a writer. I'm writing a great novel, the greatest romance of our time."

"A romantic, huh?"

"It takes one to know one." It was just like the books.

She smiled big.

"What's your name?" I asked.

"Maud. Maud Kanavkin."

Oh, it was horrible. Maud! Maud like mud like fraud like broad. Like gaudy, like laundry. Maud? Maud what?

"What kind of name is that?" I asked.

"Like yours is any better," she laughed. "David Cale. Goddamn cereal box name."

"It's a good American name," I argued.

"Sure, and I've bet you've got it written on your underwear."

"Hey now—"

"I'm only joking with you. My real last name is Carter," she said. "Kanavkin means 'ditch' in Russian. It's Chekhov." She closed her book.

"Maud Carter?" I asked.

"That's me."

"Sounds like the name of an old housekeeper."

"Maybe I am a housekeeper."

"You don't look like one," I said. "You look like trouble."

"Maybe I'm that too."

"Where are you from?"

"Indiana."

"Then where is your accent from?"

She thought for a moment. "I don't think I have an accent, do I?"

"I hear one," I said. "It's lovely. It must be that Hoosier accent. Come to think of it, I never did meet anybody from Indiana."

"That's a shame," she said. "Indiana has the best people. You know who's from Indiana?"

"James Dean."

She smiled big. "You're absolutely right. And not only him, but Hoagy Carmichael."

"And Wes Montgomery."

She stood up finally, pushed in her chair very slowly, and walked to the open chair across from me. She sat down, holding the sides of her black dress tight at her legs. A valley gave way between them and I could see the structure of her figure well. She was perfectly sculpted. She was perfectly perfect. She pulled a cigarette from her bag and put it between those red lips. She lit it and the fire of its end matched the color of her lips.

"I've always wanted to meet a writer," she said, breathing smoke out her nose. "Writers must be smart. Do you think you're pretty smart?"

"I like to think so."

"What's the book about?"

"A woman."

"What kind of woman?"

"A great woman."

"That's all you got? A great woman? How do you expect to sell a book when that's all you can say about her? That she's a 'great woman.'"

"Well, I think she's more than that," I said. "She's romantic, graceful, delicate, beautiful."

"Oh, how original. Who's going to read another book about a great guy who falls in love with a great woman?" She began to stand up.

"Wait," I said. I took her hand and led her back down to the table. "That's not it. She's not great, or romantic, she's something better all together."

"Oh, yeah?"

"Yes, something that none of the others have going for them."

"What's that?"

"She's loony. Maybe the looniest," I said. "She's the looniest woman who's ever lived."

"I think that the greatest woman who's ever lived and the looniest woman who's ever lived are probably the same woman," she said.

"I think so too," I said.

We smiled at each other. She pushed the pack of cigarettes at me and I lit one sitting across from her. Our smoke made love between us, twirling in the tumbling wind that moved down the Bowery.

Chapter Twenty-Two
How I Told Sam and Katie About How I Met Maud

Our date was set for the next night. I was so excited I could hardly contain myself. I walked to the West Side to see Sam, all filled with news, filled with life. I would be happy to see him, and I hoped Katie would be there too. They'd been worrying about me, I was sure. I couldn't wait to tell them about the progress I'd made on my manuscript and about how I'd met Maud. I stood at their stoop and rang the bell. It was nighttime now—a precious September night in New York City. I could hear the rumble of Greenwich Avenue just around the other side of the block.

Sam answered the door, happy to see me and equally irritated that I was there.

"You're alive then," he said. I hugged him. It felt good to hug him. "David's here," he called back into the house. Katie came stomping out from behind the kitchen corner. She stood and looked at me. Sam shut the door behind us.

"You stupid idiot," she said. She came over and hit me hard all across my arms and body. It didn't hurt but she hit me a lot. "You lunatic! What the hell is the matter with you?"

"You ask me that question a lot, Kate." I hugged her. She fell into my arms like a doll, neither fighting nor participating.

"You know, I had to give Mae another stack of her mail last month and she told me you were a nutcase. Told me to stay away from you."

"What we had couldn't be contained, it's true," I said. "The truest flames often burn the hottest."

"You're nuts."

"Correct you might be," I said, "but if history and literature have shown us anything at all, it is that the deepest loves often tend to manifest themselves in maladies. Our love was deep, and our sickness was madness."

"She said she was terrified for her life."

"Alright," Sam said. "Can we just be happy that Dave is alive? You should have seen him last time I did. I didn't think he was going to make it."

"I'm a new man now, Samuel. That David you once knew is dead."

"Great," Katie said.

"I'm in love," I said. "I'm in love and her name is Maud."

Katie left the room.

"Katie, wait," I cried. The bedroom door slammed.

"Maud? That's not a very romantic name," Sam said.

"No, Sam, it's not. It's a poor name. A foul and ugly name. However, you wouldn't believe the rest of this woman. She is perfect. More perfect than Mae even. Further away and closer all at once. I met her tonight. We talked for two hours, she absolutely understands me, Sam. More than you, more than Mae ever did or could have. She's just like me. She's romantic. We live in the same world, on the same plane, she and I. You wouldn't believe how we talked, it was like writing. I've never talked to somebody that gave me the same feeling as writing! It was like living inside her brain, and she in mine. It was different this time. Different than Mae, different than all the others. This didn't feel new, Sam, it felt old. Very, very old like I'd done it before."

"So really the only problem with her is the name?"

"Yes, that is right my friend. The name is bad indeed. We're going to have to do something about the name."

"Do something about it?"

"Well, I have some ideas."

"Have some ideas? What do you mean? What ideas?"

"Well, I'm not comfortable sharing just yet. We have a date tomorrow. I want to be sure it isn't a fluke. I want to be sure that what I believe to be there is actually there. If I see what I saw today—if I feel what I felt and am feeling now—we will do something about the name."

"I see."

"Both of them."

"Both of what?"

"The names. My name too."

"What's wrong with your name?"

"Oh, Sam, don't be pedestrian. Have you never considered the dullness of my name? 'David Cale.' Do you hear how stale and sterile that name is, Sam? It's a goddamn cereal box name."

"What?"

"If we're as in love tomorrow night as we were today, we're going to do something about these names."

Sam was speechless. He looked at me as if he'd never met me before. "But what about the Sylvie girl? Wasn't her only problem her name too?"

"Yes, but this is entirely different. Sylvie is a beautiful name, unusable on account of a personal bias; circumstance. Maud, *Maud* is an objectively sorry name. And my lover knows it. She would love to change it, but she has no excuse to. I'm going to show her how. I'm going to save her from that cursed name, and save myself too. The Bible says that a good name is better than any perfume, Sam."

"I don't think that's what they meant when they said that."

"The Bible has many interpretations, Sam. No matter, what's decided is decided."

"I suppose the David I once knew certainly is dead then."

"I tried to tell you, Sam. Nothing has ever done me over like this. You should have seen her, you should have met her!"

"Well, what is she like? What does she look like?"

"Imagine the blackest woman you've ever met."

"She's black?"

"No, I mean what she is."

"What is she?"

"Oh, what isn't she! She's mysterious. She's intelligent. She's exotic. She has the longest, blackest hair that rolls down her shoulders like black fire. She was in a wonderful dress."

"Black?"

"Oh, yes. You would have loved it, Sam. Had you seen her, you'd have recognized her as my one true love right away."

"What else?"

"She was cool. She had this sense of control, like I couldn't have done anything to impress her. There was this incredible sexiness to that. But she's honest too. Honest and sincere. Oh, and her accent. She has the subtlest, most erotic voice you'd ever hear."

"Where is she from?"

"Indiana."

"Indiana? They don't have an accent in Indiana. Not any different than ours anyway."

"Of course they do, Sam, don't talk silly. Who have you met from Indiana?"

"I don't know. Somebody, I'm sure."

"I realized today that I hadn't personally met a Hoosier before. Maud is the first one and she has an accent. Sam, you'll absolutely love her accent."

"What brought her to New York?"

"She's an heiress."

"An heiress of what?"

"Something about her grandfather owned a bunch of farmland. Cattle ranches and what-not. Some thousands of acres. Both her parents passed early in her life and she was raised by her grandparents. Well, just two years ago both grandparents passed and left her with all that property. She sold it all. Wanted to go somewhere to spend the money."

"I don't know if that makes her an heiress."

"That's how she put it anyway," I said.

"So she's rich?"

"Richer than Solomon."

"How's her face?"

"Sublime. Lips as red and round as burning azaleas."

"Good nose?"

"Proportionate. Unnoticeable."

"And the eyes? You know the eyes have to be just right."

The eyes. I searched my mind again and again but drew blank. It was blackness. It was me. When I saw her eyes I only saw me.

"She wore sunglasses," I said. "But I'm sure they're exquisite, matching the rest of her."

"I'm sorry?" Sam said. He stood as he said this. "You didn't see her eyes?"

"Sam, you should have seen her."

"You asked a woman out on a date without seeing her eyes?"

"She was wearing sunglasses, I—"

"She never took them off?"

"No."

"She didn't have the consideration to take them off? I'm sorry, but you can't interact with a stranger for two hours without taking off your sunglasses."

"Sam—"

"You have no clue what's going on under there, Dave. That's the whole face right there!"

"I assure you she is beautiful. I would go as far as saying flawless even. Her hair is perfect, lips and cheeks and nose all in proportion. Her body is out of a magazine. Wonderfully dressed too."

"But no eyes?"

"No eyes."

"Or brow?"

"No brow."

"You hardly know what this woman looks like!" He was pacing the room now. I could hear Katie laughing in the other room.

"You idiot!" she called out. "I hope she doesn't have any eyes."

"You have no idea what this woman looks like," Sam repeated.

"Sure I do, don't be dramatic. She's gorgeous. You didn't see her."

"And neither did you! No eye, and no brow? That's like going on a blind date. You're going on a blind date with a woman you've already met! And she's the one wearing the glasses!"

"Well, how bad can it be?" I said. I was starting to panic. "What are the chances that every last aspect of this woman—down to the freckle—is absolutely perfect, and her eyes are such an outlier that she's deemed unlovable? Chance alone says that if her genetics are favorable in nine ways then they are favorable in ten."

"I disagree," Katie said. She had entered the room again. "Nobody is that perfect. If they seem perfect and they act as if they're hiding something it's because what they're hiding is imperfect."

"She wasn't hiding her eyes," I said. "It was sunny."

"I thought you said it was evening," Sam said.

"I don't need to hear this right now—"

"There's a lot that can go wrong under there," Katie said. "I can think of plenty of times I thought somebody was attractive until they took their sunglasses off. Eyes are really important. I think you're in big trouble."

"Well if she wears sunglasses all the time then she's beautiful all the time, problem solved," I said. "Nobody will be able to tell. I'll just take her outside if I have to."

"And in the winter?" Katie said.

"Snow is bright," I said. "People wear sunglasses in the winter all the time."

"At night?" Sam said.

"We'll only meet in the day! Will you guys just cut it out? You have me all mixed up. There is nothing wrong with her eyes. I saw her. I spoke to her. She is perfect. She loves me, I know it. She's stunning. You'll see. You two will meet her and you'll see. She's the greatest woman who's ever lived."

"I can't wait," Katie said. "I'm just dying to meet her, Dave. The no-eyed cattle heiress with the charming Indiana accent named Maud. I'm sure she's a catch."

"We certainly do need to do something about the name."

Chapter Twenty-Three

Of My Delightful First Date With the No-Eyed Cattle Heiress With the Charming Indiana Accent Named Maud

We were to meet at the Roxy Hotel. It was one of my favorite places to spend a night out, a venue known for its class and Old World sensibilities. They had a fantastic piano player, the oysters were always fresh, and the table service was excellent. It was a great place for the common man to be treated like a king.

I entered the lobby, open like a garden with a tall ceiling and old turn-of-the-century paintings and decor. Dark green plants patterned the walls and ran along the handrail of the winding ramp that led to the hotel restaurant where the sound of glasses mixed with the cracking of pool balls. Everybody was dressed as they should be—no flip flops or golf shirts in the Roxy. Gentlemen wore coats and the ladies were ornamented in their best jewelry. The host received my name, found my reservation and led me to my table. It was all set. Now, all I had to do was wait.

At my table I watched the big art deco doors, waiting for my love to enter. The hosts welcomed each guest—a diverse bunch—who all played their minuscule part in the drama that played out before me, the characters in my tale of love. A man with a velvet vest, his hair back like a bomber pilot. A man and woman tied so closely together they might as well have worn the same suit. They sat together closely too, not across from each other but knee to knee at their little two-person-table. And then a beautiful blonde, single and vain. She waved off the man at the podium, stepping one slender foot in front of the other poking out of her burgundy dress. She walked straight for the bar and sat and ordered a drink. I watched the men bark as she sipped. The piano was playing now, the lights went dim. I waited and waited for Maud as pairs of people were deflected from the host to tables all around me.

A twitchy-looking goat-faced girl approached the stand. They talked for a few moments, and suddenly turned towards me. The host led her through the weaving crowd and dead-on to my table. I wondered, what on earth could this poor woman want with me? Perhaps she was confused, looking for a reservation under a similar name—Kell, or Kale, or Bacall, or Calé. Or maybe she thought she knew me from somewhere else and wished only to say hello before continuing on to her own reservation. Or perhaps something happened to Maud, and she sent a friend to tell me of her absence, or even more plausibly: a red-lipped batfish got caught in the sludge of some nuclear waste and grew a pair of legs and walked on into the Roxy Hotel looking for me.

"David," she said.

"Yes?"

"It's great to see you."

"I'm sorry?"

"Maud Carter," she said. "Your date. You are David, right?"

"Do you have any tables available on the terrace?" I asked the host.

"Unfortunately the terrace is full, sir."

"It would be, wouldn't it."

"I prefer it indoors anyway," Maud said. "It's so bright outside, the sun stays out for so long this time of year."

"It sure does," I said, "it sure does."

***

I'll give it to Sam, that hapless son-of-a-bitch, he sure can be halfwitted, but when he's right, he's as right as a gypsy woman. Those two eyes were so greatly unrelated to each other you'd have to call them two different organs. One of them was in the wrong place all together—not the eyeball, but the socket itself—as if there was some muscular lift beneath it from the nose-side persuading it to fall right off the face. The other was where it should be, though the eyeball was discolored, too big for its socket and heavily lazy. She was as symmetrical as coal. And it wasn't only the eyes. The whole crater of skin that surrounded the socket was, to use a euphemism, diseased. Black wells of sleeplessness deepened the upper cheeks, the eyebrows were unkempt, overgrown and apeish. Even the bones that protruded from the sides of the upper-nose were uneven, one almost non-existent and the other marble-like not only in shape but in its vague greenishness. She smiled big as she sat down, and I wondered what had happened to the jungle vine that she'd swung in on.

"It's great to see you," she said.

"Good!" I said.

"How have you been since the last time I saw you?"

"When was that? Yesterday? How have I been since yesterday?"

"Yes, I suppose," she laughed. "How was today?"

"Interesting," I said. "Full of surprises."

"Good surprises or bad surprises?"

"Not good or bad really, just surprises. A surprise isn't always good or bad, you know, it can just be surprising."

"Well, my day was just wonderful. I couldn't stop thinking about this."

"About what?"

"About you."

"What do you mean?"

And as she began this winding monologue that seemed to go on for an eternity, I studied deeply the imperfections of her face. I didn't hear a word she said. I only thought about what I had done. Oh, how beautiful she once was! How perfect she felt in my dreams last night! What pitiful luck of mine that this perfect woman would turn out to look like this! What was I supposed to do?

"...and I wanted to shake it off, thinking that something like this could never happen to me, but somehow I came to peace with it. Like it had been waiting for me. Like the circumstances of it all were all too strange to be a coincidence. Like the divine hand of providence plucked me from a sort of non-existence and put me on that cafe terrace last night. And I couldn't stop thinking about it. The more and more I tried to get my mind off it, the more I thought about it. It's all just so incredibly romantic, don't you think?"

"Sorry?" I said. I wasn't listening. "What was it that was romantic?"

"Oh, just that you're a writer. I was thinking about it all morning, how perfect it is that we met. I came to this city to find something like this; *somebody*. Somebody who knew about the *real world* behind the curtain of this charade people pass off as living. And when you suggested the Roxy Hotel, I just died. It's a dream. It is just like all of the books."

I couldn't believe what I was hearing. I was reminded as to why I fell in love with her the night before; she was speaking of the real world, she was speaking as a muse might, magically masterful and void of shame. It was exactly my language. Maud could understand me, she impressed me immediately.

"You're absolutely right," I said. "It is so incredibly romantic."

"All in the most romantic city in the world," she said.

"Do you think so? New York?"

"Well, what else would it be?"

"New York is certainly a great contender but I couldn't say with complete certainty..."

"What is it then?"

"Well, that's a complicated answer. My first answer would be Rome. I mean, it lends its own name to the very act. Romance in its ontology is being Roman in a sense, isn't it?"

"Oh, not anymore," she said. "Don't you think that things can take on an essence of their own while still being indebted to something else? Romance has nothing to do with Rome. Rome is a true thing and romance is...well, romance is by definition an aesthetic thing, a nature of other things, even if that nature was born from a true thing."

"That's an interesting way to think about it," I said. The sound of the piano swam between us. A playful Dizzy Gillespie tune floating just above our words.

"For instance," she said, pointing up into nothingness, "Dizzy might have *invented* bebop, but did he play it best?"

"Maybe he did."

"Sure, but maybe he didn't," she said. "Miles could be the only trumpet player to have ever existed and jazz would be doing just fine without the rest."

"But some of us prefer the way Dizzy plays."

"And some of us prefer New York City to Rome."

"Alright, let's exclude Rome and New York City."

"No problem." She smiled like she knew what she wanted to say. She was hideous. "Rome isn't even the most romantic city in Italy. I'd go with Florence or Venice before Rome."

"I'd go with Vienna before any Italian city besides Rome."

"I'd go with Seville before Vienna."

"No, no. Spain isn't romantic! Not in the same way the rest of Western Europe is romantic, at least."

"How so?"

"It just isn't poetic. Italy and Austria are both poetic. Spain is louder. Spain is prose."

"And what does Spain say?"

"Spain is tragic and serious, ancient in a vulgar, violent way. It's always trying to teach you something. Italy and Austria are about how things *feel*, Spain is about how things *are*."

"And where does France fall into this?" she asked.

"Well, of course France is poetic. France is as poetic as rain."

"So can't we agree that Paris is the most romantic city?"

"*Everybody* thinks Paris is the most romantic city. It's a bit of a trope isn't it?"

"A trope can be true."

She smiled in a certain way and she was suddenly beautiful.

"You're right," I said, "but I think *Casablanca* made Paris romantic to people who have never been to Paris, and so there is a certain...saturation."

"I love *Casablanca*."

"Of course, who doesn't, my point is—"

We looked long at each other. She wasn't so bad after all. The light was dimming, and her smile was really quite earnest there under the lobby lights of the Roxy. The piano was airy and smooth between us, letting conversation breathe just between the passing notes. At certain angles, in certain light, she reminded me of somebody. I couldn't quite put my finger on who, but her face took on the face of another as we spoke. Soon the drinks came over and we touched our glasses.

"My point is that it's hard to tell if Paris truly is the most romantic city in the world and that is why that film glorifies it as such, or if the adoration comes from the glorification in the film."

"The French are certainly the most romantic people, though, couldn't we agree on that?" she said.

"I'd have to agree. It's between them and the Italians again. Those two countries have romance figured out."

"The Italians are not that romantic, they're too fussy."

"Then who can compete with the French?"

"Not the Spanish, right?"

"No. Again, the Spanish aren't classically romantic. There's too much darkness to them. And besides, they don't have any great romantic names. Spanish names aren't romantic at all."

"French names are so romantic," she blushed.

"I know. That's one of the reasons they're the most romantic people."

"But the language is so ugly, with the spit and the throatiness. It's like they're coughing out words."

"I think that's a misconception," I said. "A lot of people think French happens in the back of the throat as in *marcher*, or *garder*, but most of it happens just below the gums, in the trenches of excess, rounded by R's and moved by vowels through the pit of the mouth. Like this: *Cela ne semble-t-il pas magnifique?*"

"*Trés bien!*"

"French on the first date!" I said.

"It is very romantic," she said. "It's just like one of the books."

She put one hand on mine, the two resting together on the table.

I was not sitting with the same woman who had come in through that door. It had been a test. It was either a farce by the devil himself or a test of integrity laid out for me by the Most High. For when we began to speak like this, in that secret coded language of all things precious and hidden from the world like romance and beauty and truth, she became as another. I couldn't say if it was my eyes or hers, but something changed. I never saw her as she was again. That goosegirl who had sat down at my table had become the woman in black once more, so sensual and sure of herself just like at the cafe the night before. And the longer we talked, the more she moved. She became ancient and bright as a star. My star, my moon, returned to me like I knew she would be. She was beautiful. She was the most beautiful girl in the world, and I knew just what I would call her.

Chapter Twenty-Four
How My Name Wound Up Becoming Dick Melish

Laying beside her on the top floor of the Roxy, my lovely little passion thing close to me after our haste decision to book the largest room on the highest floor in Manhattan's finest hotel. She's an heiress, we needed to spend the money somehow, reader. We lay skin to skin after a tormenta of touch, smoking Pall Malls and laughing at the smoke collecting at the ceiling of the room. Outside, through the vining smoke we could see Manhattan. We could see the yellowish lights of the towers birthing from the sky, black where there should have been an earth. Yellow-white lights teased the faint impressions of shapes through the blackness, tracing the holes of light like near stars, breathing light with afterglow just below the true sky, perhaps beautiful buildings in themselves out on some other island, some other astral Manhattan. Each and every star blinked for us.

There on the satin sheets of the Roxy, with the terminus of our second bottle of champagne standing upright on the mattress, we talked. We talked like we'd known each other a thousand years. Her whispers were close to my ear, I could hear every word, indistinguishable in origin from the words that populated my own mind. Every time I looked at her she was beautiful. I didn't know what I had possibly considered before, and I didn't care to find out. She was untouchable, she was exotic, she was astute, she was rich, she was arcane, she was lovely, and she was mine. There was only one real problem left.

"I've been thinking," I said.

"You always are, dearest."

Her lips fell upon the nape of my neck.

"As I've already declared, I'm in love with you. I'm madly and passionately, helplessly and glowingly in love with you…"

"And I'm in love with you!" she remarked.

"And I think you're perfect…"

"And you, sweet."

"I only have one reservation."

"What is it?"

"It's just something we spoke about the day that we met."

"Yesterday?"

"I suppose it was yesterday, wasn't it? I feel I've lived ten lives with you this night."

We embraced under the softness of the sheets and kissed. Our cigarettes burned from our free hand.

"Well, what is it then?" she pestered.

"It's only that I want to give you the best, most romantic experience possible."

"Yes?"

"And you once mentioned that you didn't find my name to be so romantic."

"Oh, dearest, don't be insecure about something like that. You can't help that."

"Sure I can," I attested. "I very much can."

"It's not your fault, you can't."

"I can."

"How?"

We looked at each other underneath the sheets.

"You don't mean?" she said.

"Yes."

"You want to?"

"Yes."

"You're sure?"

"Let's do it."

"Lets?"

"Yes, my love, the two of us together, let's change our names. Let's change them to exactly how each other prefers. The Bible says that a good name is better than any perfume. I could be called absolutely anything you'd like. Think about that! Your dream name, your dream man, and the most perfect love ever had. *Exactly* how you'd want it. Go on! Name me. What would you like to name me?"

For a moment she stared onto me like I had committed apostasy. She was surprised, and a little sad in her eyes. I held her hands and laid my face very close, so that she could see me nameless; just briefly nobody as she thought of her answer.

"I could call you anything?" she said.

"Anything, my love."

"Well, I wouldn't even know where to start. Could you help me? If you were to change your name, what would you want it to be?"

Now, I had thought about this for a long time prior to this day. As any good romantic should, I had assembled a long list of names I figured I'd call myself if I ever had to change it quickly and get out of town.

"Henry Steel," I said.

"Not a chance!" she exclaimed. "You sound like an old-time train conductor."

"You could call me Hank."

"I'd rather not."

"Okay, Clay Driscoll."

"Anything else?"

I thought hard. There was one other name that I loved, it had come to me in a dream long ago and I'd never forgotten it. It was a great name for a romantic, but a poor name for a gentile, so I saved it for last.

"Fielding Melish?" she laughed. "What kind of name is that?"

"It's a great name," I said.

"I'm not going to call you Fielding."

"Then what do *you* want to call me? This is about *you!*"

She thought for one moment, and then cracked a genuine smile.

"You'll be Richard. Richard Melish and I'll call you Dick."

"Dick?"

"Dick. After Dick Van Dyke. He was my girlhood crush. I used to watch reruns with my grandparents back in Indiana. I was in love with him. I had posters and buttons and T-shirts and dolls."

"They made Dick Van Dyke dolls?"

"I had them all."

"Fascinating."

"I was completely in love with him, and now I'm in love with you, so you shall be Dick."

"It's settled," I said. We kissed. "Do you know where Dick Van Dyke is from?"

"Of course," she said. "He's from Missouri."

"Just like me," I said.

"All the greats came from the Midwest."

"You're an angel."

"And me? What do you want to call me?"

"Well your last name is easy," I said. "We can change Carter to the more French-sounding *Cartier.*"

"Oh, French names are the best! How romantic!" she smiled. "And my Christian name?"

I looked deep into her wide eyes. We were very close, so I whispered it, as if I whispered the words right into her mouth and filled up her soul with the breath of life.

"Mae Cartier?" she said.

"It is a name, in my opinion, musical, uncommon, and expressive."

"Mae Cartier." She smiled and kissed me. "I love it. Dick Melish and Mae Cartier."

"It does have quite a ring to it."

"It does, doesn't it? It says something about us. Between your writing and my money, there's nothing we won't do. We're going to be the talk of New York."

"Think about how much more romantic this is," I said.

"You were right all along, dear. You always knew. I'm sorry I doubted you about the names. I can't believe all this!"

And we fell into each other again in that bed, rolling like wheels across each other, leaving tire tracks all up and down the roads and avenues that tied my land to hers. Nothing would ever tear us apart. Nothing could ever.

That's the story of the first night Mae and I ever spent together, and that's the story of how my name wound up becoming Dick Melish.

Chapter Twenty-Five

How I Introduced Mae to Sam and Katie

Thus began the happiest time of my life. We spent every holy second together, as close as twins, like we'd never been apart, as if we couldn't remember a time we weren't wholly consumed by one another. We discovered ourselves through discovering each other, feeling the each of us buried deep in the words we shared. We were twisted and turned in golden helix outside of ourselves; we were living forever on the wings of love. It was as if we were the only things that existed—not even our bodies existed!—solely the vague preternatural hives of consequence that we called our two selves, like columns of fire stalking tall from the bore of a train engine; we were and always had to be.

In those days we ruled the neighborhood. Mae moved into my apartment on 7th and A that summer and we never got any sleep. And we liked it. We stayed out late circusing Alphabet City until we couldn't stand, and then I'd be up early in the morning to write. While I wrote she went out "scavenging," or at least that's what she called it—that is, to capture ideas, to keep the sketchbook full. In the afternoon I'd be done writing and she'd come home and she would begin to paint.

Sound familiar? It's because it's all true, reader. Every last word of it. This is the story of how we got here. She became the muse I'd always needed to finish—and in one sense, begin—my book. I was filling page after page with blessed words about my Mae; how I saw her in that little bar on the corner of St. Mark's and A, how

I yearned for her, and how I saw her once again waitressing in that little cafe, seemingly waiting for the moment I'd come through that door and change all that she knew about life and love forever. I wrote about our nascent passion, our uncanny becoming. I wrote about my writing and I wrote about her painting. Oh, how I wish you could have been a fly on the wall during those days, reader; those seasoned autumn days with her at her canvas melting away, and myself at my desk, working like rifle fire. We opened up all the windows and drank wine throughout the day, making love and making noise between the work. It was the life I'd always dreamed I'd have. My work was incontestable, our love was growing by the moment, New York was as glorious as ever, and our home was full of sunglasses.

It was at my suggestion that Mae started her painting. She had never done it before, and she worked so hard to learn. She recognized its romantic value right away. It was a sacramental outward expression of love. She took classes and courses through the fall, shadowing some of the finest painters in New York, mastering proper technique in just a number of weeks that would have cost the common person years of their time. It did pay to be an heiress. We dined well five nights a week, drinking only the best wine, champagne, and liquor. She funded a new wardrobe for me; nothing too obtrusive, a closet full of white James Deans and a garden of blazers, jackets, and sports coats so as to appear writerly at all times. Mae wore dresses, heeled shoes, colorful jewelry, sweet-smelling things, and lipstick. When we went out together, cars crashed in debilitating awe of us.

Time seemed to pass us very quickly, as it will do when you fall in love. One day we were close and warm inside the highest window of the Roxy and the next it seemed we were feeling the first frosts of winter, deep in the gut of November, having never remembered leaving the house. It occurred to me that in the mania of our new love and the finishing of my book, I hadn't seen or even thought about Sam and Katie. The last time I'd seen Sam was the night before I took Mae on our first date and that little devil patronized me for my optimism. He thought my meeting with Mae would blow up in my face. And yet in all that time I hadn't even felt the pride—Lord, humble me—to strike down his doubts and shatter his confidence in my failure. I decided at once I had to prove him wrong. I wanted to hear him say that Mae was the most marvelous miracle he'd ever seen. I wanted him to know she was mine. And Katie too would certainly owe me the mightiest of apologies for the frankly destructive nature of her discourses over the course of our friendship. Reader, believe me when I say I didn't mean to boast in my new love, I only wanted to share the good news, but in the sharing of that news, I wanted both Sam and Katie to recognize just how good it was.

Before going to see Sam and Kate, I briefed Mae on the rather miserable disposition she would encounter in regards to my sorry friends. Lord knows that I loved them, but they had the imagination of cinderblocks, the capacity for hope of two beached whales. They were trapped in the cyclical snare of their fleeting lives. What did they have to live for? What were they chasing? They seemed all too content with operating as machinery, as slow-moving parts in a fast-moving world. It was a fact all too sensitive to make them aware of, so I only warned Mae that we were not to push and poke them on the subject of romance, for there was a chance that their own romance was failing on account of the fact that they didn't even believe in it! Sam and Katie were still good people, I told Mae. Just because they were unhappy, stubborn, and deprived didn't disqualify them from being good friends, so for that, we would see them on the grounds of friendship. Besides, if it weren't for Katie, I would have never fallen into the dizzying sequence of events that led me to my Mae anyhow. If anything, we ought to thank her together.

It was Christmastime in New York when we decided to make our way to the West Side. We bundled ourselves up, donning sweaters and scarves and mitts, and all the great romantic garments of the winter season. It was certainly cold. We walked up A to 14th Street and went west from there. Snow fell like shards of heaven. Everything was for us in those days. Everything bowed in front of us, everything changed so that we could stay the same.

We held each other as we walked, two lovers warm and close in the cold. Lights of blue and green and red and gold decorated the trees and stoops, even the streetlamps and bus stops. We saw some charity Santa Clauses ringing their bells, and a group of little children selling a sort of homemade reindeer feed. Music was in the air, and everyone was smiling; even for the cold and the slippery snow along 14th Street people were smiling. Ah reader, in case you have never been, the winter in New York is magnificent until January. Those December days are otherworldly— saved and framed in my mind for all the other days for the rest of the year. Set beside the wet gray nothing-days of March, the blistering, smelly heat of August, even the deceitfully unpleasant chill of autumn, December in New York could do no wrong.

We arrived at Sam and Katie's place in the blue-dark of the eve. It was still early, nearing suppertime, but the sun had no chance to light the earth on account of the sprawling metropolis. Occasional fumes of light seemed to break through the avenues, coming softly between a crack between buildings and disappearing in an instant with the setting of the sun. I held a fresh-cooked apple pie in one hand and Mae held a bottle of wine. The idea was to surprise them. I wanted to come to them like a thief in the night, or more like the wise men to the manger. I wanted to bear gifts, to celebrate love, friendship, and Christmas!

I knocked hard on the door, smiling, lit up like a Christmas pine. It came open quickly and Sam stood there. He looked older than I remembered him. He didn't smile nor grouch at me, he only said: "Hi."

"Samuel!" I let myself in, and my lady along with me. I embraced my old friend. "You must have thought I'd forgotten you! Let it be known it isn't true, my friend. Let it be known that I was totally consumed by another—this dashing, daring, delectable doll I call Mae—but oh, how I've thought of you in these passing weeks. We bring gifts. A feast is in order!"

"Is that right?" he said, watching us as we slipped off our shoes. "You haven't forgotten us?"

"'Forgotten' is such a strange word, don't you think? Have I forgotten you if I think about you every day? Have I forgotten you if I wish to see you, but never do? I haven't forgotten you, Sam. You know the power of these things; if there is one event that exceeds the trivialities of everyday life and forgoes the holding of responsibility in the absence we've had in each other's lives, surely, it must be the sweet purity of newlove, right? For I've been in love all this time, but don't be deceived, I've been thinking of you! Have I ever been more occupied than I am now? Only God knows. This, this is the collateral of my trouble, friend," I gestured towards Mae. "This woman here is the woman we spoke so intimately about some time ago, just at the dawn of our reddening love. We bloomed, Sam. She is me, and I am her. We are at all times one and never alone, even when we are far we are close. This is her, Sam. I've been telling you about her for years—the woman I was born to love—and now I want to show you that I've had a good reason to be absent these last months. Would you believe it, Sam? This is her. This is Mae."

Mae stuck out her perfect hand and Sam shook it quickly without smiling or saying anything.

"It is a pleasure to meet you," Mae said.

"Isn't she lovely?" I said.

"David," said Sam.

"Ah! This brings me to my next point. Before you speak again, let me announce that I no longer answer to that name. Things have changed since I saw you last. Please, if you beckon me further, my name is Dick.”

“Dick?”

“Dick!” Mae said.

“Dick,” I said. “Mae chose it. We have given each other new names, to coincide with our greatest fantasies of love. She didn’t like my name, little old David. She said it was juvenile, grainish even.”

“Sounded like the way a milk carton looks,” Mae said.

“And to match her demands, I modified ever so slightly her own identity so that we may both live in the finest sort of love, so that we may stand in its untethered light without shadows, without dark. We are metamorphosed! We agreed to do it, Sam, all for each other. So that the other may love just as they wish, and be loved in return. The sacrifice of having something as true as this.”

“David—”

“Are you listening to me at all you troubled old goat?”

“It’s hard at first, but you get used to it,” Mae said. “Go ahead, call him Dick.”

“Dick,” said Sam.

“What is it?” I smiled.

“You need to go.”

“Go? Why, we’ve just arrived. And we bring gifts. It is the yuletide afterall, can’t we at least dine, have a coco?”

“David—”

“Besides, I haven’t seen Katie, the old firecracker. Let’s see her!” I called out into the living room behind the vestibule wall, “Oh, Katie! I’ve got a bottle of red for you, you little *mostriciattola!*”

“David Cale!” she called back.

Sam closed his eyes. “Dave, you’ve gotta go,” he said.

“Sam, don’t be rash. Katie must meet Mae!”

“Mae?” Katie’s voice came from around the corner again. She was screaming. She came out of the bedroom and into the foyer where we stood. She looked at Mae. "Hail Mary!" she said. "I told you she was hiding them!"

"Hiding what?" Mae said.

"The two of you get out of my house or I'll call the police."

"Oh, Katie!" I said back.

"Leave!" she screamed.

And then I heard it. The baby. It started to wail and cry like a siren. Screeching, belly-blasting cries that tore through the whole apartment.

"Oh Sam," I said, "I'm so sorry."

"David, you have to go."

"Sam, with all due respect, it's Dick."

"Out!" Sam shouted. I'd never heard him shout like that before. The apartment was in chaos now. Sam was blood-red, and he'd snatched the gifts from our hands. Katie was shouting undetectable words over the crying of the baby whose screeches shattered my brain like the tone of a foghorn. "OUT!" Sam screamed again.

"Sam please," I yelled. "Won't you just talk to me? Come outside, let's talk."

He stood close behind me, shoving me until we both stood out on the stoop—the stoop where my Mae had stood a thousand times when she lived in that house, and there we were all over again, together and during Christmas.

Sam stood on the top now and rushed us down the steps of the stoop. He closed the door behind him and looked down at us as we shivered together on the street.

"Dick," he said. He looked at Mae and gestured across the street. There was a park just across the street from the house. "I'm sorry Mae, but could you give the two of us some privacy for a couple of minutes?"

"Of course," she said. "Sorry to cause so much trouble."

"It isn't you," Sam said.

"Nice to meet you anyway."

"You too."

She walked across the street gracefully and beautifully as always. I watched her deeply.

"David, look at me. You have to see how mad this all is."

"Sam, I'm willing to speak with you and explain to you anything you might need explained, only if you respect my wishes regarding my identity. This is no silly game, this is no temporary thing. I am in love with Mae. She is the greatest thing that has ever happened to me and she has asked that I be called Dick so that is what I will be called."

"I don't even know you."

"Oh, don't try to act like we can't understand each other, Sam. Let's talk. Only my name has changed, not my heart. I'm the same old friend you've always had."

"The friend you used to be wouldn't have forgotten that we had a baby."

"I told you already I hadn't forgotten, I was thinking of you everyday. You wouldn't believe how hectic things have been, with falling in love with Mae and all, but I haven't forgotten you and the baby."

"You came here to introduce us to a girl."

"And to see the baby. If you'd just let me back in I'd love to spend some time with the little guy."

"Girl."

"And I'd love to see Katie and tell her congratulations and that I'm proud of her...Oh, and Sam you know I'm proud of you too don't you? This was no easy feat I'm sure, getting through the pregnancy together and learning to be a father. I'm proud of you, Sam."

"Dick—"

"I know there's a lot of tension right now. I want to get you out of the house. Why don't you let us treat you to a nice meal. We'll be gone an hour. You can give Katie some space and we can talk about what has happened here between us. I know I've had some shortcomings but I want us to be in each other's lives again. Like we used to be. I want to know the baby, and I want you to know Mae. It doesn't feel right being so distant all the time does it? Answer me that, Sam, does it feel good or does it feel bad to act like we don't know each other?"

"It doesn't feel good," Sam said. He was speaking sentimentally now. "But you chose it. Katie and I have been nothing but helpful to you. We've been good friends."

"I helped you move didn't I?"

"I asked you to."

"Sam, I miss you. Let's get dinner. We'll even buy something for you to bring back for Katie so you guys don't have to cook. One hour, just down the street, come on."

"You don't deserve my time."

"I don't. But I'm asking for forgiveness. Mae has been dying to meet you. And we can straighten out this mess. I want to see Katie. I want to see the baby."

"Katie won't be happy if I go."

"Tell her you're bringing back food. She'll understand. Tell her I'm going to buy the three of you a meal and you'll be back in an hour. Or tell her that you're going to lecture me on the duties of a good uncle or whatever you must. Just tell her *something* and come with us."

He breathed long and looked out across the park and saw Mae sitting there amongst the pigeons. "Does that girl really love you, Dick?"

"You wouldn't believe our love. It's what I've always wanted."

"I'm happy for you," Sam smiled. God knows he was the greatest friend a man could ask for.

"She's amazing isn't she? Wait until you get to know her. Her accent is adorable isn't it?"

Sam laughed. "That's what you were referring to? That's the Indiana accent?"

I looked on.

"David, that isn't an accent, it's a speech impediment. She can't say her R's."

"How unrefined your ear has become from being cooped up with that baby," I laughed. "If all I listened to was crying all day I'd be hard to pick up the subtleties of the international tongue myself, so I don't blame you. In fact, before I met Mae, I didn't know there was an Indiana accent."

"I'll go tell Katie I'm going out for an hour. Stay here."

When Sam came back out he was in a coat and cap. I asked him what Katie had said and he told me it was best to not talk about it. I waved Mae back over to our side and we started down 13th Street towards Sixth Avenue. Deep in the heart of the Village we turned on to MacDougal Street and approached Minetta Tavern.

"Minetta?" Sam asked. "You want to eat at Minetta?"

"Why not?" I said.

"A little upscale, don't you think?"

"Nonsense!" Mae laughed. "It's my treat."

The host took us to a booth. There we sat on the gloss of the old mid-century upholstery. The checkerboard floor cast across the place like a palace. Pictures of old New York all across the walls. Curtains, chandeliers, easy French music like heaven.

"We always eat here," I said. "This is a proper restaurant, not one of your hip little neo-American gastropubs, or chrome cafes with that horrible music that sounds like broken electricity."

"What?" Sam said.

"We always eat at nice places," Mae said. "Minetta is romantic. It's really one of the only places we can eat, you know, people like us."

"What do you mean 'people like you?'" Sam said.

"Artists," Mae said. "Minetta has a long tradition of serving artists. Look at their pictures on the walls. Eugene O'Neil. Ezra Pound."

"Fitzgerald, Hemingway," I said.

"Even the Beats," she added.

"Capote and Cummings too."

"Minetta is our home," she said. "Between his writing and my painting we're like royalty here. We're part of something. You couldn't imagine how many drunken escapades we've had, toppled over each other in laughter in the booths of Minetta Tavern."

"What?" Sam said.

"Good evening, Ms. Cartier," said the waiter.

"Felix," Mae said.

"Mr. Melish, welcome," Felix said.

"Hi, Felix," I said.

"And greetings to your friend as well. What will it be for drinks tonight?"

Sam looked on at the three of us, puzzled.

"Champagne for all of us," Mae said. "Is champagne alright, Sam?"

"I don't need a champagne," Sam said.

"Please, Sam, let us treat you. One glass of the bubbly." I nodded to the waiter and he left us.

"I thought you were just buying Katie and I dinner," Sam said.

"A glass of champagne with your meal won't hurt anybody. Besides, you're stressed. It's Mae's treat."

Sam wiggled in his seat and looked awkwardly at Mae. "So you're a painter?" he asked.

"She's learning," I said. "She's getting very good."

"I'd never painted till I met Dick," she said. "But he suggested I take it up. I took a few classes some months ago to get a hold of the basics."

"Color theory, technique, brushstroke," I added.

"And I must be doing something right because I've already got a job painting."

"Is that right?" Sam said.

The drinks came out. We all toasted.

"She's working for the city," I said proudly.

"Painting for the city?" Sam asked.

"That's right," Mae said. "I'm helping them to cover all the graffiti on the buildings. It's everywhere, you know."

"I know," Sam said.

"So we go in the night and paint over the graffiti with much more beautiful colors, restoring the buildings back to their original styles."

"You paint over graffiti?"

"I know it's not much, but Dick says a job like this could lead to an 'in' at a gallery. Usually with a job like this, they are looking to see who has the best grasp on the artform. If you stick out, they'll push you on to the next step. My supervisor is connected with a number of galleries."

"Dick, are you still writing your book?" Sam said.

"Nearly finished, I just need to tidy up the ending."

"And what are you doing for money?"

"Well, you know I had that job working for the publishing company."

"Writing the ad blurbs?" Sam asked.

"If that's what you wish to call it. I'm through with them anyway. I'm writing the novel full time."

"You quit your job?"

"Some months ago, yes. With Mae's inheritance I've been able to work on the novel without need for an immediate income."

"Oh right," Sam said. "Something about a cattle farm?"

"That's right," she said. "I'm an heiress. A wealthy painter in love with a writer here at Minetta Tavern. Isn't it romantic?"

"I'm sorry, but I have to go," Sam said.

"Sammy, we haven't even ordered the *hors d'oeuvres* yet."

"I don't want it. I want a cheeseburger."

"They have a cheeseburger here," Mae said. "Oh, Felix!"

"I don't want their forty-dollar cheeseburger."

"We're buying, Sam, stay a while!" I said.

"How much is the champagne?" he asked.

"Who cares?" I said.

"I want to know."

"Sam, it isn't about the money, it's about the experience. Look around you, this place is amazing. It's old and smokey and romantic. Imagine how well I could write here."

Sam turned to a passing waiter. "Sir, how much does this glass of champagne cost?"

"Thirty-four dollars, sir," said the man.

"Two more here, please!" Mae called.

"You're lunatics. The both of you. Lunatics."

"Sam——"

"You haven't even asked what my baby's name is! Do you know that? This whole time you haven't even asked what my little girl's name is."

"What's her name?" I asked.

"Go to hell, Dick. And you too Mae."

"Dick, you shouldn't let him talk to me like that!" Mae cried.

"Let him go, dear. He's caught Katie's disease now. He's inconsolable."

Sam tossed the remainder of his champagne in my face, pulled thirty-four dollars out of his wallet and threw it on the table and walked out the front door.

"You never know what you're going to get at Minetta Tavern," I said. "This place is always unpredictable!"

I pulled a cigarette from my coat pocket and lit it, taking the smoke in deeply so I could feel it startle my bones. I blew it out through my nose and watched it move across the tablecloth, through the stalagmites of dishware so arranged atop the table. It slithered and twirled inside the room.

"What the hell are you doing?" asked the woman at the table beside us. "Excuse me, waiter!"

"Relax," I told her.

"You can't smoke in here," the waiter called across the room. He stomped his way over to me with his hands waving through the air like batons. "You need to leave. You can't light a cigarette in here."

"Felix, come on. I thought this was Minetta Tavern," I said, drawing again from the smoke.

"Do you know how many cigarettes have been smoked in here?" Mae said. "One more isn't going to hurt."

"Are you people out of your minds?" Felix said. A crowd began shouting at us, mostly homely, portly people with ballcaps and backpacks and cameras.

"Get out of here!" the crowd began to say.

"Somebody kick him out!"

"What in the hell is wrong with you?"

The security guard came from the front door and took me by the arms. He gripped me hard by the biceps and dragged me across the checkerboard floor. Mae followed me screaming.

"Get gone, loser!" The voices began to cry.

I shouted at the detractors. "If I live in a world where I can't have a cigarette in Minetta Tavern then I don't want to live!"

"Then go kill yourself!" one man shouted.

"I am a writer!" I said back.

"All the more!"

I got tossed out onto the sidewalk. Mae fell out the door behind me. We lay there together looking up at that beautiful red and white sign on the corner of MacDougal Street and Minetta Lane, the smoke from my cigarette still moving there from my mouth and leaching to the glass of the tavern. "Think about it, Mae," I said. "Think about how many times Bogart must have sat here on this corner looking up at this sign after getting thrown out."

"You think he got thrown out a lot?"

"If you're not allowed to smoke in Minetta, Bogey certainly got thrown out a lot. Come on, let's go home."

From there we walked up MacDougal and through Washington Square Park wondering what we'd done in our past lives to inherit such a beautiful city.

Chapter Twenty-Six
How Mae and I Grew Together in Love

Now with Sam and Katie permanently out of the picture (good riddance to their venomous souls, unwilling to give even the slightest acknowledgment to the noble things of this world. I pity their ignorance; I rage at their negligence), I had nothing and nobody to whom I owed my time save for my Mae and my Manuscript. Of course, reader, as I write this now in Paris, I remember our friendship fondly, but I remember our demise just as it happened: cold, calculated, and utterly catastrophic. It was only love now; it had always been love. So I searched on and on for the ending of my novel, the weight of its magnificence growing each day. I knew that I was writing the best work of my life.

May my Mae's divinity be attested to solely by the work that she inspires! Who on earth could write verse so bright without the help of an evershining, everliving everything at their side perpetually and ubiquitously! None other than me, with the help of my mirific Mae, moving the moon, my love and my woman, I love you like lightning. I can recall it all the same, the time passing us by in flashes, our love in light and in winter, bright spring, April sings, or one red day Octobering with you. The setting on one fine night, a Spanish restaurant. A place where I learned to love you. Between yellow walls, white tablecloths and the black heads of a hundred Chinese. The chimney warmed the room— an old building, as if we lived long ago. It was the New Year, and we celebrated. We blushed at each other from across our table, our feet wrestling beneath us, under cover from the curtain far from the audience around. You were red there, atop a walnut chair with red lips, your boxer's eyes and that precious black hair down each side of your neck. Chin atop your hands like a dream, my Mae, my marvelous muse, all flowerlike in a room ahaze.

I'll never forget that day with her, reader. We ordered the oxtail. A bottle of wine for us both. Our love drenching us—early love—the truest of all affects, alien upon us like possession. I was inside all of her. I was hypnotized across the table, looking towards her, knowing her to be me.

"What do you think of us?" These are the questions I liked to ask. We talked a lot about our love in those days. We couldn't talk about anything else. We talked about how we loved, why we loved, what we loved.

"I don't think anything," she said. "I feel love, not think love."

"You're right."

"What do you feel?" she asked.

"I feel the honeying of the lune, love."

"In the lune lies the swallowtrees, swept up and free to breeze. Like that?"

"Something like that."

"What else?"

"I feel you like a memory, like you're always there with me."

"A part of you so to speak?"

"The best part of me," I smiled.

"Not like the charade of love, right? You feel me different than that. Not just a magic trick from young to old, never feeling and always leaching. Not like what people call 'love.'"

"Middle-class love?"

"The house, the kids, the bills, the one-week vacations. Hideous."

"A vague sexual attraction."

"Oh, it is far more pronounced than vague."

We smiled together.

"We invented all of this, you know?" I said.

"How do you mean?"

"People like you and I, we are in charge of love. The dukes, the kings and queens of it. We created it. We rule love. We can't let nonlove rule love."

"We're loving as love is supposed to be loved?"

"Precisely. The spirit of love dwells in us. We created love. What do suburbanites know about love? With their children and their two big cars and their mowed lawns."

"They can't stand each other."

"But they love to know all about it don't they? They know about love from watching us love love. They watch all the films, read all the books. Anything they can get their unholy hands on. They want to trick love. Reform love. But we inform love, adorn love! They even think of us when they think of love. They don't think of them. We give love, elect love."

"They bend love and break love."

"Lend love and fake love."

Our poems were occasionally interrupted by Mae's acknowledging a peculiar happening at the table beside us. As we went on with our verses, something had garnered her attention. She couldn't help but look. Mae leaned in very close, nearly nose to nose above our candle and spoke in a whisper.

"Do you see them?"

I had seen them, but hadn't said anything.

It was another couple. Much older than us, married by the looks of the rings on their fingers. One man, thin, gray-haired, and dull-faced. His eyes were very heavy in his skull, not just the skin around his eyes, but the eyes themselves—his whole head tilted downward like he wanted to sleep for the weight of his eyes. Across from him a short woman, thin-lipped and rocking slowly in her seat, front and back. They ate in startling silence, their candle burning hot, just two glasses of water before them, untouched. They didn't speak. Very occasionally one looked at the other in the face. The man sometimes tilted his head as much as a scarecrow might in a light wind, but usually he stared on towards the table, or the abdominal center of the rocking woman ahead of him. He stopped to chew sometimes, his fork and knife playing with the food, organizing heaps of meat atop itself. A long time went on and neither of them spoke.

"We shouldn't talk too loud now," I said. "I feel bad."

"Feel bad?" Mae said.

"Well, look how miserable they are."

"Sure, but what do we have to feel bad about?"

"I don't know, I just feel bad. Like we shouldn't have so much fun in front of them."

"Feel bad? Feel bad that we are in love and they never were?"

"Were they not?"

"Could you ever look that miserable with me, knowing how much you love me now? Even if we were a hundred years old, could you ever appear *that miserable* near me?"

We looked at each other, grinning. We knew the answer.

"What do you think is going on there?" I asked. "What is their story?"

Mae loved games like this.

"Diplomatic negotiations of some sort," she said.

"Seriously," I said. "This is bizarre isn't it? They aren't fighting. They aren't mad at each other."

"They're eating."

"So are we," I said. "But it isn't as if they're making a decision not to talk. They're just...they're just nothing."

"They're nothing," Mae repeated.

"How did they get there?"

"I think I know," Mae smiled.

"Tell me."

"I think that he has poor table manners," she said.

"It doesn't look like it," I said.

"Well, they're in the process of correcting it. Look, for years he has been a bad dinner guest. He spits when he eats, he puts his elbows on the table. He spills things, he mixes meat with greens, he smacks his food. He dines like an animal and finally she's had enough."

"She's had enough?"

"She told him, 'If you don't straighten out your table manners, we can't be together.'"

"So this is a test?"

"Or practice. But here's the thing: He hates eating now. It's a chore. To behave—to make eating cerebral, it ruins it for him. She observes his every move."

"And she scolds him for his mistakes."

"Exactly."

We watched them some more. They went on eating slowly, his whole lifeless self, void of passion, void of concern, affirming a part of Mae's theory. I motioned for her to lean in again. Our faces were flush atop the candle.

"She isn't watching him," I said. "He acts just as you say, but look—she isn't concerned. She isn't holding him to any standard. It's as if they are eating alone. Look at her gaze. Out towards the window, watching passers-by. Two strangers at one table, wishing to not acknowledge one another. If this is a test, why isn't she grading him?"

"You're right," she said.

"I've got it," I said. "They aren't married to one another. They're strangers. They recently found out their spouses are cheating with the other's. So they decided to get revenge."

"They booked the dinner over the phone," Mae added excitedly, "and when they met they realized they weren't attracted to each other at all."

"Exactly. To continue on with the dinner is obligatory, but they're repulsed by one another."

"Do you think they'll continue on to the consummation?"

"I can't tell. They look awfully miserable."

"They have to, I think. To complete the revenge. They are thinking about their spouses now."

"What are the odds of that?" I asked.

"What?"

"Well, you'd think if your spouse was cheating on you, the person they're cheating with would have a spouse that you'd be interested in, right? For instance, your taste in men is similar to how I am."

"My taste in men is you."

"Sure, but play along here, doll."

"I'm playing."

"If you cheated on me, the lover of that man would probably be in the realm of my own taste, don't you think? Logic says so. It's all linked vaguely by preferences of attraction."

"I see your point."

"And do you agree?"

"I'm not sure. In our case, perhaps yes. But with these two, look at them. I don't think they're each other's type. A lot of people who marry don't even like their own spouse!"

"True," I said.

"So let's say these two are cheating on their cheating spouses, right?"

"I follow."

"Let's say they're revenge cheating. They themselves might not even meet the superficial preferences of their spouses. So there is no continuity in the logic of attraction whatsoever. Just because people are with those whom they are attracted to *in theory*, doesn't actually mean people are with those whom they are attracted to in reality. Just look around you, we see it everyday. People hate their spouses."

"So with that logic," I started, "why aren't these two just a married couple who hate each other?"

"Because that's not any fun for the sake of the game," Mae said.

We watched them some more. Even the waiters who came to refill the glasses and bus the dishware were unaware who to address and how. One waiter asked the table as a whole if they were so far satisfied. The man only shook his head yes.

Mae and I finished our own food, and ordered another glass of wine. Now we held hands across the table and looked on even deeper at the specimens beside us.

"Now I've really got it," she said. Oh how precious she was. She loved to play games and crack codes. She loved to solve puzzles and to strategize. I loved her with all of me, there in that restaurant.

"I'm all ears," I said.

"We're thinking about this all wrong," she went on. "They haven't stopped eating since we've been watching them, right? And our thinking is that they haven't stopped eating so they wouldn't have to speak, keeping themselves busy. But that's wrong, that's backwards. They haven't spoken *because they haven't stopped eating.*"

"But like I said, we can talk and eat. That's the whole thing about going to dinner with somebody! It is an art form to eat and to talk, to talk and to eat. You eat a little bit and you listen, then you talk and the other eats. It's a push and a pull, a ying and a yang. This is the dinner date, it's been going on for thousands of years like this."

"You're right," Mae said. "And this is exactly what confirms my suspicion. Think about it, Dick: *We don't talk with our hands.*"

"They're deaf," I said.

"They're deaf and really hungry."

"You're absolutely right."

"They can either eat or they can talk. They can't do both. Dick, they haven't said a single word."

"They're really hungry."

"It's their favorite restaurant."

"They can't stop eating."

"I wonder what will happen when the food runs out."

Right on cue, one waiter—a lanky, marsupial looking man, completely ignorant of the silent spectacle—laid down what we surmised were preemptively ordered desserts.

"You're kidding," I said. "They'll never talk again."

As they finished their dessert, the woman split for the restroom, leaving the man to pay the bill. As he settled up—silently—he stood, gathered both of their things and made for the door. He waited patiently there in the anteroom of the restaurant. When she emerged from the restroom, she waddled towards the table where she once sat. She overlooked it with a deep tranquility, seemingly waiting for something to happen. We watched her closely. Then, she turned her head ever-so-slightly towards us, and said, "You two really ought to keep your voices down while you're having dinner," and walked to the front of the restaurant where she met him, and they promptly exited onto 48th Street, quiet as field mice. Mae, with her shining smile, laughed and laughed until those two crooked eyes of hers almost looked straight.

It was nights like this that taught me more about love than books ever could. It was Mae, streetlight-lit Mae, walking along the rainy sidewalks of Manhattan, sparkling and smiling, happy because there was nothing to be sad about. She showed me what it was to write. To write was to perform miracles. To write was to take wind—the vanity of wind—and turn it into light. The pen is the tongue of the soul, afterall.

Oh, Mae, how our love flashes from one night to the next. To love you is to meet that buried whisper of my own inverted womanhood—the crying animus that lies chained inside me—retching for freedom. Can you feel me on the otherside? I can see you Mae, the lovely Cartier, heiress of the air, ghosting on the otherside of this glass. Reflections in slats distant and behind me as I look. "It's a mirror," you say. The light breathing on the glass just so; your own figure fleeting through its secret form. I thought I was seeing myself Mae, but it's you now, my own body strangled by glass behind the light, and all I see is you. Can you see me there? If we wait for just the right moment, just the right light, we can cross. Do you know that, Mae? I'm not bound to this world, I'm dead here. I see you in sleep, I see you in me now, Mae. Don't step too soon, lest we lose our chance. I love you. I love this glass. She hears me, I know she hears me. It's been forever Mae, inside me Mae, the other Mae was never Mae. Is there anybody who can tell me how I got here? Is there anybody but her who understands? The glass is cold, but let's cross. Come to mine so we can look back, reflections in the evening room of this vapid place. There it goes, a mirror again, until another miracle of light and time and time again and love and Mae can change us back to what we once were. Is there anybody but her who understands?

***

"It's called *Blue You*," she said. And it was lovely. "Look at you here. Rounded waves of blue, moon-blue. You're perfect here, as you are there."

"Am I there?"

"Here and there," she said.

We moved like paint that night, and I watched. I was beautiful. Still wet on the canvas, her finest yet. We didn't know the day.

We only knew us, and writing—me. Hers was painting and we'd never been born. We hadn't parents. We crawled a lot in those days. She was working under the sun and I was learning her. We passed ourselves between the past, moving parts twirling across that open kitchen of ours, her pieces leaned up against that old, noisy refrigerator so that the setting sun would come in through that one window and show her where to paint. She found me there beneath the sunnoise, and I was born again. Not painting us, but unburying us. Every time she touched the brush I either died or was born, so to thank her, I wrote. And when I wrote I knew it was love; so we made love without touch by creating each other love, moving each other love, writing each other love, and painting each other love; sat in the same room loving without looking, working and toiling was love, showing that we could, unmarked by time, unstrained by the vanity of days or what city it was we might have lived in.

"It's called *Blue You*," I said. She mouthed the words back at me.

"Who's talking now?"

"Wait, listen."

"It's beautiful," she said.

I wrote her painting long before she knew me.

"You wrote this?" She was so close now, living inside me.

"And I'm writing more. You won't believe what else I'll write for you."

So when I wrote I thought of what she'd say. And with that I came so very close to finishing what I'd started so long ago, back before I was her. And I was sending what I'd written all over the place and nobody bought it; weeks of rejects and stamps, except there was a day when one man called Fick who worked for a well-known publisher asked if I'd come and talk to him about the things I was writing.

"Do you have an ending for it?"

"Not yet. I've been working on this book for a long time. I know it's almost finished."

"It better be."

And later I spoke with Mae about the meeting.

"Did he like it?"

"He said he did."

"He'd better like it."

"He did. It's for you, everything I'm doing is for you."

We were a book now, so it was proper that we acted like one.

When the gentleman Fick from the publishing company called me back some days later he told me he found something else he'd rather pursue and wished me luck. I didn't mind. I knew what I had was good, and I knew I'd always have my Mae.

"You don't think it's me, right?" she asked me.

"Of course not."

"It's because you're writing me, and the people who are reading me aren't liking me."

"You're perfect, and I write you perfect. Don't you think I write you perfect?"

"Mhm."

"It's just that people don't want to open their hearts. They don't know writing. They are all tied up in their airport romances. Nobody can handle you, that's all. The average American buys their favorite book at 7/11."

"Don't be negative, Dick."

"I'm being realistic. It's hard. All of this is hard. I've been trying to do this the right way and I can't ever win."

We were in bed and Mae had her long hair on my chest. Her skin was rich as sand and soft too. I stroked her bare arm as morning broke through the white curtain. A silence passed between us. I was at my desk too, writing and she made breakfast, feeding me as I wrote. And then I asked her in bed if she thought there was anything I could do. Anything to relieve the weight of my suffering.

"Is there something I'm doing wrong?" I asked her. "Is there something more I can do?"

"Let me see what you're sending to these publishers. It must be something wrong with your letter."

I showed her. She read it very slowly, her eyebrows creased in concentration. She read it three or four times.

"Well," she started, "there might be one thing you can do."

Chapter Twenty-Seven

How My Name Wound Up Becoming Dick Queen

"It's just not a very musical name," she went on.

"But I like it. You've never objected before."

"It's because I love you. That's also why I'm telling you now."

"You really think it needs changing then?"

"Just the last. The first is still perfect. I really think you'll find more success with a more writerly name—Melish...Melish. Who wants to buy a book from a Dick Melish?"

"I don't see anything wrong with it."

"It sounds the way wet socks look."

"Well, then what do you suggest?" I said.

"I don't know," she said. "I don't have any ideas right now, I just think it would help you a lot. You trust me don't you?"

"Of course."

"Something slick, understated, romantic. Something memorable."

"Will you help me find it?"

"We're going to find it together. We're going to be great. You're going to be great."

We thought on it for some weeks, continuing to love and to work, not letting a small pebble in our path mimic a stone. She was right, and I knew it. For that, I loved her and for that I would always love her.

As the time went on the rejections came in faster than before. I had sent excerpts of my book to almost every known publisher in New York and nobody bit. I hadn't even had a teasing of success since Fick, and his interest didn't even last the week. I was growing more and more anxious to change my name so that I could reconcile our correspondence with the improved pitch. I knew the story was good. It had to be the name.

It was late January in the cloudy cold that we went to see the film that would change everything for me. It was *Love With the Proper Stranger.* Oh, how thrilling and tender that picture is; a fresh, modern-day romance, both topical and controversial, though romantic at heart. It features the eternal and most perfect Natalie Wood and the unmatched Steve McQueen as two stranger-lovers in a bind. I could write a novel in and of that film itself, but I'll try to contain my praise and analysis to only the remainder of this chapter.

'Love With the Proper Stranger' (1963; Dir. Robert Mulligan)

A dollish shop clerk and an irreverent jazz musician navigate a delicate situation in which she discovers she's carrying his child, while he can't even recall the hazy, boozish night of their one and only meeting. Both of them, financially depleted and emotionally complicated for their own reasons, band together to scrape up the sufficient funds for a "doctor" to remedy their "problem." As they spend time together, they learn that they just may love each other too. Wood plays the intelligent, love-wanting Angie Rossini, a woman made afraid by her own desire for tangible, boneshaking romance in the age of sterile gender relations and feigned social freedoms. She waits her whole life for that moment of "bells and banjos:" the meeting of a man that stirs her so far free she forgets she was ever imprisoned. She never thought what she was looking for would come in the form of Rocky Papasano (McQueen), a drifter and a playboy, seemingly unconcerned with love until he realizes just what he would do to make Angie feel desired in an undesirable situation.

I won't reveal anymore of the plot, so that the reader may watch it unimposed and revel in its glorious unwinding, but needless to say Mae and I just spilled out over this film. We stood in the theater—the little Roxy Theater—and clapped and clapped until there wasn't anybody else left to scold us. We especially marveled at Wood's immaculate performance. My tragic Natalie! How cruel was Death for hoarding your talent for himself! Her performance in this particular picture captures so perfectly just what kind of actor and woman she really was. She was the archetypal Mae. Her movement as graceful as dance, her voice strong, her sensibilities confident. Mae adored her and I did too. We wept as the credits rolled, thinking not of the favorable ending of the picture, but of the tragic finish to one star's life at the hands of misfortune.

Now regarding her co-star, Mae and I were so delighted by the tender display put on by McQueen that we even considered getting ourselves into the same sort of conundrum as theirs, only to stage a struggle and an atonement of sorts to exhibit just how deep our love for one another really was. Though after further discussion, it seemed like a sort of anachronism; an unnecessary introduction of a post-pill paradigm into our delicate, yet functioning ecosystem. I digress.

The reason I have written this review in the first place, reader, is to frame the context for the single best thing we took away from seeing the picture, coming straight from the lips of Mae following the program: "Why don't you take on Steve McQueen's name? You admire him so much, it could be a sort of living homage."

I loved it. It was like a badge of honor. He was a great romantic lost to history, bound to be brushed over and forgotten in the near future if something wasn't done to seal up his esteem and keep it alive. Not to mention, a great Midwesterner; a Hoosier like Mae.

Though, to be sure to show tribute without defilement, I elected to modify his great name ever so slightly, just to be found innocent of any perceived disrespect.

"That is a most brilliant idea, my love. However," I started, "in my mind there is room for only one great McQueen in the world and he has already said his piece and gone, *may God rest his soul.* To honor him without disgracing him, I think that I'll change my meandering last name to Queen. Just Queen."

"I love it," she said. "One part Van Dyke, one part McQueen."

"One part Missouri, one part Indiana."

"One part you, one part me."

And we kissed until we fell back onto the velvet seats of the cinema where we kissed some more. The reddish lights coming up, illuminating our raucous love, which then took us to the floor where we kicked and moaned between the seats like sea lions until the theater usher came and demanded that we leave the premises before he called security. We promptly left and held each other tight by the hand, running into the darkening street, a new life, a new chance. And that's the story of how Mae and I got banned from the Roxy Hotel, and that's the story of how my name wound up becoming Dick Queen.

Chapter Twenty-Eight

A Brief Interjecting Chapter on the Content of My Query Pitch That the Reader May Recognize From My Novel, Based on True Events Already Related in Chapter Twenty-Four of This Document

With my new name established I began immediately sending out query letters to publishers once again. I had no doubt in my mind that my problems were solved, seeing my new, shiny name there on the page. Rallied by my newfound confidence, I sent over one hundred hand-written, personally signed and sealed queries the first week after my renaming. I expected nothing but resounding approvals from these publishers on account of my agreeable new name, and the virtuosic nature of the included excerpt.

I feel now it would be responsible of me to share with the reader just which part of my manuscript I was sending as a query to the publishers—not only to reinforce my point on the impossibility of it being the cause of the rejections I had received—but also because it does in fact play a distinctive part later on in this volume.

Now I personally felt that this scene—the first night in the hotel with Mae—was one of the strongest offerings from my novel, which is why I almost always used it as the sample piece for my query. The reader will surely recognize this snippet from the identical version published in my novel (which the reader should have read before reading this book), but I want to relay it again here if only for the sake of juxtaposing it against the scene in *this* book that tells the *true* story of that fictionalized account in my novel. As the reader should understand, there are naturally ways to modify a true story to better fit the style of a novel with commercial intentions while still retaining the core truths within. Let this suffice to explain the blatant differences that the reader may have already sensed between the two accounts.

Note: If you are for some reason still reading this book before you've read that book, you've gone way too far and might as well finish it.

The Sample:

She was lying on her stomach now, the gentle curves of her body so alluring in the low, teasing light.

"What's your name anyway?" I said.

"Mae."

"Mae. It's a lovely name."

"I don't even want to know yours."

"Let me tell you."

"If I'm supposed to know it, I'll find out somehow."

We kissed some, brought close by the jest of our love. I couldn't believe who I saw there on the pillow next to me. It was her, the woman I'd longed for since seeing her for the first time a year ago.

"You know," I said, "I've watched you on that corner for so long. Night after night I've watched you, there on St. Mark's and A. It feels like I know you. Like I've always known you."

"You should have said something."

"You were always with another man."

"Don't talk about him," she said. Her eyes cast away from me, towards the outerdarkness of the window. I stroked her shoulder; her delicate white shoulder that rose like a wave above her body as she laid her weight on one hand and hip, sidewinded beside me, beneath me; I loved her then, just like in the dreams I was having about her, I knew I loved her.

"I could live in this hotel with you forever, away from everybody," I said. "I don't know if anybody could ever understand how I'm feeling now."

"Don't tempt me like that. I would love to live here. Look at this place, it's like a palace."

How precious she looked when she surveyed that room—that spectacular room at the top of the Roxy Hotel. A chandelier reflected the lamplight off each of its hundred crystal teeth, lamps like torches were mounted to gold-furnished plates that lined the walls as they might have in Rome or Babylon.

"Who says we can't?" I said. "I'll bring you to this room every night for the rest of your life if it means you'll love me."

"No more watching me from that corner?"

"I'll never need that corner again. It was only a means to see you."

And she fell atop me for the third time that night, running me like machinery, Maeing me back into those long tender dreams I had of her before I had her, wondering if they were in fact premonitions of this moment or all moments I would spend wrapped up betwixt her and the moment next, crestfallen to all things unMaeish or profane; her light inside me, flesh of my flesh, bone of my bone blushing like Morn: yea, all heaven and happy constellations on that hour shedding their selectest influence; the earth giving sign of gratulation, joyous the birds, fresh gales and gentle airs whispering it to the cityscape above, and from the wings of those virgin birds flung rose, flung odours of majesty, betraying the evening star downst forever in a flash of our flesh. Here, passion I felt first.

Chapter Twenty-Nine

How I Got a Meeting With a Publishing Company
Because of My New Name

It was only six days after I'd begun sending in my manuscripts as Dick Queen that I got a reply from Passion Publishing about my work. It was by the grace of divine fate that this name was bestowed upon me! I was sure of it now. I had been misnamed at birth by two Midwestern parents who held undeserved affection for one birth-agent's Great Uncle, and thus bestowing that common name upon their first child for reasons uncontested, and now forgotten. His place and title so rightly restored now twenty-seven years later: Dick Queen! The world's next great writer of romances.

To call Passion's reply to my inquiry enthusiastic would be an understatement. Rather than describe what I believe they were feeling, I'll transcribe their reply here:

Dear Cherished Writer,

We have received your inquiry regarding your untitled manuscript and we are happy to share that we are incredibly interested in pursuing this project further. We love the sample text that you have provided and have full respect for an author's vision when it comes to courageous, ground-breaking writing such as this. We strive to give everybody from all walks of life a chance to publish their art here at Passion, and your book seems to have just what it takes to be one of the year's flagship releases, granted you wish to pursue a relationship with us. Upon an in-person meeting and the delivery of a finished manuscript, Passion is prepared to fully fund this project, as well as future endeavors the author may have in mind. Please don't hesitate to call our office and schedule an appointment at your soonest convenience.

Best,
Roger Hale,
Editor-in-Chief
Passion Publishing

I called Passion immediately after receiving their reply and scheduled a meeting for the next day. They were dying to meet me. I sat Mae down at our kitchen table. She was as beautiful as ever, smiling, long-haired and doveish. I held her hands in mine, our gaze inseparable.

"Mayflower," I started.

"Tell me," she begged. "You're so intense, what's going on?"

"It's all happening, my love. All thanks to you."

"What is it? What's happening?"

The faintest shade of worry in her eye, that innocent confusion, how lovely she was.

"It's Passion Publishing. They want to meet. I've gotten a reply. They love it. They love the book. They love you."

"They love me?"

"All that I've written about you, about us, they love it. I'm going to meet with them tomorrow."

"This is incredible!" she threw her arms around me. Tears swelled in those untethered eyes, swimming around like two marbles in a shot glass.

"It's all because of you, dear," I said. "You made the change, and now look how quickly I've gotten a reply."

"You think it's because of the name?"

"Well, surely! Don't be silly, Mae. Years of failure under other identities and now immediate success."

"That's nonsense, they're in love with your writing, darling."

"Whether you're right or wrong, I want to tell you that from this day forward everything will change. We will be living the life we've always dreamed of. And once I finish this book, we're going to get your paintings into a gallery. Hell—with the money they'll be paying me, we'll buy our own gallery!"

"All for my paintings!" she laughed.

"Of course, my love. We can live anywhere we'd like from here to Rome. We'll work on every continent in the world and discover a new one ourselves if we feel like it. Our work will be side by side in all the great magazines, our love preached throughout the world! And all because you—in your ingenious sense of omnipotence, you impossible goddess you—told me that success would come should I change my name."

"Oh, don't give me so much credit," she said. "You are an amazing writer. You're an artist, a visionary, a genius. They love your work, not your name. You should be proud of *the work*. It is completely outrageous to think they have called you just because of your name."

★★★

"Queen Dick."

The receptionist was a portly woman with a slight southern drawl. I looked around the waiting room and saw some of the other clients had peeked up from over their reading material as I stood.

"Queen Dick," she called again.

"Yeah, yeah, yeah," I said, approaching the desk.

"You Queen?" the receptionist said as I inched closer.

"It's actually Dick," I whispered. I put my hands on the desk and leaned in. "First name Dick, last name—"

"Oh, shoot, I'm sorry," she said, laughing. She started to convulse with restrained cackles for a moment but then straightened herself out, busying herself at her desk. "It's just that this list of appoint-ments is organized by last name. So I—"

"Understood," I said. "No hard feelings."

"Mr. Queen, Mr. Hale is ready for you."

The door let off a buzzing noise and then a click.

"Just through the brown door and proceed to room 904."

The door was open so I let myself in. An older Hispanic woman was setting the table with coffee, fruit, cheese and crackers, and laboring with the curtain rods when I entered. It was a sterile looking room, the walls plastered with outdated corporate-looking posters showing off various book covers—some classics, some new releases I didn't recognize. It felt like I was in a kindergarten class for adults who liked books.

"Hi," I said. "I have a meeting with Mr. Hale."

"Meester Hale be right in," she said. "I go now. You need som-ting more?"

"I'm just fine, thank you."

"Okay, Meester Hale come now."

I looked out the window onto Midtown Manhattan. The streets buzzing like a beehive, all speckled in drab colors and long lines of yellow snaking through the avenues. I tried to look southward, past the shoulders of the brick buildings and out to the East Village, to see if I could see it. I thought perhaps I could see the big oak that stood across from my building in Tompkins Square Park. It was a long way down the island, and it all looked quite similar, almost like looking out of an airplane window.

"Knock knock," said a voice behind me. I turned from the win-dow and saw two tall men in suits enter the room playfully. "I'm sorry, sir, I don't mean to startle you," one of them said.

"No problem, you didn't startle me," I said.

"I'm Roger Hale, and this is Vice-President of Domestic Market-ing here at Passion, Gage Ellsbury."

"Pleasure to meet you."

We shook hands.

"Where's Queenie?" Hale said.

"I'm sorry?"

"Pardon me. We've been calling her that around the office the last few days. We really love the piece."

"Calling who that?"

"Dick Queen. We've been calling her Queenie. Just a little pet name. We like to be friendly with our clients."

I looked on.

"You know, every editor on this floor has read that excerpt and they're *clawing* at each other to get their hands on it," he said.

"Everybody wants it," said Ellsbury.

"Sir, I—"

"In fact, I've already sent it over to my contact at the Swoon. She wants to publish the excerpt as a teaser as soon as possible. She was asking about doing a full review actually; breaking the book."

"Great, but, sir—"

"Sorry, what was your name, by the way? Are you an agent or partner or what?" said Hale.

"Sir, I'm Dick."

"You too?"

"Two Dicks are better than one," laughed Ellsbury.

"No, I'm sorry for the confusion," I said. "I am Dick Queen. I'm the author of the piece that you've read."

The two men sat still, studying me for a moment, a time just long enough to notice. Before I could break their concentration, Hale spoke up.

"I'm so sorry for the mistake."

The other continued to look at me inquisitively, seemingly spending great amounts of effort at my jaw, my hands, my ears.

"It's a great piece," said Ellsbury reluctantly.

"Thanks," I said.

"Well, there are all sorts of snacks here, please help yourself," said Hale.

"Drinks too," said Ellsbury. "Coffee, sodas, we can do special orders too. Just a push of the button."

"Thanks," I said.

Hale flipped through a manilla folder excessively. It wasn't thick enough with paper to flip through, but he went on searching and searching, remarking to himself with little moans of aggravation so as to tell us that the meeting would formally begin once he had found what he was looking for.

"It's a nice building," I said.

"Yes, we like it here," Ellsbury said. "And where do you live Mr. Queen?"

Hale shot him a look.

"It is 'mister' isn't it?" Hale said.

"Oh, I'm terribly sorry, what do you prefer? How should I address you?" said Ellsbury.

"I'm sorry?" I said.

"We understand if you wish to be free from the constraints of labels," said Ellsbury.

"Or if you have your mind perfectly made up," added Hale.

"I'm not sure what you're—"

"We are more than accommodating to what you need," said Hale quickly.

"Are you insinuating—"

"If there are any publishing companies more open-minded than Passion, I've yet to hear about them," Ellsbury said.

"Excuse me!" I shouted.

Hale put down the folder.

"Gentlemen, correct me if I'm wrong," I said, "but I'm under the impression that there has been a sort of dire confusion regarding the nature of this meeting. My name is Dick Queen. I wrote the excerpt that you read. You replied to me and said you loved the piece and were very interested in working with me. I am a man—a man named Dick. I was named after Dick Van Dyke. My family was once called McQueen, as in Steve McQueen, but my grandfather decided to drop the 'Mc' after years of facing prejudice for his Irish heritage. This is simple. I'm writing a romance; a no-frills romance about a writer—a man—looking for and finding love in New York City. The excerpt that I sent you is from that book. Now, I was under the impression that we were here to meet about that and that you were aware of all this, but it seems that you two have utterly no clue as to what is going on at this meeting you invited me to."

The two men were stunned. Their hands rested on the table, side by side. I couldn't even confirm that they were breathing for a few moments there, nearly opting to stand up and walk out before their petrified eyes. Hale broke the stalemate with a series of violent blinks, and finally turned to his partner. Ellsbury spoke first.

"I'll be frank with you Mr. Queen, and I'm sorry to put it this way, but we thought that...you were a woman...well, not just a woman..."

"We thought perhaps you were a hooker," said Hale.

"A whore," said Ellsbury.

"A whore?" I said.

"A long-time streetworker, veteran of the vice, willing to share her story."

"Why on earth did you think that?" I said.

"Well, honestly, a lot of it had to do with the name."

"The name?"

"Yes," said Hale. "And not only that, but the excerpt. I mean, you send in this bit about meeting on a corner, and lovers in this hotel room together..."

"The Roxy at that," said Ellsbury.

"That's high profile shit," said Hale.

"You thought I was a hooker?" I said.

"Not in the negative connotation. We're very open-minded about this sort of thing. We thought maybe you were a celebrity escort or something," said Hale.

"Hey," said Ellsbury, "*I* thought that. You thought he was a transvestite."

"A transvestite?" I said.

"The name, again," said Hale. "Put yourself in our position, Dick."

"It's really a bold name," said Ellsbury.

"Look, I hate to poke fun at a person's name, but it did help you in the long run. 'John Smith' doesn't even make it through the slush pile, no matter how good a writer he is. Now, 'Dick Queen' on the other hand! There is just something so brave about that."

"Your cover letter didn't have any gender indication, so I guess we just assumed."

"You see, those are the sort of stories we're looking for—a whistle-blower, a seasoned trick-turner with a story to tell. A sort of *behind the curtain* look at sex-work."

"That sort of stuff is really popular right now, you know with the feminist movement and such."

"It's really brave."

"Well I'm sorry to disappoint you," I said, "but can we just put the misunderstanding aside and carry on as planned? I mean, this doesn't change the fact that you liked the writing, right?"

"Well—" said Hale.

"You read the excerpt," I continued, "you thought the writing was good. So why not publish the book? I have the manuscript here. It only needs a final chapter and I think I'm cracking the code on that. It'll be done any day now. It's all coming together very nicely, I could just use a little encouragement. You like the writing. You said so yourself that the writing is good."

"Look, Dick," said Hale.

"Whatever advance you were willing to give Dick Queen the cross-dressing hooker you better be willing to give to Dick Queen the writer," I said. "I've worked for years on this book."

"Dick, listen," said Hale. "Can I call you that?" He was calm again, back to almost not breathing. He held a pen softly in his hand and tapped it on the table between us.

"That's my name."

"You're a good writer."

"You're a great writer," said Ellsbury.

"But what you're doing isn't really what we're looking to publish right now."

"You don't even know what it is that I'm doing!" I said.

"A writer in New York City falls in love?" Ellsbury said. "Isn't that a little done?"

"There are a thousand books with that plot, Dick," said Hale.

"Yes, but this one is different—"

"Dick, I'm sorry. We're looking for something—"

"Something what?" I asked.

"Something, well, brave. Something about the things you can't say out loud. Something about identity. Something to really stir the pot."

"Something that represents the unrepresented," said Ellsbury.

"There is a really big market for that sort of writing right now," said Hale.

"Those two statements contradict each other!" I said. "How can something—"

"What you're doing," said Hale, "...it just...it can't be sold."

"Why not!" I said. I stood up and paced the length of the table. "I'm a fine writer! I study writing! All I do is read and write. I don't do anything but this. I *can't* do anything but this. I don't have friends. I don't have hobbies. All I do is read and write! Isn't there something to that?"

"Where did you go to school?" Hale asked.

"I didn't."

"You want to be a writer and you didn't go to school?" Ellsbury said.

"If I went to school I wouldn't have had any time to read or write," I said.

"This changes everything," Ellsbury said.

"How does this change everything from sixty seconds ago when you were disappointed that I wasn't a hooker?"

"Listen, Dick," said Hale again. He stood now. He took off his glasses and set them on the table and shook his head. "I don't doubt you're a good writer and a hard worker, it's not that. It's just, that's not what book publishing is about. I'm sorry. We're looking for something exciting, explosive, brave. Something that already has a built-in market. There are standards in our industry and what you're doing doesn't pass those standards. It isn't selling. I'm sorry."

"You keep using that word, 'brave,'" I said, "but you're not making any sense. If there is a built-in market for something, then how is it brave or new? It would be brave to publish *good writers* regardless of their—"

"Anything that opens up a vulnerable discourse about the nature of sex or the fragility of masculinity is brave," said Ellsbury proudly. "We are a very open-minded publishing house and—"

"Oh, give me a break!" I said. "If *Disney* is getting rich on the same creed you're calling 'brave' then the ship has sailed! Those writers aren't brave, they're golddiggers. Be a man, write a book about a whale!"

I was angry now. I was pacing faster, my blood was scolding me. I knew what I wanted to do.

"Mr. Queen, I'm sorry, but I think this meeting is adjourned. Our apologies for the misunderstanding. I want to say we really did like your manuscript and I hope that—are you...are you smoking in here?"

I was.

"You phonies are going to have to throw me out of here kicking and screaming." I blew a long wall of smoke out towards the men. I stood on the table and kicked the folder out from beneath Hale's hands. "*Vive les livres!*" I shouted.

It wasn't long before security had me by the arms. I blew smoke in their faces too as they dragged me through that heinous hospital looking hallway, laughing as I went, laughing until I couldn't hear the shouts of Hale and Ellsbury behind me anymore. The joke was on them and I knew it. No matter what they published, no matter how much money they made, they wouldn't have my book. They weren't deserving of it, and I was glad they didn't have it.

"Bye Queenie," called the bulbous receptionist from her desk. "Give the king my regards!"

I wasn't sure what to make of her final remarks, but what I did know was that something had to change.

Chapter Thirty
How Mae and Me Decided to Take Our Life to Paris

How she consoled me, my Maest of all; may she make home within me, without me, mystical as Mary who does Mae me when they maim me, yesterday and today. Her miracles unmatched, may she amaze me, forever and after. In her arms, dusk quiet, it's New York again. I told her all and she put this boy to bed. Can't we find anything that works for us, My Mae? Can't we win just once?

"You can't let it hurt you," she spoke to me. "They know nothing of beauty, nothing of art. They're businessmen after all, Dick."

"But how can they be so clueless?" I asked. "To love my writing, to commend it even! And to betray me on the grounds that I am not a whore? What world are we living in, Mae? What madness is this universe? Can we step away from our tedious little lives, our self-righteousness, for just a moment and realize that I just got rejected because I'm not a whore? How did we get here? Is beauty a sin? Is there any virtue in construction rather than deconstruction? Can anything just be good for the sake of goodness anymore?"

"You can only prove them wrong. You can only work harder, and show them their own folly through your success. You're great. I always tell you that you are great."

In that bed, in the blue winter room of Avenue A, we lied together for hours. The sun was smoldering behind clouds, the park across the street singing songs, the avenue lit up below us, a jolly fever in the air, though none of it had reached our sorry room. What spiral revelations dawned on me during this winter's eve, locked in Mae's arms, silently ruminating on what had transpired, remembering the hours perspired in that very bedroom, working and performing magic, pulling rabbits out of hats, fighting all the desires of my body to finish mine own work. I was depleted that evening. The feeling that all of God's creation was also a tool I could use to make sense of the mysteries of the world, to find them and to write them, to love them in sickness and in health, till death do us part; it all left me that day. The world was not a beautiful place, it was a senseless place. It wasn't made for me, I was condemned to it. The people snowstepping on the avenue below didn't understand, the poor subway rats could never understand. The buffs at Passion were the aggressors of this world, representing the void, the passionless pit of pain, problem-passing devils comfortable and celebrated even for their pillaging of our perfect Garden here upon Earth. Pity me, O Lord. For what can I do next? Do you even understand? Or is it only Mae?

I stroked her dark hair and tried to look her in the eyes. Those evading orbs of hope, the only straight things in this crooked world, and that was really saying something. I loved her so. I couldn't live without her, I knew that, reader, but in this moment of weakness I wondered for the first time, what was it that we were trying to do after all?

"Don't say that!" she shouted. She broke our peace.

"It just isn't making sense to me," I said. "What is all of this? Who do we think we are?"

"We don't think we are anybody, Dick! We *are ourselves* and we are wonderful! We have everything here!"

"Don't give me that again, Mae. Listen to me: What if there is something better than this? What if we've been fooling ourselves?"

I was convincing myself as I spoke.

"What could be better than this?" she asked.

I didn't know. But I thought about it, and I suppose I lied.

"What if we got out of here?" I said. "What if we moved out of the city?"

"And did what?"

"What if we got real jobs? What if we contributed something?"

"Real jobs?"

"What if we bought a house? Somewhere in Jersey or Pennsylvania. Maybe even farther out. What if we went home? To Indiana?"

"You want to move to Indiana?"

"What if we had children? Mae, listen to me: What if we are missing something? What if this writing and this painting and this…this thing in our heads, what if it's just striving after wind? What if it is all meaningless? What if it is all vanity? What if we're the fools, and the joke is on us? Have you stopped to think about this at all? We spend all this time wondering what is wrong with the world but has it ever occurred to you that the whole world might wonder what is wrong with us?"

"Dick!"

"My name is David! You have to listen to me, I'm seeing it all, I'm having visions, I have clarity."

"You're losing your mind, Dick, please—"

"When was the last time you sold a painting? Tell me. When was the last time you even painted anything? I think it's all in our head, Mae. I don't know if we're even doing this at all. I don't think we are who we think we are."

"What are you saying? Do you hear yourself?"

"When was the last time anything that we're doing even resembled a career? We don't make any money."

"We don't need to!" she cried. "I have money. I have money forever."

"But sitting around and living off your money is meaningless! We don't *do anything*, Mae! We don't actually live. We could have an income, we could have a home, we could have a family. Isn't that what life should be about? Don't you think we've been missing the point all along?"

She hit me. She hit me hard. The sky had come dark now and the low glow of a lamp lit her face so goldenlike, I could just see her perfect cheeks and red lips below the shadow of her forehead. She held my arms and looked at my stunned face. There wasn't a hum in the air. It was silent, still, like I'd come out of a dream. I looked at her and I loved her more than ever. I couldn't talk even if I tried, my tongue was locked, and tears worked behind my eyes. I squinted hard to keep them from moving.

"Dick," she said. She was crying. "I want to show you something."

Mae stood, floating from the bed towards the far wall where an easel was, covered by a sheet. She looked as perfect as ever there standing at the foot of her shadow, identical in the dark room to that long umbratic twin. "I made this for you," she said. She pulled off the sheet and there it shone like the sun, the perfect portrait of her and I, mixed and ensouled as one, love incarnate in color and in light. She stood near it and the tears came to each of us at once.

"Mae, my God, it's beautiful."

"I've been working on it for a long time now, and I finished it today while you were at your meeting. It's us. It's our love. Since you have written us so wonderfully, I wanted to paint us."

Reader, I withhold no veracity when I tell you I bawled like a baby that night. All night, until dawnbreak I bawled. I rolled around in that bed like a sick animal and cried strange noises I'd never even known I could make. I was exorcising something. I was ridding myself of that delusional demon I had spewed in my trance. All that hogwash about families and jobs and New Jersey—save me Lord! How could I have been so senile? It was the closest I'd ever come to insanity, reader, and it was Mae who saved me. She pulled me out of what could have been an inescapable hole of lifelong pain and sorrow.

As the sun rose that morning, and my snow-white Mae wiggled from her sleep, I lay there still sleepless, and it all came to me. I knew then what must be done. All along we were chasing something that didn't exist. We were playing checkers instead of chess. We were living in black and white when we could have been in technicolor. We were mistaken. We were handicapped. We were stunted completely because of one simple fact: We were living in New York City when we could have been living in Paris.

***

The plans were made, the tickets were bought, the dates were set. I was to finish my book in Paris, leaving New York's strangling arms behind us once and for all. We would leave on the 18th of February. It was all for the better, and Mae understood it very well, trying to convince me even on our first date that New York paled in comparison to Paris, the very heartbeat of all romances, the ventricles of the literary world. For what sense is it to try and do an angel's job in a slave's country? The bloodsucking shamelessness of New York City was no place for a writer anyway. Who could work in such conditions as these? For all that it's worth, New York is the Whore; no, America is the Whore! There are no principles in America, only slogans. There are no real profound beliefs, only blind loyalty. Loyalty to brand, to country, to man, to money. America has no backbone, it only goes from fad to fad, dressing itself in the latest style, swearing by the latest oaths with fingers crossed behind its back and its teeth out. The poor, lonely America with its beggars cup out before it, how desolate will it be when you've killed all your geniuses? This America believes it is a free country, yet it is horrendously bound to its own mythos. According to Americans it is a religious country, but only until the vagrant needs a dollar.

According to Americans it is a country with strong family values, yet it humiliates and degrades the Latino, whose values surpass her own tenfold. According to Americans it is a rich country but all I ever hear about is how badly she needs my money. This nation is a place of business. What an infinite bustle. I am awakened most nights by this nightmare of business. It interrupts my dreams. There is no sabbath. I think that there is nothing—not even crime—more opposed to poetry, philosophy, to life itself, than this incessant business. For that, we decided to take our lives to Paris.

From the first mention of the proverbial city Mae was sold. She could see the vision as well as I could. Both of us living high in the windows of that Parisian cityscape, painting everything; Mae, our us together shining with words and color, our life a parable, inosculate in essence, both of me stardancing across the nocturnal Seine in uttermost love, no New York-nothing, no trashcan animals, flailing sounds of death overhead, suffering slaves of Sodom, the dour horror of American dreams dismembered and sold for fuel somewhere on Roosevelt Avenue. My poor Mae, how did she ever survive that apocalypse?

The days passed as we awaited our day of exodus. I prepared my farewell to the city, the city that taught me how to write. I loved it for that, but it had become a jealous lover. It would let me write, but wouldn't allow me to be a writer. It would let me love, without being a lover. New York had always been a contradiction in that way, it demanded something from you. For what it gave you, it always bartered back more, and it took a long time until you came to realize what it had stolen from you.

I knew Paris would allow me to finish my book. What a fine novelty great American stories have always been for the well-in-taste European market. They don't care anything for capital or for sustainability of sales. They complain not of "target audiences" or "obscure motives," their tastes are refined as such, able to handle the density of Sir Henry James when the Americans couldn't, willing to publish Joyce when the Irish wouldn't, and happy to house Burroughs when the world said we shouldn't. As the day approached, we had just one thing we knew we wanted to do before we left.

***

It was February 14th, the day of St. Valentine, and we waited along Second Avenue in a harsh flurry beneath the marquee. We were already running late for the showing on account of a slow waiter at the restaurant where we dined.

There it was in lights along the theater wall: *Casablanca*. I couldn't believe we were doing it. For years I'd come alone, suffering great trials of will, great hours of hardship watching and yearning, and now, I had with me my very own Ilsa. What could conceivably be more romantic than seeing the finest picture of all pictures with the finest girl of all girls on the finest day of all days? It had all come full circle for me, my humble beginnings, my ambitious plans, my curious habits, my tragedy, oh! my undeserved tragedy! But what relief I felt when I walked past that ticket booth with my arm around Mae, bustling into the theater, hearing that orchestra thrashing, the narration starting, the red-dotted lights of the theater steps guiding us to our seats, and Paris in bold black letters filling that screen. Oh, my Paris! My home, just four short days away. What a sendoff this would be, to bury—no, *to cremate* our love affair with the unfaithful, promiscuous American wench called New York City, and move onto the princess of all great cities, the reigning regal room of romance since before the days the great romantics had ever written their first words.

This film, in its grandeur and timelessness, teaches one great lesson:

Don't do it. Don't dare leave Paris.

For that love you once had, breathing so freshly and freely will never be the same. Your love will go stale. It will wax cold. Even a war of global proportions should not be grounds for dissolving true love. And Rick, that hard-nosed romantic-at-heart knew it all too well. He'd have rather stayed there in Paris and died as a martyr for love than to have lived what he lived out in Casablanca. He sent her off so that he didn't have to live with the past any more than he already had. And now there we were, Mae and me, ready to make that adventure our very own.

It was a true and proper celebration of love. I couldn't remember the last time I was so happy, watching my Mae take in and relish each perfect scene, the struggle, the pulling and pushing of love between hearts, all dangled and exposed in the open air for the public to see. What love they had!

When the curtain fell I kissed Mae and she held me warm in her arms.

"I love you, Dick," she said. "I can't wait to begin this adventure with you."

"I love you too, Mae," I said.

"Even in Paris?"

"Even more in Paris."

We walked hand-in-hand out of the theater and into the lobby.

"I'm going to use the bathroom, and then we'll get a move on," I said.

"Sure," she smiled. "I'll be right here."

It was just a moment after I'd unfastened my pants at the urinal that he walked in. I didn't see him at first, as I was looking straight ahead at the cinderblock wall atop the urinal. I only heard his steps, light as a ducktrot, a sort of pattering, a waddling wash of a sound. I stood and relieved myself of the forty-eight ounce fountain Coke I'd indulged in during the film. How amazing a film that was! I couldn't shake its greatness, as if I had been bathed in its glory and I'd yet to dry. Rick's infinite words bouncing around in my head; the look in Ilsa's eyes when she realizes she still loves Rick despite her best efforts. All of it pummeled me as I stood beside him at the basement bathroom urinal there on Second Avenue. At once, as I heard him fumbling with his own equipment, I had no choice but to let some energy out.

"So," I said, "did you like the film?"

Nothing but the sound of my relief and the faint buckling of denim and brass. I thought I may have heard him curse under his breath.

"Ah," I said. "Not a romance guy then?"

"Excuse me?" he asked.

"The film. *Casablanca.*"

"You're talking to me?"

"Yes." I was embarrassed. "My apologies. I just wanted to know if you enjoyed the film. I loved it, see, and I'm just bursting with energy. I wanted to know if you loved it too."

"Yeah, yeah, I loved it. It's one of my favorites."

"And mine," I said with glee. I finished up my business there at the unit and turned slightly for the first time. There he was—or should I say, there he wasn't—I hadn't noticed it before. He was perhaps only a third of the height of a normal man.

"Oh, I'm terribly sorry," I said.

"For what?" he jeered.

I guess I didn't know what I was sorry for. Perhaps that I hadn't noticed his affliction before.

"To disturb you," I said.

"Oh, golly," he said, "you didn't disturb me." He spoke a little out of breath. He was struggling. "It's just that I can't believe they still haven't put a smaller urinal in this damn bathroom. I've talked to management about it a dozen times. I'm a member here. Do you know that? I come here at least five times a month, and I spend a lot of money every time. I'm buyin' snacks, drinks, popcorn, and when I come in here to take a leak, I gotta lean back and let loose like I'm firing off artillery shells."

"I'm so sorry," I said again.

"You'd think they'd look out for their loyal customers."

"You'd think they'd at least put in a step stool."

"Even that," he said. He hadn't begun yet, he was still finding the angle, tip-toeing and measuring his shot. A peculiar little man he was. To say he wasn't a midget would be outright lying, but I'm not familiar with the codes of discernment between midgets and dwarves so I'll leave it at that. But, Lord, was he a small person.

"What if I gave you a hand?" I asked.

"Excuse me?"

"Don't be shy! I can lift you. Imagine how great it would be to do your business right in front of the ceramic there, hands free."

"Lift me? I don't know about that...I mean—"

"Think about it!" I said. "Let yourself go. I'll come up behind you, turn my head and lift you, that way you can go just like the rest of us. Staring up at the wall, no backsplash in your face."

"That really would be nice." He began to feel sorry for himself. "I really need to go. I drank a forty-eight ounce Coke in that theater."

"So did I. Ruined me."

"Imagine what it does to me," he said.

"So what do you say?"

He thought for a moment, anxiously. His hands were at his member, he did a little hop in place. "Shoot, let's do it."

I came up behind him, took him around the abdomen and brought him up to my own chest. I turned my head and he fumbled with his belt.

"I'm Dick, by the way," I said.

"Rick," he said.

"Rick? Just like in the movie."

"That's right," he said proudly.

I heard that sweet sound of relief finally run against the porcelain. He was getting lighter by the passing second.

"It's my favorite movie, ya know," he said. "I used to watch it at home, all by myself on Valentine's Day, but this year my fiancée and I got to come see it together. It's her favorite too."

"I don't believe it," I said. "I used to watch it alone too and this is the first year that I'm here with my girl."

"Well, Happy Valentine's to the both of you," Rick said.

"I was particularly admiring the soundtrack this time around. I mean, I've always loved it but, just how perfect it all is together! I wish I could have an orchestra follow me around all day, scoring my life. Imagine how much better things would be."

"Don't even get me started," said Rick. He was finishing up. "Hey, if you don't mind, Dick, give me a little shake would you?"

"Not a problem," I said. I held him tight around the body and moved him up and down and back and forth with some commanding force.

"Ow!" he shouted. "A little gentler on the ribs there, Dick."

That's when it finally hit me. I couldn't believe it.

"Alright you can put me down now," Rick said.

I looked at him closely as I held him. It was all coming together in my head, but I had to know for sure.

"By the way, Rick," I started, "is your fiancée still here?"

"Of course she is. She's just outside waiting for me."

I didn't know if I should ask or not. I figured we'd get Rick buckled up and washed and I'd find out soon enough. I set him down, watched him fix himself up, tucking his plaid shirt back into his pants, and then I picked him up again to use the sink. We caught ourselves in the mirror and tried not to stare. We looked like an old Vaudeville act.

"Alright, Dick, you can put me down now."

"Sure."

"Thanks a lot for everything. That was really great."

"Sure, no problem. Listen," I said, "would you mind if I met your girl? I mean you're such a nice guy, maybe my Mae could meet your lady and we could all stay in touch."

"Shore," said Rick. "I don't see no problem with that. Sounds fun."

We stepped out together into the half-light of the lobby, it was beginning to crowd from the other theaters letting out. Still through the window I could see the blizzard coming down, sick-colored streetlights, a sort of jaundiced looking glow lighting Second Avenue for the pedestrians bustling through the cold of the eve. A few taxis lined up at a red light, the smoke from their exhaust mixing up with the falling snow. Rick beside me waddled his best through the coming crowd, and there sat on a bench together were our two lovers, my Mae, and his most extraordinary looking bride-to-be, one Callie David. There she was, where she always had been and where I should have expected her to be, in the lobby of the theater across from me. How had I forgotten her? Blinded by my own love for Mae, perhaps, or otherwise displaced from my mind on account of my failed attempts to offer my love to her; that shining star Callie, nominal twin, born from the same somewhere, interfated once again, and somehow, unsurprisingly, involved with the likes of another very little man with a fascinating infatuation with *Casablanca.*

"David!" she shouted.

"David?" said Rick.

"Callie!" said I.

"Callie?" said Mae.

"It's Dick," said Rick.

"Rick's right, it's Dick," said I.

"It's Dick?" said Callie.

"It's Dick," said Mae.

"I'm Ilsa," said Callie.

"Ilsa?" said I.

"Ilsa," said Rick.

"Like the film," said Ilsa.

"You're kidding," said I.

"I'm not," she said.

"Rick, this is Mae," said I.

"Mae," said Rick.

"Rick," said Mae.

"We were just talking about you," I said to Ilsa. "Rick mentioned that he had his fiancée here, and gosh, I thought what a coincidence it would be."

Ilsa blushed.

"I suppose everybody does have their type," I said.

"And thank God she does," said Rick, now taking Ilsa's hand from below. "So how do you two know each other?"

"It's a long story," I said. "We've seen each other here at the theater. We've...well, in a way we've been through a lot together."

"So you've gone and changed your name then?" said Ilsa.

"Sure," I said. "Mae and I did it together. We thought it was a lot more romantic."

"Probably would help with getting noticed as a writer too," Ilsa said. "That old name was so...I don't know, stale."

"Well, you'd think," Mae said. "You wouldn't believe how wrong you are."

Ilsa squinted.

"It's another long story," I said. "And you? You've obviously—"

"Yeah," said Ilsa. "I mean...listen Dick, no offense..."

"None taken!" I said happily. "This is great! All of us here together."

"I guess I met Rick, oh, I don't know…two months after I last saw you, and we just knew it."

"We just knew it," said Rick.

"You understand, Dick," Ilsa said.

"I do, of course."

"Once I found out he loved *Casablanca* as much as I do, I suggested I change my name. To have a little bit of magic with us everywhere, all the time. So I became Ilsa."

"I've always been Rick," said Rick.

"My legal name is Richard now too," I said. "Mae calls me Dick because she loves Dick Van Dyke."

Mae blushed now.

"And I do think Dick is a better author's name."

"It's true," said Ilsa. "So much *zing*."

"Well, I'm glad you found what you're looking for," I said to Ilsa.

"And same to you," she said. She was smiling big. Everybody was really happy. "It seems that Mae here is everything you could ask for. We were talking while you were in the restroom. You're leaving for Paris then?"

"We are," I said. Mae stood by me now, we held each other tight.

"Isn't it romantic?" Mae said.

"It's a wonderful city," said Ilsa. "I envy those who can handle its…its power."

"Its vigor," added Rick.

"I'm sorry again," I said. "I know it still must hurt."

"It will always hurt, but I have Rick now. We always have Paris in a way."

"That's beautiful," said Mae.

"Well," said Ilsa. She was sniffling a little bit and wiped her nose with the glove she'd just feathered on. "Do you think you'll marry there?"

Mae and I both laughed.

"I don't know," I said. "We haven't quite gotten that far."

"The first priority is for Dick to finish his book," Mae said.

"Oh you must be close!" said Ilsa. "You've been going at it for such a long time."

"I'm just at the end," I said. "The two lovers will be starting up a new life in Paris. I just need that final puzzle piece to fall into place and I can finish it."

The four of us stood there as people walked around us from all angles. The silence was louder than the passers-by now. Rick, the poor little guy, was right in the crossfire of one of Mae's two bad eyes, its gaze sunken like a stone and honed in on him so that he nervously looked to and fro, up and down, until finally Ilsa spoke up.

"You know what," she said. "I...I mean I feel awful saying it, but you must admit that what happened to me all those years ago does make a pretty good story."

"I've thought the very same," I said. "With all due respect."

"It's a great romance," Rick spoke up.

"It really is quite a tale," I said. "One of the fondest romances I've ever heard."

"I can't say he wouldn't be proud of it," Ilsa said. "He loved a good tragedy. He was such a good man, and as romantic as they come."

"By all accounts, he certainly was," I said.

"I suppose I wouldn't mind if...you know, if you wanted to."

"If I wanted to what?"

"If you wanted to incorporate his story," she said. "It would be awfully romantic if he—"

"Oh, Ilsa, I couldn't."

"I insist, Dick."

"Ilsa, you don't have to."

"I think he'd want it. Really."

"You think?"

"What is more romantic than that?" added Rick.

"A candlelight dinner on the Seine," said Ilsa. "An unfortunate accident…"

"In an act of romantic martyrdom at that," said Rick.

"It would be the perfect ending," I said. "Two lovers optimistic for their new life abroad, having experienced the full glory of love's gifts, a proposal is made…"

"And then the dagger in the heart," Ilsa said. She was talking through tears.

"Or a snail in the throat, rather," Rick said, solemnly.

"It hurts so much, but it's so beautiful," Ilsa said. "It would be a great end to a great story."

"Love is not the only face of romance," I said. "You once told me that."

"Often it is tragedy that prevails," she said.

"God rest his little soul," I said, and we all said *Amen*.

I knew then exactly how my story would end.

Chapter Thirty-One
How My Name Wound Up Becoming Dick du Quesne

"Well, think about it, Dick," Ilsa said. "Use it if you want, I don't mind. I think it's serendipitous how all this turned out, you know, with us seeing each other like this all the time, and now the two of you moving to Paris afterall."

"I think it is too," I said. "I'll certainly think about it. And I want to thank you for ever having talked to me in the first place."

"I'll look out for the book," she said, smiling. She hugged me and we left each other with a soft kiss of the cheek. Mae bent down and offered the same to Rick. The ladies hugged, and then Rick and I shook hands. We all smiled a lot, and went out the same door, Rick and Ilsa turning left to go uptown, and Mae and I moving to the right towards 7th Street. The snow was really picking up now, and the wind roaring, loud as a jet engine. We must have walked about six paces south before I heard Ilsa's voice over the roar of the storm.

"Dick!" she called out.

Mae and I turned together.

"What is it?" I asked.

"What's your new last name anyway?"

"It's Queen," I shouted.

"After Steve McQueen?"

"That's it!"

"It's good, but...Dick Queen?"

"I know, I know," I shouted. "We're working on it."

"If you're going to Paris you'll need something a little more French-sounding. Why not Dick du Quesne?" she said.

Mae looked at me and kissed my cheek soft and warm.

"We love it," Mae shouted to Ilsa.

"We love it," I said too.

"Send me a copy!" Ilsa said. "And, oh Dick!"

"Yes?"

"I can recommend a great restaurant for the two of you...it's right on the Seine."

"*La Limace Volante*, no?" I shouted.

"That's the one," she said. "Just don't order the snails!"

And that's the story of how my name wound up becoming Dick du Quesne, and that's the story of how I came to write my book.

THE END